D1266181

SNOWBOUND

Also by Blake Crouch

Abandon

Desert Places

Locked Doors

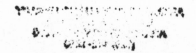

SNOWBOUND

BLAKE CROUCH

Minotaur Books New York

This is a work of fiction. All of the characters, organizations, and events portrayed in this novel are either products of the author's imagination or are used fictitiously.

www.minotaurbooks.com

Library of Congress Cataloging-in-Publication Data

Crouch, Blake.
  Snowbound / Blake Crouch.—1st ed.
     p. cm.
  ISBN 978-0-312-42573-9
  1. Missing persons—Fiction. 2. Human trafficking—Fiction. 3. United States. Federal, Bureau of Investigation—Employees—Fiction. 4. Gangs—United States—Fiction. 5. Gangs—Mexico—Fiction. 6. Organized crime—Fiction. 7. Domestic fiction. I. Title.
  PS3603.R68S66   2010
  813'.6—dc22

                                                                2009047487

First Edition: July 2010

10 9 8 7 6 5 4 3 2 1

For Jordan Crouch
I love you, brother

ACKNOWLEDGMENTS

In September of 2007, my great friend and uncle, Greg "Zig" Crouch, took me to Redoubt Mountain Lodge on Crescent Lake in the heart of Alaska's Chigmit Mountains. It was one of the best times I've ever had, and I am profoundly grateful for that invitation. If there is a more spectacularly scenic place on earth, I haven't seen it. The isolation and beauty of Redoubt became a huge inspiration for this book.

John Grove also made that trip possible, and Ryan and Heather Richards, who run Redoubt Mountain Lodge, were superb hosts and guides. Neither of them, nor any of the staff or guests who were at Redoubt when I was there are characters in this book. Except for Zig.

A heartfelt thanks to Linda Allen, who went so far above and beyond to get this one off the ground.

Michael Homler, my editor, made this book better in a thousand ways.

Anna Cottle and Mary Alice Kier, as always, provided wise counsel and tireless support.

Anne Gardner at St. Martin's Press is the best publicist I've ever had, and these words are totally insufficient acknowledgment of the hard and brilliant work she has done to spread the word about my books.

And finally, back at base camp, hugs, kisses, and lots of love to Rebecca, Aidan, and my new daughter, Annslee Gray Crouch. I love you.

The Wrong Stars

ONE

In the evening of the last good day either of them would know for years to come, the girl pushed open the sliding glass door and stepped through onto the back porch.

"Daddy?"

Will Innis set the legal pad aside and made room for Devlin to climb into his lap. His daughter was small for eleven, felt like the shell of a child in his arms.

"What are you doing out here?" she asked, and in her scratchy voice he could hear the remnants of her last respiratory infection like gravel in her lungs.

"Working up a close for my trial in the morning."

"Is your client the bad guy again?"

Will smiled. "You and your mother. I'm not really supposed to think of it that way, sweetheart."

"What'd he do?" His little girl's face had turned ruddy in the sunset and the fading light brought out lighter strands in her otherwise-midnight-dark hair.

"He allegedly—"

"What's that mean?"

"Allegedly?"

"Yeah."

"Means it's not been proven. He's accused of selling drugs."

"Like what I take?"

"No, your drugs are good. They help you. He was selling, allegedly selling, bad drugs to people."

"Why are they bad?"

"Because they make you lose control."

"Why do people take them?"

"They like how it makes them feel."

"How does it make them feel?"

He kissed her forehead and looked at his watch. "It's after eight, Devi. Let's go bang on those lungs."

She sighed but didn't argue. She never tried to get out of it.

He stood up, cradling his daughter, and walked over to the redwood railing.

They stared into the wilderness that bordered Oasis Hills, their subdivision. The houses on No-Water Lane had the Sonoran Desert for a backyard.

"Look," he said. "See them?" A half mile away, specks filed out of an arroyo and trotted across the desert toward a shadeless forest of giant saguaro cacti that looked vaguely sinister profiled against the horizon.

"What are they?" she asked.

"Coyotes. What do you bet they start yapping after the sun goes down?"

When Devlin had gotten into bed, he read to her from *A Wrinkle in Time.* They'd been working their way through the penultimate chapter, "Aunt Beast," but Devlin was exhausted and drifted off before Will had finished the second page.

He closed the book, set it on the carpet, and turned out the light. Cool desert air flowed in through an open window. A sprinkler whispered in the next-door neighbor's yard. Devlin yawned, made a cooing sound that reminded him of rocking her to sleep as a newborn. Her eyes fluttered and she said softly, "Mom?"

"She's working late at the clinic, sweetheart."

"When's she coming back?"

"Few hours."

"Tell her to come in and kiss me?"

"I will."

He was nowhere near ready for court in the morning, but he stayed, running his fingers through Devlin's hair until she'd fallen back to sleep. Finally, he slid carefully off the bed and walked out onto the deck to gather up his books and legal pads. He had a late night ahead of him. A pot of strong coffee would help.

Next door, the sprinklers had gone quiet.

A lone cricket chirped in the desert.

Thunderless lightning sparked somewhere over Mexico, and the coyotes began to scream.

TWO

The thunderstorm caught up with Rachael Innis thirty miles north of the Mexican border. It was 9:30 P.M., and it had been a long day at the free clinic in Sonoyta, where she volunteered her time and services once a week as a bilingual psychologist. The windshield wipers whipped back and forth. High beams lighted the steam rising off the pavement, and glancing in the rearview mirror, Rachael saw the pair of headlights a quarter of a mile back that had been with her for the last ten minutes.

Glowing beads suddenly appeared on the shoulder just ahead. She jammed her foot into the brake pedal, the Grand Cherokee fishtailing into the oncoming lane before skidding to a stop. A doe and her fawn ventured into the middle of the road, mesmerized by the headlights. Rachael let her forehead fall onto the steering wheel, closed her eyes, drew in a deep breath.

The deer moved on. She accelerated the Cherokee, another dark mile passing as pellets of hail hammered the hood.

The Cherokee veered sharply toward the shoulder and she nearly lost control again, trying to correct her bearing, but the steering wheel wouldn't straighten out. Rachael lifted her foot off the gas pedal and eased over onto the side of the road.

When she killed the engine, all she could hear were the rain and hail drumming on the roof. The car that had been following her shot by. She set her glasses on the passenger seat, opened the door, and stepped down into a puddle that engulfed her pumps. The downpour soaked through her black suit. She shivered. It was pitch-black between lightning strikes and she moved forward carefully, feeling her way along the warm metal of the hood.

A slash of lightning hit the desert just a few hundred yards out. It set her body tingling, her ears ringing. *I'm going to be electrocuted.* There came a train of earsplitting strikes, flashbulbs of electricity that illuminated the sky just long enough for her to see that the tires on the driver's side were still intact.

Her hands trembled now. A tall saguaro stood burning like a cross in the desert. She groped her way over to the passenger side as marble-size hail collected in her hair. The desert was electrified again, spreading wide and empty all around her.

In the eerie blue light, she saw that the front tire on the passenger side was flat.

Back inside the Cherokee, Rachael sat behind the steering wheel, mascara trailing down her cheeks like sable tears. She wrung out her long black hair and massaged her temples, trying to alleviate the headache building between them. Her purse lay on the floor on the passenger side. She dragged it into her lap and shoved her hand inside, rummaging for the cell phone. She found it, tried her husband's number, but there was no service in the storm.

Rachael looked into the back of the Cherokee at the spare. She had no way of contacting AAA, and passing cars would be few and far between on this remote highway at this hour of the night. *I'll just wait and try Will again when the storm has passed.*

Squeezing the steering wheel, she stared through the windshield into the stormy darkness, somewhere north of the border in Organ Pipe Cactus National Monument. *Middle of nowhere.*

There was a brilliant streak of lightning. In the split-second illumination, she saw a black Escalade parked a hundred yards up the shoulder.

Thunder rattled the windows. Five seconds elapsed. When the sky exploded again, Rachael felt a strange, unnerving pull to look through the driver's side window.

A man swung a crowbar through the glass.

THREE

Will startled back into consciousness, disoriented and thirsty. It was so quiet—just the discreet drone of a computer fan and the second hand of the clock ticking in the adjacent bedroom. He found himself slouched in the leather chair at the desk in his small home office, the CPU still purring, the monitor switched into sleep mode.

As he yawned, everything rushed back in a torrent of anxiety. He'd been hammering out notes for his closing argument and hit a wall at ten o'clock. The evidence was damning. He was going to lose. He'd closed his eyes only for a moment to clear his head.

He reached for the mug of coffee and took a sip. Winced. It was cold and bitter. He jostled the mouse. When the screen blinked back on, he looked at the clock and realized he wouldn't be sleeping anymore tonight. It was 4:09 A.M. He was due in court in less than five hours.

First things first—he needed an immediate and potent infusion of caffeine.

His office adjoined the master bedroom at the west end of the house, and passing through on his way to the kitchen, he noticed a peculiar thing. He'd expected to see his wife buried under the myriad quilts and blankets on their bed, but she wasn't there. The comforter was smooth and taut, undisturbed since they'd made it up yesterday morning.

He walked through the living room and into the den, then down the hallway. Rachael had probably come home, seen him asleep at his desk, and gone in to kiss Devlin. She'd have been exhausted from working all day at the clinic. She'd probably fallen asleep in there. He could picture the night-light glow on their faces as he reached his daughter's door.

It was cracked, exactly as he'd left it seven hours ago when he'd put Devlin to bed.

He eased the door open. Rachael wasn't with her.

Will, wide awake now, closed Devlin's door and headed back into the den.

"Rachael? You here, hon?"

He went to the front door, turned the dead bolt, stepped outside.

Dark houses. Porch lights. Streets still wet from the thunderstorms that had blown through several hours ago. No wind, the sky clearing, bright with stars.

When he saw them in the driveway, his knees gave out and he sat down on the steps and tried to remember how to breathe. One Beamer, no Jeep Cherokee, and a pair of patrol cars, two uniformed officers coming toward him, their hats shelved under their arms.

The patrolmen sat on the couch in the living room, Will facing them in a chair. The smell of new paint was still strong. He and Rachael had re-done the walls and the vaulted ceiling in terra-cotta last weekend. Most of the black-and-white desert photographs that usually adorned the room still leaned against the antique chest of drawers, waiting to be rehung.

The lawmen were businesslike in their delivery, taking turns with the details, as if they'd rehearsed who would say what, their voices so terribly measured and calm.

There wasn't much information yet. Rachael's Cherokee had been found on the shoulder of Arizona 85 in Organ Pipe Cactus National Monument. Right front tire flat, punctured with a nail to cause a slow and steady loss of air pressure. Driver's side window busted out.

No Rachael. No blood.

They asked Will a few questions. They tried to sympathize. They said how sorry they were as Will just stared at the floor, a tightness in his chest constricting his windpipe in a slow strangulation.

He happened to look up at some point, saw Devlin standing in the hall in a plain pink T-shirt that fell all the way to the carpet, the tattered blanket she'd slept with every night since her birth draped over her left arm. And he could see in her eyes that she'd heard every word the patrolmen had said about her mother, because they were filling up with tears.

FOUR

Rachael Innis was strapped upright with two-inch webbing to the leather seat behind the driver. She stared at the console lights. The digital clock read 4:32 A.M. She remembered the crowbar through the window and nothing after.

Bach's Four Lute Suites blared from the Bose stereo system, John Williams playing classical guitar. Beyond the windshield, the headlights cut a feeble swath of light through the darkness, and even though she was riding in a luxury SUV, the shocks did little to ease the violent jarring from whatever primitive road they traveled.

Her wrists and ankles were comfortably but securely bound with nylon restraints. Her mouth wasn't gagged. From her vantage point, she could only see the back of the driver's head and occasionally the side of his face by the cherry glow of his cigarette. He was smooth-shaven, his hair was dark, and he smelled of a subtle, spicy cologne.

It occurred to her that he didn't know she was awake, but the thought wasn't two seconds old when she caught his eyes in the rearview mirror. They registered her consciousness, flickered back to the road.

They drove on. An endless stream of rodents darted across the road ahead, and a thought kept needling her: At some point, he was going to stop the car and do whatever he was driving her out in the desert to do.

"Have you urinated on my seat?" She thought she detected the faintest accent.

"No."

"You tell me if you have to urinate. I'll stop the car."

"Okay. Where are you—"

"No talking. Unless you have to urinate."

"I just—"

"You want your mouth taped? You have a cold. That would make breathing difficult."

Devlin was the only thing she'd ever prayed for, and that was years ago, but as she watched the passing sagebrush and cactus through the deeply tinted windows, she pleaded with God again.

Now the Escalade was slowing. It came to a stop. He turned off the engine, stepped outside, and shut the door. Her door opened. He stood watching her. He was very handsome, with flawless brown skin (save for an indentation in the bridge of his nose), liquid blue eyes, and black hair greased back from his face. His pretty teeth seemed to gleam in the night. Rachael's chest heaved against the strap of webbing.

He said, "Calm down, Rachael." Her name sounded like a foreign word on his lips. He took out a syringe from his black leather jacket and uncapped the needle.

"What is that?" she asked.

"You have nice veins." He ducked into the Escalade and turned her arm over. When the needle entered, she gasped.

"Please. If this is some kind of ransom—"

"No, no. You've already been purchased. In fact, right now, there isn't a safer place in the world for you to be than in my possession."

A gang of coyotes erupted in demonic howls somewhere out in that empty dark. Rachael thought they sounded like a woman burning alive, and she began to scream until the drug took her.

FIVE

They started arriving after four o'clock in the afternoon. By five, Rachael's disappearance was the lead story on all the local news stations, even in Tucson and Phoenix. When six rolled around, there were more cars parked along No-Water Lane than when the Hasslers had hosted their last Fourth of July barbecue.

Come 7:15 P.M., more than forty people had crowded into Will and Rachael's modest adobe home in Ajo, Arizona. They packed the den, the living room, the kitchen, even spilling out onto the deck. It was a strange assembly, all these people drawn to a tragedy in the making. The ambience mirrored the hushed formality of a postfuneral gathering, with the glut of food and alcohol, whispered conversations, the absence of laughter. And it struck Will as he sat on the sofa holding Devlin, surrounded by those he loved, friends he'd not seen in years, neighbors he rarely spoke to, that these people had come to hold vigil with him. They were waiting to hear that she'd been found, though everyone knew that people weren't found alive when they went missing near the border, if they were ever found at all.

"Will?" He broke from his trance and looked up at Rachael's mother standing by the built-in bookshelves, a glass of bourbon in her hand.

Debra bore a strong resemblance to her daughter, right down to her trim figure and black hair. From across the room, they could've been mistaken for sisters. Closer up, her silver roots showed and the added decades of living in these desert borderlands and the punishment of the sun became evident in the leathering of her face, which more resembled hide than skin.

"I couldn't remember if you took ice or not," she said.

"Yeah, I do. That's perfect." She handed him his fourth Maker's of the evening.

"Can I take her?" Debra motioned to her granddaughter, who had fallen asleep in Will's arms, and he'd have let her, but she was near bulletproof with Valium and vodka.

"I need to hold her, Mom." As he sipped the whiskey, his face flushed with heat and he theorized through the bourbon-embroidered fog that maybe Rachael's funeral had already happened and he'd blocked everything out—the eulogies, the stern-faced pallbearers, his daughter in hysterics as she watched her mother's casket being lowered into the ground.

He staggered to his feet and carried Devlin back to her bedroom. She was beyond exhaustion now. So was he. He tucked her in, knelt on the floor, spent several moments watching her sleep, feeling a sharp pinch in his gut every time he breathed. After awhile, he got up, headed for his bedroom. His and Rachael's bedroom. He shut and locked the door after him, opened the sweater chest that stood at the foot of their bed.

He found it near the bottom—a tattered sweatshirt that Rachael wore religiously when the weather turned cooler. It was navy blue and had years ago evinced the name of her alma mater, the washing machine having long since stripped away the white lettering.

He brought the sweatshirt to his face and smelled his wife.

On his way back to the den, he stopped at the guest room. Someone sobbed loudly behind the door. He opened it. There were no lights on, but as his eyes adjusted, he discerned the ponderous form of Rachael's sister, Elise, curled up in the corner beside a dresser.

"You all right?" he asked. It took her a moment to catch her breath. Looking out the window above her head, he noticed strange lights in the front yard.

"She's dead, Will. I can feel it." He shut his eyes and braced against the concussion of her words, could have struck her for giving voice to the malignant prediction on all of their minds. "Can't *you* feel it, Will?" He closed the door and went back into the den, grabbed his whiskey from the end table.

One giant swallow and he'd reinforced that beautiful cushion that was padding him from reality, the room humming now, just a few sips shy of spinning.

He was en route to the front door to investigate those lights in the yard when someone caught him under the arm.

"Hey, Will. You hanging in there, guy?" He couldn't recall the man's name, and then he realized why. It was a neighbor, but they'd never met. Will recognized him only because the man was usually washing a white Lexus in his driveway on Saturday mornings whenever Will and Rachael drove past his house on the way to the gym.

He was Will's age, Latino.

"I'm sorry, what's your name?" Will asked.

"Miguel. We always exchange waves when you and your wife pass by my house. I saw the news, all the cars out there. Thought I should come by. If there's anything I can do. . . ."

Will could feel his eyes welling, and whether it was prompted by the whiskey or the totality of this terrible day, he was suddenly overwhelmed by the kindness of this man he knew only through gestures.

"Thank you, Miguel." He wiped his eyes, cleared his throat. "Why don't you go get something to eat, something to drink. They've got a whole buffet thing going in the kitchen."

When Miguel was gone, Will opened the front door and stepped onto the porch.

He whispered, "Oh God." The cushion evaporated. The crushing load of Rachael's absence ripped the breath out of him and he crumpled down on the steps, thinking, *So this is really happening.* It had become a parking lot out in the street. He spotted a news van one block over, a large satellite dish perched on its roof. And in the long grass of the front lawn, a dozen people stood in a circle between the yuccas and saguaros, their faces lighted by the candles in their hands, flames quivering in the evening wind blowing in from the desert.

He sat watching the circle of flames, the sky deepening into dusk, his stomach hurting so much that he could manage only the shallowest of breaths as he strained to hear their words.

A woman's voice reached him: "Dear Lord, You say that where two or more are gathered in Your name that You are present. Well, here we are Lord, and we're asking for the deliverance of Rachael Innis."

He struggled to his feet and stumbled toward them through the grass. He hadn't prayed in years, since they'd found out their daughter was sick. A standoff fuckoff with God. That ended tonight.

SIX

Will slipped away from the circle of candles and started back toward the house to check on Devlin. Though he'd wanted to, he hadn't prayed aloud. It had been a long time and he was rusty at talking to God, particularly in the presence of strangers.

As he reached to open the front door, it swung back. Rachael's mother was standing on the threshold, distraught.

"There's a detective in the living room, Will. He wants to talk to you."

For some reason, Will had expected a younger man, perhaps his age, with a buzz cut and stern, distrusting eyes. Having dealt with many cops as a defense attorney, he'd come to regard them as authority junkies, an unimaginative and reactionary bunch prone to forming fast, unmovable opinions. But at first glance, the detective on his couch proved none of his prejudices. The man was sitting between two of Rachael's girlfriends from yoga class, his hands flattened out on his knees, gazing with a Zen-like calm at a framed photograph over the mantel—a picture from their Grand Canyon vacation two summers ago. He was an older, clean-shaven gentleman with stark white hair and clear blue eyes, and when he saw Will, he rose to his feet, buttoned his jacket, and flashed an appropriately restrained smile.

"Mr. Innis," he said as they shook hands. "Detective Teddy Swicegood. You've cross-examined me in court a few times, if I'm not mistaken. But don't worry. Won't hold it against you. I'm so sorry to be here under these circumstances."

He had at least four inches on Will, and his wizened face belied the strength of his handshake and the lean, solid build beneath the Sears suit.

"You have news?" Will asked.

"It's pretty crowded in here. There someplace we can talk in private?"

"Yeah. You want a drink?"

"I wouldn't object to a whiskey."

Will poured a pair of whiskies and led Swicegood through the sliding glass door. There were a half dozen people on the deck, most of whom he didn't recognize, sitting on chairs dragged out from the breakfast table and eating off paper plates like they were at a cookout.

The two men walked down the steps and crossed the grass to a weathered fence that ran the length of No-Water Lane and separated the backyards of Oasis Hills from the desert.

Will leaned on the fence, steeling himself, and said, "Just tell me. Don't beat around—"

"We've got APBs out everywhere across the Southwest and we're working with the Mexican authorities, as well."

"You haven't found her?"

Swicegood shook his head.

"But you think she's alive."

"I don't know."

"Your opinion?"

"Mr. Innis, it's just too early to be—"

"Please. Take off the fucking kid gloves."

"That's a bad stretch of highway she disappeared on. Notorious for drug running, human trafficking. It doesn't look good."

The words hit Will like drops of acid, and it struck him that following a tragedy, grief comes in waves, each bigger than the previous, each carrying a new component of pain. They stood there drinking bourbon, looking south across the desert toward Mexico, where only a tinge of light lingered in the sky, lying across the horizon like the last thread of day.

Then it vanished and stars appeared, numerous and vivid. A coyote cried. He heard the rustling of a large animal, probably a mule deer, running through the sage. Will thought about Rachael, somewhere out there, maybe alive, maybe not, and he knew he wasn't even close to the pain yet. But he could sense it lurking on the outskirts. It would be waiting for him in the morning when he opened his eyes to face this nightmare all over again.

A match flared. Swicegood lighted a cigarette, blew out the flame. He licked his thumb and forefinger and squelched the heat from the glowing match head before flicking it into the grass. He took a deep drag and sent a train of smoke curling into the desert.

"I was wondering, Mr. Innis, is there someone who could watch your daughter for a little while?" Will had been leaning on the fence. Now he turned and faced the detective. His head wasn't clear. It took a moment to locate the exact words he wanted.

"Why would she need to be watched?"

"I thought you and I could ride over to the station. Have a little talk."

The air between them turned electric.

"What about?"

"I'll be waiting in my car. It's parked behind the news truck with the satellite on top. You go make sure your daughter's taken care of, then come on out."

Will knocked back the whiskey and set the empty glass on the fence post. The darkness seemed to tilt. He felt clammy, sweat beading on his face.

"Shit." He staggered ten feet away and retched into the grass, stood hunched over, looking back toward the house at all the silhouettes moving like ghosts behind the windows. He took in the dark stillness of the desert, the wet chill of the grass blades brushing at his bare ankles. He wiped his mouth. "You're serious?" he asked.

"I am."

"Do I need to bring a lawyer?"

"I don't see why at this point. I just need you to answer a few questions. Help me sort something out. So, my car. Five minutes."

SEVEN

Javier wanted coffee—strong and scalding—and as if his desire had conjured its own object, the sign for a freestanding Starbucks appeared a quarter mile ahead, beside a gas station just off the interstate.

It made him nervous, leaving the woman alone, but she was reasonably secure, more than reasonably drugged, and if he was going to reach Idaho without drifting off and killing them both, caffeine would be required.

Into Starbucks and the intimate odor of the beans and the chromed shine of mugs, French presses, and espresso machines as world music throbbed through speakers in the ceiling.

He counted nine people in line ahead of him.

Rachael floated in a warm, dark sea. It seemed to take years just to open her eyes, and when she did, the world was awash in blinding streaks of light, echoes of jumbled sounds. She moaned softly, though not from pain, but a burning euphoria.

She sat in the front seat of the Escalade, restrained only by a seat belt. The car was stationary but idling. She managed to rotate her head toward the empty driver's seat.

Looking through the tinted window in front of her, she tried to get a handle on her surroundings, but the slightest movement blurred light and distorted objects beyond recognition. With her head swimming, it took extraordinary willpower to keep her thoughts from derailing into dreamy and meaningless directions. She possessed a dim awareness that she was in trouble, but she couldn't remember what kind, or the events that had preceded this moment. All she knew was that she needed to get out of the car before the driver came back.

As Rachael stilled herself, the outside world eased into focus. She made out the bright lights of a familiar chain, the Escalade parked near the entrance.

Inside, she spotted a line to the cash register. The man who had been driving the Escalade stood at the end, watching her.

From his place in line, Javier had a view through the storefront glass, saw the woman was no longer draped unconscious in the front passenger seat, but struggling to sit up.

A customer collected her drink, the line shuffling forward.

The next couple ordered lattes and items from the pastry case, beside which he now stood, watching the hands of the heavyset barista reaching for two pieces of crumb cake.

He glanced outside. The woman was looking down, having probably noticed what he'd done to the seat belt.

Next customer, a truck driver.

"Just coffee, darlin'."

Good man.

Then a woman after some high-end water, a twenty-second transaction, swipe of the credit card, Javier feeling a jolt of anticipatory excitement at the caffeine coming his way and getting back on the road again, as that redneck with the braids loved to sing.

She reached to undo the seat belt, but the button had been wrapped several times in duct tape. Too groggy and weak to tear it off, she lifted her arm instead, and on the fourth attempt, she touched the switch on her door that lowered the automatic window.

The tinted glass descended quickly into the door. Night air swept in, reeking of gas and oil. In the near distance, an interstate droned with the ceaseless hum of traffic. The air was far too cool for southern Arizona, and through the fog of the drug, she wondered how far she was from home.

Just a family ahead of him now—mom and dad, teenage girl, young boy who'd been stealing glances at Jav ever since he'd walked into the store.

Dad: coffee.

Boy: hot chocolate.

Girl: latte.

Javier glanced at his Escalade, saw the window sliding down on the passenger side.

Mom: "I'll have an iced, skinny, venti, ten-pump chai latte, hold the whip."

Javier glared in the general direction of the register as a tremor of murderous irritation pulsed between his temples.

The barista, grinning, said, "Could you say that one more time, and just a tad slower."

"Iced. Skinny. Venti. Chai latte. Ten pumps. Hold the whip."

"I have to charge you for the extra pumps."

"That's fine."

"It's my second day, so let me be sure. When you say 'skinny,' you mean—"

"Nonfat milk."

The barista grimaced, bracing for the deliverance of bad news. "We just ran out."

"Oh no." Mom slumped in devastation as Javier calculated that his BP had risen to 130/90, the tips of his ears tingling.

"We have two percent."

"How about one?"

"Sorry."

"What if you made it with water?"

"Water?"

"Instead of steamed milk."

"Um, I've never heard of doing that, but I guess I could. You're the customer, right?"

It wasn't going to stay inside like he'd hoped, and he knew enough about himself to realize that if he just stood there watching the fuse burn down, he'd end up doing something combustive and reckless, like that time in Juárez.

Javier opened his mouth, not to say what he really wanted, just to cool himself off, a quick pressure release to get things back to baseline.

"Have you ever tried coffee?" he asked brightly, the family turning as one to see who'd spoken. Javier smiled, felt the hate exuding through his teeth, hoped it overshot them. "They have their Anniversary Blend available tonight. And all you have to say is, 'Anniversary Blend, please.' None of this complicated ordering. And do you know what? All the barista has to do is take a cup, or a mug if it's for here, and fill it up. And then you are done and the next person can order."

"I'm taking a long time, aren't I?" the mom said. "I'm sorry."

"This is your favorite drink?"

"Guilty as charged. I have two chai lattes a day."

"Ah."

"May I buy your coffee? For the inconvenience?" He couldn't tell if she meant that she was really sorry, or that he was a giant asshole, but he admired her for treading the line so well, even as he despised her.

"No, thank you."

A family emerged from Starbucks, carrying a tray of drinks.

Rachael leaned over and hung her arms out the window, resting her chin against the strip of weatherproofing. She raised an arm, let it drop with a bang against the door.

The adults had already passed by without noticing her.

She raised her arm, let it bang again. The young boy glanced back, and when he saw her, he stopped, his eyes narrowing.

Help me. He cocked his head and stared at her. Rachael's face was lying against the door, her skin milky, sweating, her eyes crossed.

"Help me," she mouthed.

The boy approached the door.

"Help me," she whispered. "I'm not supposed to be here."

"You look funny," he said. "What's wrong with your eyes?"

Rachael fought to keep them from rolling back in her head.

"Donnie, let's go, pal! You're holding up progress!"

"Dad, there's something wrong with this woman!"

Oh thank you. Thank you. Rachael was on the brink of losing consciousness again, the heroin raging through her blood. She lost the boy to swirls of trailing light, made her eyes bring him back into focus. He looked to be Devlin's age, and now a man was standing beside him, looking down at her, his brow furrowed. He was soft and round, a young father yet to shed his baby fat, filling out his khaki shorts and yellow polo shirt. His mouth was moving, but it took her a moment to connect the movement of his lips to the sounds they made.

". . . need a doctor or something?" *Get me out of here.* ". . . person who's driving you inside?" *Oh God. Please.* ". . . can't understand a word you're saying."

The brown-skinned, blue-eyed man who'd taken her walked up behind the boy and his father.

Rachael tried to lift her eyes from his boots—they appeared to have been fashioned from the pebbled black-and-yellow skin of Gila monsters.

The boy said, "What's wrong with her?"

Javier smiled. "It's a personal matter, son." He stepped between them and gently lifted Rachael's head off the door, kissing her cheek as he did. "Let's go back to sleep now, honey." Rachael moaned, fighting him with everything she had, which wasn't anything. He opened the door, raised the window, shut the door. When he turned back around, the boy and his father were still standing there. The window lowered again.

Rachael said, "Help me," and groaned loudly enough for everyone to hear.

"What's going on here?" the boy's father asked.

Javier sighed, looked down for a moment, studying an oil stain on the concrete.

"What's going on," he said finally, "is that my wife is addicted to heroin. She's loaded right now. This far"—he held his thumb and forefinger an inch apart—"from a lethal overdose. I'm driving her to a detox program in Salt Lake."

"Oh, I'm sorry. That must be so difficult."

"It is. I can only take it a day at a time."

"We're sorry to have disturbed her. Come on, Donnie."

"But she asked for help, Dad."

Javier squatted down, stared at the boy.

He'd already identified all of the exterior surveillance cameras.

"I want you to remember this night always," he said. "Because that"— he jerked his thumb back toward the window as Rachael banged her arm against the side of the door—"is what drugs can do to you."

"God bless," the boy's father said, and he took his son by the shoulders and guided him back toward a minivan parked on the far side of the gas pumps.

Javier climbed behind the steering wheel of the Escalade. He looked at Rachael, who was slumped forward into the dash.

"Do you have any idea what you just did?" he said.

Inside the minivan, Rick Carter was distributing the Starbucks beverages to his wife and children. He had a long night of driving ahead of him, and with a little luck and no delays, they'd arrive in Albuquerque some time tomorrow afternoon.

He'd just swallowed his first sip when he heard a knock at his window.

He turned, saw the man from the Escalade standing there, felt a small knot blossom in his stomach. For half a second, he debated just putting the car into gear and pulling away.

"What do you think he wants?" his wife asked.

"Guess we'll find out." He lowered his window several inches. "May I help you?"

Javier glanced at the children in the backseat, at the man's pretty wife. The car smelled of Starbucks.

"Do you have a cell phone with you?" Javier asked.

"Yeah, do you need to—"

"Have you called nine one one?"

"Um, no, why would—"

"You're sure?"

"Look, I don't understand what you're—"

Javier jerked the door open and shot the man in the face, fired two quick bursts into the backseat to silence the screaming, and stared at the woman, who'd crushed her recycled cup in her left hand, the burning chai steaming off her fist.

"Enjoying your iced, skinny, venti, ten-pump chai latte, hold the whip?"

He shot her in the throat and shut the door.

EIGHT

They didn't speak on the short ride to the Pima County Sheriff's Department, and the building was practically deserted when they arrived. Swicegood led Will past the unattended reception desk, down a hallway, and stopped in front of a door with stenciled white letters that read INTERVIEW 1. Inside were a small table, three chairs, and a tape recorder. A video camera angled down from one of the corners in the ceiling, the lens pointed at the table.

Swicegood said, "Get you some water? Coffee?"

"I just want to get this over with and get back to my daughter."

"Sure." Swicegood eased down into a chair across from Will, tossed a thin file on the table. Will was sobering up fast, his heart beating wildly in his chest. "I'm going to record this," Swicegood said, starting the tape recorder. "You're aware of your rights?"

"Of course I am." Swicegood went through them anyway, and when he'd finished, Will said, "I waive those rights."

Swicegood leaned forward. "You're an officer of the court, correct?"

"You know I am."

Swicegood smiled. "I wonder if you could just clear something up for me. Your wife never came home last night, correct?"

"That's right."

"You said she was working at a clinic in Sonoyta."

"Yeah."

"What time was she due back?"

"Between ten and ten-thirty."

"Okay, so here's my question. At what point does a loving husband become concerned when his wife doesn't come home?"

"I don't understand what—"

"When she's an hour late?"

"Look—"

"Two? Three? Four hours?"

"Okay, I see where you're going—"

"I suppose for you, it's somewhere beyond the six hour-mark, but we'll never know, because you never called nine one one, did you?"

"Would you let me explain?"

"Please do."

"I was supposed to do closing arguments at a trial this morning. I was up late last night working on them."

"How late?"

"I fell asleep after ten, at my desk. When I woke up, it was four. I went looking for her in the house. I was horrified. Highway Patrol showed up before I had a chance to call nine one one."

Swicegood inched closer. "Will, I've been a detective going on thirty years now. And crimes? They're always emotional. You've represented some of the lowlifes I've put away, and you know that in the heat of the moment, when rage and adrenaline take over, criminals do stupid, stupid things. So I just have one question for you. Did you make any mistakes?"

"I don't know what you're—"

"You think you did it perfectly, don't you?"

"Excuse me?"

"You've got a million-point-five life-insurance policy on your wife."

"My daughter has cystic fibrosis. If something were to—"

"I'm sorry to hear that, but still, quite a chunk of change. How was your marriage, Will?"

"Good. Great."

"Really? Because I spoke with the next-door neighbors this evening. The Tomlins told me you two put on quite a show on your back porch several nights ago. Shouting, swearing, the works."

"You've never had a fight with your wife? Congratulations."

"What was it about? The fight."

"Money."

"Money."

"Things are tight. You have any idea what health insurance costs for someone like my daughter, who has a terminal disease? It can stress a marriage."

"Well, it won't be a problem anymore, will it?"

"What?"

"Money."

Swicegood got up without a word, turned off the tape recorder, left the room. When the door closed, Will looked at his watch: 10:47 P.M. His hands shook. His throat closed off.

He's trying to pin this on you. You could lose your wife and *daughter.* His eyes ran over as it hit him—Devi could become an orphan. What broke him more than anything, even the prospect of prison and what would happen to someone like him on the inside, was the possibility that he wouldn't be there for his daughter when the disease finally claimed her. The reality that Devlin would probably die within the next five years was something he looked square in the eye every day. But what he imagined as he sat in that interview room was a dismal morning several years in the future at the maximum-security facility in Florence. A guard would walk down the long corridor to his cell, rouse him, tell him through the bars that his daughter had passed away in the night. He couldn't fathom anything worse than that. *Devi is not dying alone. You cannot let that happen. She is your purpose. Your heart.*

The door to the interview room opened. Swicegood sat down across from Will, set a steaming Styrofoam cup of coffee on the table.

He said, "Before we continue, let me say this. This is my job. I operate on instinct. Go where it says go. That's what I'm doing right now. If you didn't have anything to do with this, I am so, so sorry. All right, back to business."

He started the recorder, seemed softer, calmer. Will straightened himself in the chair.

"Look at me, Will." Everything faded into a distorted darkness except for Swicegood's eyes. They worked like magnets on Will's, holding his gaze, his focus, with such intensity that it hurt him to blink. "Somewhere inside of you," the detective said, "you want to tell me the truth. Been doing this a long time. I've seen it in many pairs of eyes, and I see it in yours." His voice had dropped in pitch and evened out into a soothing monotone that might have lulled Will toward sleep were it not for those blue magnets. "Do you know how good it would feel to just say it, Will? The relief? You know how much easier it would make things for you and your daughter? You're young. You talk to me now, we might have some wiggle room with the DA." Will felt the gravitational force of the detective's eyes trying to coax something out of him. The air buzzed with Swicegood's desire to hear it, and Will suddenly understood how a person could make a false confession. Anything to make that buzzing stop. "But once I've got a body, Will, it's over for you. Life. Or maybe they strap you to the execution table in Florence, put a needle in your arm. I hope you buried her deep, because the coyotes will find her. Sniff out the rot. Dig her up. And someone will stumble across the bones, and that'll be that. But I don't need the body. You know why? Because everyone knows she's dead. And the little secret about juries? About society? They want closure. Wrongs righted. Threads tied up. People like you swept away into prison, out of sight, so they don't have to think about depravity while they're tucking their little ones into bed at night. You want to take a chance on a jury? You want to stand there on verdict day, your knees quaking, your life, your daughter's, in the hands of twelve strangers who might be willing to trade reasonable doubt for closure? You up for that, Will?"

Will stood up, trembling with rage. He didn't know if his wife was alive or dead, and this man was accusing him of her murder.

"I didn't kill my wife, and I don't know where any of this is coming from. You charging me, Teddy?"

"Where'd you bury her?"

"Are you charging me?"

Swicegood cleared his throat. "I'll be talking to the DA first thing in the—"

"Then I'm done here. Am I free to go?"

Swicegood chewed his bottom lip. "For the moment."

"Take me home right now. I don't want my daughter waking up and not finding me there."

Swicegood stopped the recorder. When he pushed his chair back, the Styrofoam cup tipped over, black coffee spilling across the table, falling in a thin dark stream onto the floor.

NINE

Will whispered into his daughter's ear, "Wake up, Devi." She stirred, turned away from him. He sat her up in bed. In the blue glow of the night-light, he watched her eyes open slowly.

She looked around the room, then looked at her father. "Where's Mom?"

"She isn't here, honey. Now listen, this is important. We're gonna get you dressed now."

"But it isn't morning yet."

"I know. We're going on a special trip."

"Where?"

"No more questions."

In the darkness, Will helped his daughter dress.

"I'm going to carry you," he said. "I need you to be very quiet. Don't make a sound."

He picked her up, walked to the bedroom door, and slowly pulled it open. The hallway was dark, quiet. He crept down it, heard Rachael's mother snoring in the guest room.

Rachael's sister, Elise, was asleep on the sofa in the den. The creak of the front door opening made her shift, but she didn't wake.

Three A.M is one of the few comfortable hours in Ajo in the summertime, a cool, fleeting reprieve. The Beamer's trunk was already packed with suitcases. Will put Devlin in the front seat, buckled her in. He climbed behind the wheel, shifted into neutral, let the car roll silently to the end of the driveway before shoving the key into the ignition.

"Where are we going, Daddy?" Will looked at his daughter, shook his head in disbelief at all that had changed in twenty-four hours, at how quickly, when the wrong stars align, it all comes apart. *You will not die alone.*

"I don't know yet," he said. And he turned the key and put the car into gear, driving slowly and without headlights through the subdivision.

The highway north out of Ajo was empty and shining in the moonlight. Aside from his wallet and a suitcase of clothes, he'd taken only one other thing—Rachael's college sweatshirt.

They would not see their home again.

TEN

Two days later, Rachael awoke on a small, hard mattress. She sat up in a tiny room, barely the size of a walk-in closet, and illuminated by only a single bare lightbulb that swung from the ceiling.

Her head pounded and her mouth was dry, but she felt alert again.

The walls and the floor were covered in thick yellow foam. She saw five jugs of water in a corner, and beside them, a box filled with bags of potato chips, apples, candy bars, and packs of crackers. She heard a humming sound beyond the soundproofed walls.

She stood up, found it difficult to keep her balance, as if the floor were shifting beneath her. She looked at the foam walls again and thought, *I've been committed. I imagined the kidnapping. The crowbar through the window. I've gone mad.*

Rachael grabbed a jug of water and carried it back over to the mattress. She sat down and took a long drink, wondering if they were watching her right now.

But if I'm in the asylum, why am I still wearing this black suit?

There came a sudden blast that sounded vaguely like a foghorn. It blew once more, and as she considered it, there was something about the constant humming that unnerved her, and the way this place shifted beneath her. She looked up at the ceiling. No soundproofing foam there. Just shiny metal. And the dimensions of the room suddenly made perfect sense. So did the subtle rocking movement, the humming, the low drone, the horn. *This isn't a psych ward. I'm in the trailer of an eighteen-wheeler.*

She wept, and her body shook with tremors.

Ghosts Present

ELEVEN

The man who was now Joe Foster floored the old Chevy down the hill into town. It was mid-October, the Colorado sky blue-screen blue, fresh snow gleaming above twelve thousand feet in the La Platas, the aspen and cottonwoods turning gold across the foothills. Five miles west, the profile of Mesa Verde shimmered in the Friday-afternoon sunlight. He could see the glint of cars crawling south on the high road that snaked through the park.

He drove into the small town of Mancos, pulled his pickup over to the curb, and cut the engine. It was still a few minutes shy of 3:00 P.M. and so quiet inside the truck, he could hear the trees chattering around him. A gold aspen leaf fell on the windshield wiper, twitched for a moment until a breeze pushed it up the glass and airborne again.

She would have liked this little town, he thought.

He spotted his daughter moving with the throng of students down the stone steps of the K–12 school. She was walking with two friends, a backpack slung over her shoulder, caught up in some breathless adolescent debate. The group of girls stepped off the sidewalk into the grass and formed a tight circle. Making plans, he imagined. Promising to call one another. Propagating silly rumors.

He watched his daughter through the cracked windshield. He could have watched her all afternoon. The truth was, he'd never expected her to reach her sixteenth year. For a long time, he'd dedicated himself to preparing for the worst-possible outcome, including plans to end himself when she was gone. But then something had happened. Or actually, not happened. She *hadn't* died. She got sick several times a year. She'd been scary sick twice, but she always bounced back. The cocktail of meds and the chest physical therapy were working, and every day she was healthy felt like a sentence commuted, an execution stayed.

Now she was coming toward the truck, but as he slipped the key into the ignition, a woman intercepted his daughter on the sidewalk.

He sat up. His daughter had stopped, and she was talking to a tall woman in a navy skirt, white blouse, the matching jacket folded over her arm. His daughter shook her head. He couldn't hear what they were saying. He reached to open the door, but his daughter was on her own again, moving quickly toward the truck, the woman walking in the opposite direction. She pulled open the squeaky door and climbed inside.

"Hey, baby girl." She'd picked out a new name, but he rarely said it, called her "baby girl" or "sweetie," or nothing.

"Hey, Dad."

"Who was that woman you were just talking to?"

"She didn't say."

"What'd she want?"

"Asked me my name, if I lived around here."

He cranked the engine, the noisy truck now vibrating beneath them.

"Why'd she want to know that?"

"I don't know. I blew her off, told her I had to go. You think she's a cop?"

"I don't know."

"Can I drive home?"

"Not today, honey." He shifted into drive and pulled out into the street, cruising slowly past the school, looking for the woman who'd approached his daughter. "What color hair did she have?"

"Brown. She was pretty." The upperclassmen were flooding out of the building now. They were taller. It made it difficult to spot the woman. "What's wrong, Dad?"

She wasn't there. Just a bunch of kids.

"You know we have to be very careful," he said.

"Are we gonna leave again?"

"I don't know yet, sweetie. Not tonight at least." He spun the steering wheel, did a 180 in the street, and headed back up the hill, out of town, toward home.

TWELVE

The farmhouse stood in a grove of blue spruce, a mile and a half south of
town. There was a little pasture out back, and the Mancos River formed
the east border of the property. They could hear it from the house during
spring runoff.

Now it was full-on dusk. Through the open windows, the night air swept
in, carrying the scent of decaying leaves and sour apples and the odor of a
dairy farm.

The girl got the pillows from the game closet while he queued up the
DVD. They were near the end of *Vertigo*. Movies helped to make the therapy more bearable. They'd seen more than thirty Hitchcocks together this
way. The man sat down behind his daughter and she leaned forward into a
pillow and watched Jimmy Stewart kissing Kim Novak in the eerie green
light of the hotel room.

With cupped hands, he began to pound on her back. After five minutes,
he told her to cough. She switched positions, now lying on her side.

Not long after she was born, he and his wife had started calling her their
"salty baby," since whenever they kissed her forehead, they'd taste salt. His
wife happened to mention this to the pediatrician, and he promptly ordered
a sweat test, which came back positive. They had no idea, but overly salty
sweat is a major indicator of cystic fibrosis.

The girl was diagnosed when she was two years old, and every day for
the last fourteen years, the man had given his daughter CPT, chest physical
therapy. The therapy broke up mucus in her lungs, made it easier for her to
breathe, helped to stave off infection. CPT had long since become just another part of the routine, like brushing their teeth.

When they were finished, the girl sat at the table in the kitchen, working
through her geometry problems. The man went outside. The truck had been

running loud and hot, and he figured an oil change was long overdue. He crawled under the truck and lay on his back, struggling to unscrew the oil cap. Sometimes a car would pass on the nearby country road, but otherwise, the silence remained undisturbed.

The night grew colder as the moon rose over the foothills. An occasional breeze stirred the firs. From the next farm down, he could hear cows groaning at the moon, their bells clanging.

He finally got the cap off, smelled the scorched oil as it drained into the pan.

Another car was coming, which made three in the last ten minutes. Busy night.

The car was slowing now. He heard it stop at the end of his driveway. A city car. A rental perhaps, not the big rumbling gas guzzlers most of his neighbors owned.

The tires began to turn. *What the hell?* He wriggled himself out from under the truck and came to his feet, stood there shielding his eyes from the headlights as the car rolled toward him down the gravel drive.

It stopped behind the Chevy. The engine quit. The headlights died. For a moment, he couldn't see a thing, temporarily blinded. A door opened. Slammed. Footsteps moved toward him. The man thinking, *Now you've fucked up. Should have left this afternoon. Packed a suitcase, gotten the hell out of here.* He backed away as his eyes readjusted to the darkness.

"You blinded me with your brights," he said, "so I can't see too well right now. Who's there?" The footsteps stopped. He could see the shape of his visitor now, light from the front porch falling across her face.

It was the woman who had approached his daughter after school.

"Sorry to blind you," she said. "I must have driven past your mailbox three times before I saw it."

"Who are you?"

She offered her hand. "Kalyn Sharp." She was his height, maybe a few years younger, with straight brown hair, pronounced cheekbones. He couldn't determine the color of her eyes in the poor light, and he didn't take her hand.

"What do you want?"

"Are you William Innis?"

Surging blast of adrenaline. "No."

"Well, I have a picture of Mr. Innis here in my purse. You could be twins."

"You need to leave." He turned away from the woman, started back toward the house.

"Mr. Innis!" she called after him. "Please!"

He went inside, let the screen door bang shut behind him.

"Who's out there?" his daughter asked.

"Go finish your homework in your room." She recognized something in her father's voice—nonnegotiable fire. The girl gathered up her textbook and notebook and headed down the squeaky hardwood floor of the hallway.

The man stood at the kitchen sink, ran the tap, scrubbed the oil and grease from his hands with hot water and soap, trying to piece together exactly what he would do, what they would need to take, what they could leave. As he looked up to see if the car was backing down the driveway, there was a knock on the door.

He walked over, stared through the screen at the woman standing on his porch.

"Out here in the boondocks," he said, "when someone tells you to get the hell off their property, it's usually a wise thing to—" Now she was holding something up against the screen, and when he saw it, his stomach turned.

FBI credentials. A crippling weakness spread into his knees.

What are you willing to do to stay with your daughter?

"Relax," she said. "If I were here to take you in, you'd already be in handcuffs."

"Then what do you want?"

"I believe you're innocent, Mr. Innis." Her words stopped him cold.

"And why is that?"

"Because your wife . . . Rachael. She wasn't the first. Or the last."

THIRTEEN

As Will filled a pot with water from the tap, he glanced over his shoulder at the FBI agent seated at the kitchen table.

"How'd you find us?"

"Year and a half chasing down your aliases. What are you using now?"

"Joe Foster." The pot was full. He set it on the stove, turned up the gas, took a seat at the kitchen table across from Kalyn. The woman had draped her coat over one of the chairs, laid her briefcase on the hardwood floor. "Which field office you out of?" Will asked.

"Phoenix. So, I've been dying to ask—why'd you run?"

"My daughter has cystic fibrosis. I had to assume her mother was dead, and this Ajo detective had a giant hard-on for me right out of the gate. I figured there was a decent chance I was going to be charged. I don't know how familiar you are with CF, but it's a terminal disease. Most people who have it never see their thirtieth birthday. I wasn't taking a chance that my daughter would die without me there by her side."

"But she's okay now?"

"We've had three good years. That's not to say she won't get sick again."

"How are you making a living?"

"Web design. I work out of my house."

"Must be hard, knowing what everyone thinks of you. What they think you did."

"Look, we have a new life now, and it's pretty good. I know what happened the night my wife went missing. My conscience is clear."

"You shouldn't have run."

"If you aren't here to arrest me, what is it you want?"

Kalyn reached down and lifted her briefcase. She opened it, pulled out a manila folder. The first thing she handed Will was a map—New Mexico,

Arizona, SoCal. Red X's had been marked in four locations across the Southwest.

"What's this?"

Kalyn scooted her chair beside his, laid down a photograph of a woman smiling, with ski slopes in the background. Reflective sunglasses. Enormous down jacket.

"Suzanne Tyrpak. Disappeared in July of 2000 between Gallup and Albuquerque." She dropped another photograph on the table. "Jill Dillon." She pointed to an X on the southern border of Arizona. "Disappeared in August 2001, outside of Nogales." Another photograph. Will's wife stared at him. Beautiful, devious Rachael smile. He remembered taking the picture on the south rim of the Grand Canyon. "Rachael Innis. Disappeared in Organ Pipe Cactus National Monument, July 2002. Here's the last one." She laid a photograph carefully beside Rachael's picture. "Lucy Dahl. Disappeared August 2004 on the interstate between El Paso and Tucson."

A strange silence settled in the house. Chimes clanging in discordance on the front porch. Will feeling like it wasn't just Kalyn and him in the kitchen. Ghosts present. He glanced down at the photographs, lined up side by side, and a chill pushed through him.

"Oh my God," he said.

"You noticed."

"These women could be sisters."

"I know. The dark eyes. Curly black hair."

"Is that a coincidence?"

"I don't know, but I'll show you what isn't." Kalyn took four more photographs from the folder, spread them out. A Lexus. Honda Civic. Ford Explorer. Rachael's Jeep Cherokee. In each photograph, the driver's side window was busted out. "You can't see it here, but the right front tire on all of these cars was punctured."

"So this is like a, um—"

"An MO. Yes."

"Were any of these women ever found?"

Kalyn shook her head. "Your water's boiling."

Will got up from the table and took two mugs from the cabinet.

"I have peppermint, green tea, and Earl Grey."

"Peppermint, please." Will dropped the tea bags into the mugs, and as he poured the boiling water slowly over them, Kalyn said, "I think I know who took these women."

Will set the pot of water back on the stove, turned off the gas, his hands trembling now.

He stared at the floor and took deep breaths. "You think? Or you know?"

"I'm about eighty percent sure. Let me ask you something. You were a defense attorney. You somewhat familiar with how the cartels operate?"

"Sure."

"Ever heard of the Alphas?"

Will carried the cups of tea over to the table and sat down. "No, what's that?"

"There used to be an antidrug paratroop and intelligence battalion called the Special Air Mobile Force Group. These were Mexican soldiers, but they were trained at the School of the Americas. In 1991, a large contingent of this elite military force deserted and went into business with the drug traffickers. I guess the profit margins were too lucrative. Today, they're known as the Alphas, a gang of high-paid mercenaries, primarily tasked with protecting loads of cocaine, heroin, and marijuana smuggled into America by the Gulf Cartel. No one knows how many there are, but estimates run from one hundred to two hundred members. They're superbly trained, and they operate more like commandos than your run-of-the-mill cartel thugs. They're fiercely loyal. Their handiwork is obvious. State-of-the-art weapons. Military-style cover and concealment tactics. And they're brutal. Currently offering fifty-thousand-dollar bounties for the assassination of U.S. law-enforcement officers.

"Now I have contacts and informants in every border town in the Southwest, and I've learned that a handful of the Alphas dabble in human trafficking. Let me tell you, information about them is damn near impossible to come by. My informant in Nogales wouldn't even say this one guy's name out loud. He insisted on writing it on a piece of paper. And he wouldn't have done that, but he's a tweaker. I bought this name for two grand."

"What name?"

"Javier Estrada. You know it?" Will shook his head. "You sure? You never represented this guy or—"

"No. You have a photo?"

She shook her head.

"And what makes you think these Alphas are involved?"

"Couple of things." Kalyn sipped her tea. "First off, there was something about the crime scenes that always bothered me. No blood, and aside from the bashed windows, no sign of rape or violence. And it seemed to have been done very professionally. Plus, the bodies never turned up. That always bugged me. If these women were just killed and dumped, wouldn't you think that at least one body might have surfaced by now? Serial killers tend to want their victims discovered, but these women literally vanished."

Will leaned back in his chair, blew ripples across the surface of his green tea.

"What makes you so certain it's this guy? Javier." He didn't like the way the name felt as it rolled off his tongue.

"My informant used to be a mule for the Gulf Cartel. He worked with Mr. Estrada on several assignments. Said that once, over a bottle of mescal, Javier told him about snatching a woman on I-40, between Gallup and Albuquerque."

"Suzanne Tyrpak."

"Yeah."

"So why hasn't he been arrested?"

"It's a bit more complicated than it sounds."

Will sipped his tea. "You need something from me," he said.

Kalyn nodded. "You've said you don't recognize his name, and I believe you. But maybe if you saw him, something would click. I need you to come to Phoenix with me and ID him when we pick him up."

"What about the outstanding charges against me?" Will asked.

"I'm working on it. Officially, we aren't having this discussion, and I never came here."

"Why is that?"

"Not everyone in the Phoenix Field Office is so gung ho to devote money and manpower to these murders. There's more pressing business, and since this isn't directly drug-related, it's a second-tier priority."

"Have you contacted the other women's families?"

"Tyrpak's husband killed himself three years ago. Dillon's husband won't talk to me. He's got a new wife, new baby, wants nothing to do with the past."

"I can understand that."

Kalyn gathered up the photographs and the map and shoved them into the manila folder, dropped it all in her briefcase. She stood up.

"So when would this happen?" Will asked.

"I was kind of hoping we could go in the morning."

"Tomorrow? That's sooner than—"

"You're still a fugitive. What's to say you won't disappear tonight when I leave?"

"I thought you believed me."

"I do. Not sure I'm ready to put my career on the line for it, though. Besides, would you rather sit around waiting, anticipating?"

"I'd have to bring my daughter."

"Fine."

"That truck out there is all I've got, and it won't make the trip to Phoenix and back."

"You can ride down with me. I'm staying at the Mesa Verde Inn. I'll come by at seven to pick you up."

Will stood. "We'll be here."

Kalyn lifted her briefcase, reached out, and this time, Will took her hand.

"You're still tortured," she said.

"Yeah."

"Comb the Internet for news items about her every day, don't you? Anonymous calls to police stations across the Southwest to see if any bodies have turned up?"

"I just need to know what happened to her, and how it happened. It kills me not knowing where her body is. It's stupid, I know. It shouldn't matter, but it does. You know what I mean?"

Something in Kalyn's eyes told him that she did.

"It was good to meet you, William Innis."

"Will."

He walked her out to the car.

When she was gone, he stood in the driveway in the dark, breathing in the cold chill of the autumn night.

Then he crawled under the truck to finish changing the oil.

FOURTEEN

Will knocked on the door.

His daughter yelled, "*What?*" and he walked in, saw her sprawled on her back on the bed, staring at him upside down, the cordless phone held to her chest. "What?" she whispered.

"I need to talk to you. Now."

"About that woman?" she mouthed.

He nodded.

She brought the phone back to her ear, said, "Christie, I gotta go. Okay. Okay. You tell me what he says. Bye, sweetie."

Will pulled the chair out from the desk and sat down.

"Who was that woman?" she asked.

"Her name's Kalyn Sharp, and she's an FBI agent."

His daughter sat up quickly. "Are they taking you, Dad?"

"No, honey, no. She believes me."

"It's about Mom."

"She thinks she knows who killed her."

She took a sharp intake of breath. "Who?"

"This man . . . look, that's not important. She thinks maybe I've seen him before, back when we lived in Ajo. She wants me to try to ID him. So we're all going down to Phoenix first thing in the morning. We'll ride with Ms. Sharp. Honey, it's okay."

His daughter turned over and wept into her pillow. Will climbed in bed with her. He pulled her into his lap, ran his fingers through her hair.

After awhile, she rolled over and wiped her eyes, her face red, tear-streaked.

"This FBI woman really believes you didn't hurt Mom?"

"Yeah," Will said. "She knows I didn't."

She sniffled, wiped her nose.

"I want to ask you something," Will said, "and you can tell me the honest truth. I won't be mad, no matter what you say."

"What?"

"Did you . . . do you ever wonder if I had something to do with what happened to Mom?"

His daughter stared at the poster on the ceiling, at the two lava lamps glowing on her desk, at the piles of clothing scattered across the floor. She pried off the black curls that had stuck to the tears on her face and finally looked her father in the eye.

"It would be a lie if I said I never wondered."

He nodded, shoved back the emotion those words had detonated inside of him. What hurt him more than anything was the fear he knew his daughter must have lived with, wondering if he was this monster, responsible for her mother's death.

"That's okay," he said. "I understand."

"I only mean that *sometimes* I wonder. Not that I think you did it. And I haven't wondered in a long time."

"Baby girl," he said, "look in my eyes." They'd sheeted over with tears. "I'm not sure if I ever said this to you, but I'm going to say it now. I did not kill your mother. My wife."

"I know, Dad."

"I loved her. And if I thought for a second there was anything I could do to get her back, I would."

"I believe you."

They embraced. As they pulled away, she said, "Is there a chance Mom's still alive?"

"I don't think so, sweetheart."

"But anything's possible, right?"

"It's been five years. I don't want you walking around with your hopes up, okay?"

The phone rang. She grabbed it, glanced at the caller ID. "I have to take this, Dad."

Will chuckled at that. "I love you, Devlin," he said.

"Dad," she whispered, "you just said my old name."

"I know. It's okay now." Will got up and walked out of the room, shut the door softly behind him as Devlin said, "Hey, Lisa, what up, girl?"

He walked through the old farmhouse, closing windows. There would be a heavy frost in the morning.

Just the possibility of closure, of returning to some semblance of his old life, thrilled him. He hadn't seen his parents, his sister, or any of his friends since he and Devlin had fled Arizona, and the pain their disappearance must have caused was always with him. Every day, he'd check friends' blogs, Facebook and MySpace pages, Google his and Devlin's name to see if people still searched for them. If they were still mentioned. Still thought of. Still remembered and missed.

And he desperately missed his work, his real work—practicing law. He missed being in a courtroom, missed picking a jury during voir dire and the nerves of verdict day.

Though he knew it wouldn't return Rachael to him, he still wanted all the vestiges of his old life back. Perhaps going down to Phoenix with Kalyn would be a step in that direction.

He sat at the kitchen table, sipping his cold green tea, couldn't stop thinking, *Tomorrow, you face the man who killed Rachael.* He was nervous, but more than anything, just anxious to put it all behind him. Figured he and Devlin were due a little peace.

Jav

FIFTEEN

A t 2:30 P.M., after a seven-hour drive down from the high country of southwest Colorado, Kalyn pulled her Buick Regal beside an overflowing
Dumpster and turned off the engine. They all stepped out into the potent
October heat, crossed the parking lot, and stopped at the cluster of mail-
boxes so Kalyn could collect her mail.

Four cinder-block buildings boxed in the dirt courtyard where Devlin
stood, each containing eight apartments, four on top, four below.

A rusted swing set had collapsed nearby. One roller skate and a deflated
soccer ball sat in a sandless sandbox. Between the constant drone of air con-
ditioners and the roar of the nearby interstate, peace and quiet did not appear to thrive here.

They approached the north building and entered the stairwell.

A jet airliner thundered overhead on its descent toward Phoenix Sky
Harbor International Airport.

Their footfalls clanged up fourteen metal steps and they emerged onto
the open second-floor walkway, where Kalyn stopped at the third door.
Apparently, the brass lettering had fallen off or been stolen, because the
number 22 was scrawled above the peephole in red Magic Marker.

She unlocked the dead bolt and led them in. Even from the foyer, Devlin
could tell it wasn't much of a home. Small living room. Smaller kitchen.
White walls in desperate need of several coats of paint. Cramped hallway
leading back to the single bedroom.

It must have been over ninety degrees inside.

"Sorry about the heat," she said. "My AC went out two weeks ago, and
I just haven't been around to replace it." Sheaves of paper had been spread
across the coffee table, the sofa, in numerous piles on the floor. Devlin
counted three bulletin boards in the living room alone. One had been

covered with what appeared to be crime-scene photos. Another displayed the organization of the Gulf Cartel, with maps of various corridors of the United States, certain highways and interstates highlighted.

"I apologize for the mess. As you can see, I'm a bit of a workaholic."

Devlin was already sweating. Kalyn grabbed three diet Cokes from the fridge, and they sat on the sofa, fanning themselves with sheets of paper, sipping the cold soft drinks.

"So here's the plan," Kalyn said. "We leave Devlin here, and Will, you and I drive over to Mr. Estrada's residence, see if you can't make that identification."

"I thought I was just going down to look at a lineup. That's what you—"

"No, you're going to do what we call a ride-along. Don't worry. You'll be up front with me. It'll be fine."

"But I thought you already—"

"Look, we can't pick him up unless you ID him."

Devlin looked at her father.

"Will my daughter be safe here?" he asked.

"She'll be fine. She can watch TV. I don't have cable, but you can get the network stations."

The last thing Devlin wanted to do was sit in this hot, disgusting apartment all afternoon.

"I want to go with you," she said.

"You heard Miss Sharp."

"Dad!"

Her father stood up, said, "Come with me, Dev." He glanced at Kalyn. "I need to talk to her for a minute in private."

Devlin followed Will outside and shut the door. They stood by the railing overlooking the downtrodden courtyard.

"Listen to me," he whispered. "I know you don't want to stay here, and I don't blame you. The thing is, I'm not exactly sure what's going on yet. This just feels off, but she has us in a bind. If you get scared, if anything happens while we're gone, you call me on your cell. I'll come back here and get you."

"I just wanna go home. I'm missing a sleepover at Lisa's tonight."

"I know, baby. I'm gonna take care of this, and then we're out of here. We'll fly back to Colorado if we have to."

"You promise?"

"I promise. You're earning major points today."

"You'll take me shopping in Durango?"

"Yes."

"On a spree?"

"Okay."

"Three hundred dollars."

"Two fifty."

Devlin smiled, said, "All right. I'm not gonna let you forget."

SIXTEEN

Fifteen minutes from her apartment, Kalyn turned into the driveway of a five-story office building and pulled into a parking space near the entrance.

"He's here?" Will asked.

"No, this is the Phoenix Field Office. I just have to run in and grab something."

Kalyn left the Buick running and hustled into the building.

She returned five minutes later, hopped in the car, sped out into traffic.

The road into Scottsdale was lined with palm trees.

"So how's this going to work, exactly?" Will asked.

"I have to be honest," she said. "I'm not wild about doing it this way."

Will laughed nervously. "Makes two of us."

"First, we have to see if he's home. If he is, I'll arrest him, bring him out to the car. You can give me a thumbs-up, thumbs-down on whether or not you recognize him."

"What if I don't?"

"This is the guy," she said.

"But what if I can't—"

"Can I trust you with something?"

"I guess." They were passing strip malls at the rate of ten per mile.

"Here's the dilemma. Mr. Estrada is wanted for a whole host of things, many of them much easier to prove than human trafficking. You ID him early on, we can go that route. Maybe we get some answers. If you don't, well, somebody else gets a crack at him. Border Patrol. Phoenix PD. DEA. Mexican authorities. And then we can forget about ever getting him prosecuted for what he did to your wife, or finding out what happened to her. I really don't like where that leaves you in terms of the pending charges."

"Is this how it's normally done?"

"No."

"Is it legal?"

Kalyn glanced at him. "Something you should know about FBI agents."

"What's that?"

"We're always by the book."

They were driving through residential neighborhoods now, the houses on steroids, lavish and ridiculous.

"How'd you become an agent?" Will asked.

"I was a cop right out of college. Did that for four years, went to law school. Then the Academy. Typical route."

"Did you always know—"

"Look, I can't do the 'Is this what you always wanted to be when you grew up?' conversation right now. I'm trying to get my head straight for this takedown."

They rode in silence for another few miles, and then Kalyn turned into a gated community. At the guard station, she flashed her badge and creds. The gates opened, and they drove into one of the swankiest neighborhoods Will had ever seen, six- and seven-thousand-square-foot homes being the runts of the bunch, private security gates, driveways that looked like Jaguar and Porsche dealerships.

They followed Superstition View Boulevard up the lower flanks of a brown mountain turreted with rock outcroppings and desert flora. The properties were exquisitely and exotically landscaped. Hundreds of species of cacti. Yuccas. Rocks in place of grass.

A mile past the guard station, Kalyn pulled over to the curb.

"This it?" Will asked.

"Next house on the right. You got your cell with you?"

"Yeah."

Kalyn took hers out of her purse. "Give me the number." She programmed Will's number into her phone, then turned off the engine and opened the door.

"Wait. I thought—"

She tossed him the keys, said, "Leave your cell on and hop in the driver's seat."

"No, I want to know exactly how this is—" She shut the door and walked quickly up the road, disappearing behind a row of hedges. He scooted over behind the wheel. With the AC off, the heat soon became unbearable.

Will was sweating again. This felt all wrong.

He turned, looked through the back window. The road had risen several hundred feet above the city of Scottsdale. He had a commanding view.

Thirty miles to the east, mountains soared over the desert, looming mythi-
cally in the afternoon sunlight.

He thought about Devlin, hoped she'd found something to do to pass
the time.

His cell rang. Kalyn calling. "Hey," he said.

"Bring the car into the driveway now." There was noise in the background.

"Did you—" She hung up. Will shoved the keys into the ignition and
cranked the engine. He gave the Buick a little gas, edged toward the driveway, readying himself to see the man who'd taken Rachael. Surprisingly,
he wasn't angry, just nervous and scared, wanting to get this over with, get
back to Colorado with Devlin.

When he turned into the driveway, he caught an eyeful of the sprawling
multi-level residence, lots of steel, glass, and adobe, like something that belonged in a textbook on modern architecture. A virtual forest of saguaros
and organ pipe in the front yard. Two cars in the driveway—a black Land
Rover and a silver Lotus.

He pulled up behind the sports car, palms sweating on the steering
wheel. *Where are you, Kalyn?* Every passing second, this whole thing was
feeling worse and worse.

The front door finally swung open. He exhaled, dizzy. *Here we go.* But a
boy walked out. He had dark hair and eyes, light brown skin. Next came a
thin blonde wearing hot pants and a purple halter top, red-faced, barefoot,
her hands cuffed behind her back.

They walked down the steps and onto the sidewalk, Kalyn following, a
gun in her hand. *What the fuck?* Will watched as they all approached the
car. Kalyn opened the door behind the driver's seat and the boy and the
woman got in, the woman crying, the boy silent, stoic.

Kalyn climbed into the front passenger seat and slammed the door.

"You got no right!" the woman said.

Kalyn got onto her knees and faced the backseat. She looked at the boy.
"What's your name?" she asked. He glanced at his mother. "Don't look at
her. I asked you—"

"Don't you fucking think about talking to my son like that, you piece
of—"

"Raphael," he said, his voice still prepubescent.

"How old are you?"

"Eleven."

"Raphael, I want you to do me a favor and buckle your mother's seat belt
for me." He leaned over, fastened it. "Now buckle yourself in." When he'd
done that, Kalyn leaned down and snapped a second set of handcuffs

around the boy's slender ankles. "That too tight?" He shook his head. "Start driving," she said to Will.

"They under arrest?"

"What does it look like?"

"This isn't how you said it'd go."

"Roll with it."

"I don't feel comfortable—"

"Drive, Will!" He shifted into reverse, backed down the driveway.

"You're dead," the woman said. Glancing in the rearview mirror, Will could see her eyes narrowed and raging, eyeliner running down her cheeks. "Jav will take you apart. You have no idea what you just did. You just killed yourself, your family, friends, anyone who ever knew you."

"Where is he, Misty?" Kalyn asked.

Misty spit in her face.

Will turned onto the main road and headed downhill toward the guard station.

"Where's your father today, Raphael?" Kalyn asked, wiping her face. "At the Boulders?"

He said nothing.

Will didn't see it happen, but he heard the bone crunch.

"Fuck!" Misty was wailing, and looking in the rearview mirror again, he saw blood pouring out of her nose. Raphael was crying, too, Will swerving.

"You can't do that! I have rights, you bitch!"

"I know the wife of Javier Estrada better not say one word to me about rights. Now I'm gonna crack your son's head right the fuck open in front of you if you don't tell me where your husband is."

"Kalyn, what are—"

"You can't do that!" Misty screamed.

Kalyn raised the Glock.

"The Boulders."

Oh my God, Will thought. *Oh my God.* They were nearing the guard station and the front entrance. Kalyn turned around and sat down in her seat.

"By the book?" Will said under his breath. "Was that by the book just now?"

The gates parted. They passed through. Will punched the gas, boiling inside, and he hadn't gone half a mile before he stomped on the brake and pulled over to the curb. He turned off the engine, opened his door, and jumped out into the brutal heat.

Kalyn got out, too, slammed her door. They met at the front bumper.

"Let me see your badge right—"

"Just listen."

"You broke that woman's nose, threatened to hurt her son. Let me see your—"

"I used to be an agent."

"*Used* to?"

"Listen to me, Will. Please."

He glanced back into the car. "I'm out of here," he said. "I'm done with this."

She grabbed his arm. "I was an agent up until a year ago. They wouldn't let me open this case. I investigated anyway. Used Bureau resources."

"They fired you."

"No one was doing shit to find out what happened to these women."

"They fired you."

"Yeah."

"Well that's . . . that's just great. You've manipulated me into this."

"I can't get Javier on my own. I need you."

"So does my daughter."

"I know you're scared," she said. "I understand that. But we are *this* close to finding the man who took your wife. *This* close."

"She's gone. Dead. I have a daughter to raise. He isn't worth prison."

"Is your wife?"

"What are you talking about?"

"What if she's alive, Will?"

"She isn't. It's been five—"

"But what if she is? Isn't that possibility worth this? Look, I lied about Javier. Nobody has anything on him. Just me. And today is our chance to talk to him."

"You threw away your career for these women? That makes no—"

"You remember the pictures I showed you last night?"

"Yeah."

"Lucy Dahl? Remember her?"

"Yeah, so?"

"Her maiden name was Sharp. She was my younger sister. Putting it together yet? Now, Javier is the man who took your wife. My sister. Wouldn't you like to know where they are? Wouldn't you like to ask him a question or two?"

"Yes, but—"

"Well, no one else is gonna get that information for you, and this is the price. This is what it costs. So man up."

"I've never done anything like this, and I can't risk prison."

"Well, unless you figure this out, you're already going away for your wife's murder."

"What's that? Blackmail?"

"I'd hate to, that's the truth, but I'll turn you in, Will. Maybe I get back in with the Bureau. Maybe I get some interest in my sister's case. Don't think for a second I won't if you jeopardize my getting my hands on Javier." Will stared at a passing car, the air above the pavement rippling with heat. "I have you by the balls, Will. You got no other play."

"We talk to him," Will said. "That's it. We only talk."

SEVENTEEN

Five minutes later, Will pulled the Buick into the parking lot of an abandoned mall that appeared to have been gutted by fire in the recent past. It was 4:00 P.M., the light beginning to lengthen. Kalyn helped Misty and Raphael out of the backseat, removed the handcuffs from the boy's ankles, and led them at gunpoint through one of the shattered front windows of a Belk Store, Will following close behind.

It was dark inside, and smelled like a fireplace. Kalyn had brought a flashlight, and she swept the beam through the store as they followed one of the aisles past the footwear section, the south wall scorched black, the odor of melted plastic and glass and linoleum growing stronger. Clothing racks still populated the store, most laden with singed, molding clothes. Will didn't know if it was the stench of the place or the fear of the situation, but he felt sick to his stomach.

"What are we doing here?" Misty asked. Her question went unanswered. "My nose is burning."

In the far corner of the store, they came to the children's department.

"Head back toward the dressing rooms," Kalyn said.

Misty was crying again. They arrived at the door to the last dressing room, which Kalyn pushed open. On the floor lay two sleeping bags, a stack of paperback books, four flashlights, two cases of bottled water, and a canvas bag brimming with nonperishable food.

"What's this?" Misty asked.

"Sit down, both of you." Kalyn uncuffed Raphael and Misty, then recuffed their hands to two of the metal legs of a bench that was bolted to the floor. She put the water and the food and the flashlights within reach.

"You're gonna leave us here?" Misty asked.

"Think how terrified the women your husband kidnapped must have been."

"I don't know what you're talking about."

"Right. Am I going to find him at the Boulders?"

"Yeah."

"You do not want to lie to me."

"I'm not."

"If you've told me the truth, the police will come get you tonight. If you haven't, I will, and God help you." She looked at Raphael. "Nothing's going to happen to you, okay? I need you to be brave for me for a little while longer."

As Kalyn and Will walked out of the dressing room, Misty screamed after them, her voice filling the dark, empty store.

EIGHTEEN

Now Kalyn drove, speeding north up Scottsdale Road.

Will stared out the window, and despite the fear, he had to acknowledge that there was a part of him that wanted very much to be here, to see Javier Estrada.

He pulled out his cell.

"What are you doing?" Kalyn asked.

"Calling my daughter."

Devlin answered on the first ring, "Hey, Dad."

The sound of her voice crushed him. "What are you doing, baby girl?"

"Watching a cooking show on PBS."

"How is it?"

"Awesometastic," she replied, echoing her mother's sassy spunk. "You almost done? Kalyn's channels suck even worse than ours."

"Not yet."

She paused, said, "Did you see him?"

"I can't talk right now, honey. I'll tell you about it later. Just wanted to check in."

He closed the cell.

North of Scottsdale, they passed through the gates of the Boulders, thirty-six holes of legendary golf links, sculpted into desert foothills.

"You play?" Kalyn asked as they approached the clubhouse.

"Used to."

"So how do we find this guy if he's somewhere out there?"

"This is a very nice course. I'm sure he needed reservations, so the pro shop would be the place to start."

Kalyn pulled into a parking spot and they walked together into the pro shop. The man behind the counter was forty-something and tanned to golden perfection, his brown hair gilded by sunlight. Will could also see that he was brimming with attitude, that rare, sophisticated superiority effused by those with just enough talent to be the local pro but who lack some crucial ingredient to win their PGA card. His name tag read Dan.

"Help you with something?" he said. Kalyn reached into her purse, took out her expired FBI ID, let it flip open, carefully watching Dan's eyes. They weren't really reading it, just registering the shock of seeing FBI in bold blue letters.

Kalyn snapped it closed. "I wonder if you could help us, Dan. We're trying to locate a gentleman named Javier Estrada. I believe he may be playing here right now."

The club pro stepped behind a computer, began typing.

"You don't need a warrant or anything for this?" he asked.

Busted, Will thought. *You better handle this with grace, Kalyn.*

"No, sir," she said. "Now if I wanted to know how many times he'd played in the last month, or access to his locker, that would require a warrant."

"What's this all about?" He was still typing.

"I'm sorry, I can't go into that. Do you know Mr. Estrada?"

"I've given him several lessons in the last month. He tips very well."

"Look at me, sir." Dan looked up. "I'm not going to tell Mr. Estrada whatever information you give me, and you'd be wise not to discuss this with him. He's a dangerous man." Dan's eyes cut back to the computer screen.

"He had a one-thirty tee time on the north course," he said.

"Can you tell exactly which hole he's on right now?"

The door to the pro shop swung open.

"No, but he should be getting—" Dan glanced up, his tan paling. He caught himself, smiled broadly, now looking past Kalyn and Will. "Javier!" he said. "How'd we do today?"

"Seventy-seven."

Will heard pride and a faint accent in the man's even voice. Javier Estrada walked up and stood beside Kalyn, decked out in knickers, Payne Stewart–style, the sides of his white-collared shirt darkened with sweat stains. He was fanning himself with a golf cap.

Will wandered away from the counter and Kalyn discreetly followed, hanging on to his arm as if they were just perusing the clubs and golf bags.

"Seventy-seven?" Dan said. "No. I don't think I believe that."

"That thing you showed me? The wrist turn thing? You are a beautiful genius."

"Well, I'm happy for you, Jav. That's good stuff. Good stuff."

"I'd have shot seventy-five except for that par five on the back."

"Fifteen?"

"I four-putted. That green was much slower than the others."

"You know," Dan said, leaning forward confidentially, "yours isn't the first complaint I've heard about that green today. Between you and me, one of the groundskeepers overwatered it."

"Who? Which groundskeeper?"

"Brian."

"Brian cost me my personal best."

"We still on for a lesson Monday afternoon?"

"Absolutely. Give me a bucket of balls. I need to straighten out something on my sand wedge before I head home."

Kalyn pulled her Buick around to the side of the clubhouse so that they had a view of the driving range. The sun was setting, turning the rock formations pink, the fairways gold.

"I have to admit," Will said, "seeing him here, dressed up like a golfing dandy—it kind of undercuts the badass, Alpha mystique."

"Your cell on?" Kalyn asked.

"Yeah."

"Program my number." She gave it to him. "The moment he starts packing up to leave, call me." She grabbed her purse, opened the door.

"Where are you going?" She got out, left Will sitting in the hot silence, fifty feet back from the range.

With his smooth, fluid swing, Javier was putting most of his balls on the nearest green. After awhile, he took out his driver, set up a tee. He settled into his stance, stood there shifting his hips, staring down at the ball, nodding his head. He did this for fifteen seconds, then brought the club back and swung. Will heard the impact of the huge titanium club face meeting the ball. Javier followed through, froze, then looked up, watching as the ball arced toward the back of the range.

Sitting there, watching this kidnapping, drug-running murderer, Will felt surprisingly calm. *It's because you don't really think you'll go through with what you're about to do.* Javier drove the last ball and slid his driver into the golf bag.

Will opened his cell, called Kalyn. "He's hoisting his bag onto his shoulder right now."

"Wait there. I'm coming back to you."

Will closed the cell, Javier walking toward him now. Will could hear the crunch of his golf spikes on the pavement. Javier passed by his window. Smell of cologne and sweat. He wore RayBan sunglasses, and Will didn't like not knowing where the man was looking. Glancing in the side mirror, he watched until Javier disappeared around the clubhouse. Then he stared through the windshield, but he couldn't concentrate, kept watching the side mirror.

Calm down. Calm down. Calm—

Someone knocked on the driver's side window. He flinched. It was Kalyn. Will unlocked the door and she opened it and climbed in behind the wheel.

"What'd you do?" he asked.

She cranked the engine, shifted into reverse. "You'll see."

NINETEEN

The new Escalade slowed as it neared the entrance to the Boulders, right turn signal blinking.

"What'd you do?" Will asked again.

Kalyn cut her eyes at him, grinned wickedly. The Escalade pulled out onto N. Tom Darlington Road. They followed.

"Do me a favor," Kalyn said. "Reach in my purse and pull out the Glock. You've held a gun before, right?"

"Yeah, at Webelos camp about twenty years ago." Will lifted out a small black semiautomatic handgun. "Loaded?" he asked.

"Yep. Now very gently, pull back on the slide. You see a round?"

He saw the copper-tipped brass casing. "Yeah."

"You can put it back." Will looked up through the windshield, saw Javier's SUV fifty yards ahead, but something was clearly wrong with it, the Escalade drifting toward the shoulder.

"Why's he swerving?"

Kalyn smiled again.

"Oh God," he said. "You didn't."

After another half mile, Javier pulled over onto the shoulder. The way it dipped forward and to the right, Will could tell the vehicle's right front tire was flat. Kalyn slowed down, and twenty yards past the front bumper of the Escalade, she veered over onto the shoulder.

She turned off the engine, said, "You ready for this?"

"No."

"Listen. You just do exactly what I say, and it'll be fine." Will looked in the side mirror, saw Javier's door swing open. "When we come back," Kalyn said, "I want you to drive. Javier's gonna be beside you. I'm gonna be in back with the gun." Kalyn reached into her purse and pulled out the Glock. Will saw Javier squatting down by the deflated tire, sunglasses in one hand, running the palm of his other across the rubber tread.

Kalyn holstered the Glock in a shoulder rig, which was concealed by her jacket.

"There's no turning back once he's in the car, Will. You understand that, right?"

Will took a breath, opened the door, and stepped outside.

Traffic was light, and with this stretch of road still five miles outside of Scottsdale, the landscape was predominantly sunlit desert as far as Will could see. He steadied his hands as they approached the Escalade, trying to process everything that had happened in the last two hours, marveling at how fast it had come to this.

Kalyn ran her tongue against the roof of her mouth, moistening it so she could speak. He had to buy it, or they could forget the whole thing. She rubbed her hands against her wool skirt.

Javier looked up when they were fifteen feet away, and Will watched Kalyn work up a big smile. She was originally from Texas, and she conjured up the accent she'd fought so hard to shed.

"Got yourself a flat tire there?"

Javier nodded, and Will tried to read him, but he wasn't smiling or scowling, just receiving information. He wondered if he had a gun on him, would have staked the savings he didn't have that the man had something lethal in the Escalade, probably under the seat or the dash. Javier let loose a lukewarm smile, not a shred of warmth to it. Will was praying Kalyn's accent was so appalling, she'd offended whatever sensibilities he had, thereby distracting him.

"Did you run over something sharp?" Kalyn asked. "You got a spare?"

He sighed. "Yes. I have a spare." He was still staring at her, his eyes processing her face. "Could you tell me something?" he asked.

"What's that?"

"I'm certain I've seen you today. Could you tell me where?"

"I never seen you before in my life. I was just stopping to help a—"

"Ah, yes. The pro shop. You were speaking with Dan when I came in from my round." At light speed, Javier's eyes cut to Will, then back to Kalyn's face. "This is the gentleman you were with?"

Will estimated that they were seven feet apart, wondered how fast Javier could move. *Blink of an eye. Draw, Kalyn.*

Javier said, "Your palms are sweating."

Draw.

"Your hand is anxious to reach for the gun under your jacket. My concern, being that I don't know you, is that you would try to do it quickly and accidentally shoot me before I've given you actual cause. So let's circumvent that possible outcome. Take two steps back. Then slowly draw your weapon. Here are my hands. I'm unarmed. I will not move."

She stepped back, reached into her jacket, drew the Glock, holding it low as she moved around behind him. "Get on your knees," she said. He did. "Now put your hands behind your head and interlace your fingers." Will was feeling confident in Kalyn's ability to control the situation now, the Escalade keeping them shielded from the view of passing cars. From an inner pocket of her jacket, she took a pair of handcuffs and snapped them over Javier's right wrist. "Lie flat on your stomach, with your hands behind your back."

Javier made no argument, carefully prostrating himself on the pavement.

She locked the cuff around his other wrist.

"Get up on your feet slowly." He rolled over onto his back, sat up, then stood up. "Approach your car, lean against it, and spread your legs." She frisked him, found nothing but his wallet and a BlackBerry in the knickers pockets. "Now walk to *my* car."

TWENTY

The passenger door opened. Javier Estrada ducked his head and climbed into the front seat.

"Buckle his seat belt," Kalyn said. Will hesitated. "He's cuffed; he isn't carrying any weapons. It's fine." Will felt Javier's eyes taking inventory of his face as he leaned over and pulled the seat belt across the man's chest and locked it into place. Kalyn shut the door, opened the one behind it, and climbed into the back. "Javier," she said, "just so we're clear, you have a Glock pointed at your spine through the seat. Drive, Will. Don't speed, don't run stop signs, and for God's sake don't get us into a wreck."

It was the weirdest silence Will had been a party to—no radio or talking, just three strangers in a car, driving through Scottsdale, Arizona. Javier stared straight ahead. Will watched him out of the corner of his eye at the stoplights, the man at ease, collected.

As they neared the interstate, Kalyn said, "Take Highway Sixty east."

Javier spoke for the first time since getting into the car, "Ah, the Superstitions. Am I right?" No one answered. "I've done business out there. That was an excellent takedown, by the way. Creative. Outside of the box. And the accent. Beautiful. You realize my mistake. I very nearly averted this entire situation. I keep a forty-five Smith & Wesson under my seat, and I actually started to reach for it before getting out of the car. Out of habit, you see. But I didn't. Had I"—he caught Kalyn's eyes in the rearview mirror—"you would be dead." He looked at Will. "And so would you."

They sped east, the sun sinking fast into the horizon, molten in the mirrors, on the glass and chrome of passing cars, the mountains in the distance getting bigger, vivid and deeply textured in the fading light.

"I have a question for you," Kalyn said. "Did that situation back there ring any bells?"

"I don't understand."

"Well, I almost brought along a bat, or a crowbar . . . something to bust out your driver's side window. Maybe, if I'd done that, you would have realized what was happening."

Javier shook his head. "I'm sorry. I don't see your point."

"No worries. You will."

The sun was just a flaming sliver in the west as Will drove past the ranger station into Lost Dutchman State Park.

Kalyn told him to park at the first picnic area.

It was late. Only two other cars. Both empty. No hikers in sight. Beyond lay miles of darkening desert and, farther back, the Superstitions, the summits catching light, the bases cloaked in mist.

Will turned off the engine.

Total silence, save for the wind. The car rocked imperceptibly.

"So," Kalyn said, "have you figured it out yet?"

Javier smiled. "Do not flatter yourself to think you are the only ones who would like to be in this position with me. I have plenty of enemies. But friends also. And it is my friends, my brothers, the threat of them, that make my enemies wise to keep a respectful distance. In short, I am not fucked with. This is unheard of. You are not law enforcement," Javier said, "though perhaps once you were. Will here is shitting himself. You're trying, so far, to be impersonal, but I sense the rage in you. At me. I don't know why. You will tell me?"

Kalyn reached into the front seat and dropped four photos in Javier's lap.

"Line them up, Will, so he can see."

Will arranged the photographs, two on each leg. Suzanne Tyrpak. Jill Dillon. Rachael Innis. Lucy Dahl. Javier looked down at them. Looked up. Shrugged. Kalyn pulled out her cell, flipped it open. Will saw her pressing buttons. She handed the cell to him, said, "Show him." On the miniature screen was a digital picture of Misty and Raphael in the back of the Buick. Will hesitated. "Show him." He held the cell to Javier's face. Javier registered the image, then looked out the side window toward a distant forest of saguaros.

"You two," Javier said, his voice low, deliberately measured, "may be the bravest people I have ever met."

"Why don't you look at the photos in your lap again," Kalyn said.

"My family, they're alive? Unharmed?"

"For now."

Javier nodded. "I would like to speak to them."

"Not possible."

"Then I don't think we have anything to talk about."

Kalyn moved into the middle seat so she could see Javier's face. "Look at me," she said. "I'm going to tell you something, so you understand how serious we are. So you have no doubts of what we're ready to do to you, Misty, *and* Raphael. Those photos on the right? That's Rachael Innis, Will's wife, and Lucy Dahl, my sister. So please believe me when I tell you that if you continue on this track, you and your family will have a very long, very bad night."

"And if I were to provide the desired information?"

"They live. We aren't like you, Javier."

"And me? Either way, whether I tell you, whether I don't, you will kill me, no?"

"You tell us what we want to know, and I leave you here, handcuffed to a picnic table. Maybe someone finds you tomorrow. Doesn't matter. By then, we'll be gone."

"I don't know that I believe you. If the tables were turned around the other way, I would get the information I needed, and then I would murder you."

"What'd I just say? We aren't like you."

He looked out the window again, said finally, "I am afraid you won't be pleased with my information, as I am only a small variable in the equation."

"Just tell us what you know."

As he spoke, he watched the color of the desert move through darkening shades of purple, noticed the mist slithering up the mountains. "It has been the same way every time. A man named Jonathan calls me and says, 'They want another one.' And so I begin looking. There are parameters of course. Caucasian. Big dark eyes. Black hair with abundant curls. Beautiful. They like my taste, I suppose. Perhaps I have a counterpart somewhere who specializes in blondes or redheads. When I find her, I follow her for several days. I learn about her. Patterns, habits. Then, when I feel it is time, I call Jonathan, and I tell him. When she's in my possession, I call Jonathan once more. The time and place are set."

"Where?"

"I think I will wait to tell you that. Suffice it to say that a journey of considerable distance is made. We meet. Jonathan is a large man, a truck driver. The woman is put into a trailer, and that is the last I ever see of her.

Anywhere from five to ten days later, a deposit is made into one of my off-shore accounts. A larger deposit each time. I require this. I do not speak to Jonathan again until he calls and says, 'They want another one.' "

Kalyn wiped her eyes. She could barely form the words, and they came as a whisper. "How many women have you taken?"

"Five. It is not my typical line of work, but the money is good."

"How did Jonathan find you?"

"Various channels. The first time we did business, he mentioned an important name. The right name. I took a chance."

"Are there other people like you, people who Jonathan uses?"

"I have no idea. Ours is not a relationship of questions."

Will said, "Look at me, Javier." The man looked at him. Will reached down, lifted the photograph of his wife. "I want to hear about the night you took her." He was trembling with fear, rage, sadness.

Javier looked at the photograph. "That was some time ago."

"Five years. My daughter misses her mother."

"I first saw her coming out of a clinic in Sonoyta. That's all I remember. And that it was raining and the sky full of lightning on the night I took her."

"How was she?"

"Afraid," Javier said. "They all are. I try to calm them. They're drugged for most of the trip, but not mistreated, if that's what you're asking. Not by me at least. You don't pay what I am paid for damaged product."

Will swung. There was a pop. Javier fell back into the door and spit out a tooth.

"Easy, Will," Kalyn said.

Javier licked the blood from a cut on his bottom lip, smiling, his eyes shining, and for a moment Will was convinced the man was mad.

"Did that feel good?" he asked. "I imagine it did."

"Is Jonathan the man who's buying these women?" Kalyn asked.

"I would think not. Like me, he's just a well-paid mule."

"Then who? Where are they being taken?"

"Maybe to Mexico. Maybe they're shipped on boats to other parts of the world. Thailand. Eastern Europe. I am a blind appendage in the operation, and intentionally so."

Will looked at Kalyn, his right hand throbbing.

"Javier," she said, "that was the wrong answer." She opened the door, stepped out of the car, opened Javier's door. "Get out."

Javier didn't move.

Will leaned over, pushed him out of the seat. Javier fell onto the pavement. Will got out, walked around the hood, finished dragging him the rest of the way out of the car.

Kalyn said to Will, "If you want to wait in the car, I'll understand."

"I'm with you now."

"Then drag him onto the trail. I don't want blood on the pavement."

Will grabbed Javier under his armpits and lifted him. The man was heavy, solid muscle. Twenty feet took almost a minute. Will finally collapsed in the dirt, sweating, out of breath.

The sky was now a dark, rich navy, with just a shrinking bar of red in the west, the saguaros silhouetted against it. Will surveyed the parking lot, the road. The only lights, a collection of them, emanated from the park's campground, a mile away.

Kalyn said, "Roll onto your back." Javier rolled, looked up at her, the right side of his face swollen, his jaw broken. "What would you do if you were me?" she asked.

"We would be in a warehouse in Tempe. Acid would be involved. There is also this thing I do with a soldering iron and a powerful magnet."

"I only have this gun." She aimed it at his crotch.

"One moment," he said, though his voice completely lacked fear. "If you do that, I will be in no shape to make the phone call."

"What call?"

"As it so happens, I received word from Jonathan a month ago. I am still in the searching phase."

"You haven't found anyone?"

He shook his head.

"Sit him up, Will." Will propped Javier against the toppled trunk of a dead saguaro. Kalyn took out Javier's BlackBerry, turned it on, found the address book. "This him?" she asked. "Jonathan?"

"Yes."

"What would you text him?"

"I wouldn't. He lives behind a steering wheel. We speak."

She squatted down beside him. "When he's on the line, you tell him you already have a woman, and that you're ready to meet."

"In return?"

"You keep your penis a little while longer. Do this right, I leave you here. Maybe you see your family again."

The Superstitions were now just a black wall in the backdrop.

"Here, hold it to his ear, hit 'Talk' when I say." Kalyn handed the Black-Berry to Will and aimed the Glock between Javier's legs. "Transparence is key, Javier. If you launch into Spanish, if you say things to Jonathan that don't make sense, that sound suspect, I will pull the trigger. Clear?"

"Yes. You are handling this all very well."

"Do it, Will." Will pressed the button, held the BlackBerry to Javier's ear. They waited; then came the static sound of the ring. On the third, someone answered—the voice husky and low over the speakerphone. Will could hear the voice on the other end, but he couldn't make out the words.

"It's Jav. I have someone. . . . No, I have them already. . . . They're with me right now. . . . Yes, I can do that. . . . Okay. . . . No, that's plenty of time. . . . All right, I'll see you then."

Javier nodded. Will broke the connection.

"That was it?" Kalyn asked.

"That was it. So. I tell you the information and you both walk away?"

"That was the deal," Kalyn said.

"And my family stays unharmed?"

"In twelve hours, I call the police, tell them where they are."

"The exchange is in two days," Javier said.

"Where?"

"Interstate Eighty-four, exit fifty-six, twelve miles outside of Boise, Idaho."

"What's there?"

"An abandoned drive-in movie theater."

"And you're supposed to meet Jonathan there?"

"Monday night. Eleven o'clock."

"What's he look like?"

"Long red hair, bushy beard, weighs over three hundred pounds. Smells terrible."

Something rustled a ways off in the underbrush.

"Look at me," Kalyn said. "You've been responsible for the deaths of more than a few people. Am I right?"

"Yes."

"Ever looked one of their loved ones in the eye? Accounted for what you'd done?"

"I don't believe so. This situation has been unique in many ways."

"I want to know if you feel remorse."

"It is not personal what I do. I did not take your sister because I desired to do her harm."

"No, you took her for money. But you did cause—"

"Let's not pretend I am in any way like you. You ask about remorse. You would like me to say that I deeply regret harming your sister, his wife. I can say these things, but they would be untrue. I would know it. You would know it. My line of work does not allow for remorse. Tell me what you were. I'm guessing DEA."

The whites of his eyes stood out in the growing darkness.

"FBI."

"You're very good, Kalyn. I would have enjoyed killing you."

"How many of you are there?"

"How many what?"

"Alphas."

He chuckled. "Not as many as people think. Some who believe they are Alphas are not."

"How many?"

"Fifty-seven at the moment."

"Any gringos in the bunch?"

"Just two."

"Come with me, Will."

He followed Kalyn back to the car, stars now visible.

"You believe him?" Will asked, leaning against the hood. It was the first time since arriving in Phoenix five hours ago that he wasn't overwhelmed by heat.

"Yeah, actually. I'm going after Jonathan."

"The trucker?"

"You be up for that?"

"I don't know. What about Javier? You comfortable just leaving him here?"

"No."

"Well, what's the alternative? Take him with . . ." Will felt something tighten in the small of his back. "No. No way."

"I dug a hole three days ago. About fifty yards out."

"Kalyn—"

"Alphas aren't the kind of people you walk away from. You understand what I'm saying? They'd use every resource tracking us down. Kill friends, family to get to us."

Will shook his head. "Not in cold blood, Kalyn."

"You can wait here, Will, for all I care. I'll take—"

"No. Not like—"

"Oh fuck."

Will didn't even see the draw, just a blur of movement, then Kalyn standing with her feet shoulder width apart, a two-handed grip and the Glock out in front of her, sweeping back and forth, aimed into all that darkness.

"You see him?" she whispered.

Will kept staring at the trunk of the dead saguaro, as if the man might rematerialize, but he wasn't there.

"No."

"Get in the car, passenger seat. Right now."

Will turned and opened the door, got in and shut it as Kalyn climbed behind the steering wheel.

She flicked the locks.

For a moment, with the interior lights on, they were blinded to the nightscape beyond.

"Keys."

Will handed them over and she fumbled with them for a moment before jamming one into the ignition.

The engine cranked. She flicked the headlights to high beam, shifted into drive.

The brights shone out into the desert, and the first thing Will noticed was the glimmer of metal near that dead saguaro where they'd questioned Javier.

"You see that?" he said.

"What?"

"By the cactus. He got out of the handcuffs."

Kalyn eased her foot onto the accelerator.

"What are you doing?"

The car lurched forward, crossed twenty feet of pavement, then rattled into the desert.

"He can't have gone far," Kalyn said, dodging jumping chollas and shrubs of Mormon tea. "He had what? Thirty seconds? At a dead run, might have covered—"

"Two hundred meters."

"Really?"

"I ran track in college. He's in great shape."

Something darted out from behind an ocotillo—just a cottontail, two bunnies in tow.

"See the arroyo up ahead?" Will said.

"Yeah."

Kalyn braked, the Buick sliding through the dirt. She reversed, then drove on again in a slow, wide circle, the headlights scanning the desert.

Thirty seconds later, they were stopped again at the arroyo's edge.

"Think he went down in there?" Will asked.

Kalyn pulled her Glock out of the shoulder rig.

"No," Will said.

"He's out here. We either get him now or spend the foreseeable future looking over our—"

"Don't go out there."

"I'll be fine." She shook the Glock. "He doesn't have one of these."

She threw open the door, got out.

"Kalyn."

"He's not supernatural, Will. Bleeds like you and me. Stay here."

She slammed the door. With the interior lights on, he couldn't see Kalyn moving away from the car, only heard her footsteps crunching through the dirt.

Just the headlights now, blazing into the desert, and the last thing he saw before they went dark was a roadrunner streaking between chollas on the far side of the arroyo, a snake twitching in its beak.

TWENTY-ONE

Kalyn was at least a hundred yards out from the car before she realized she'd forgotten the flashlight in the glove compartment. She stopped beside an ancient saguaro, gnarled and rotting to death. With no wind, the silence screamed, though after a moment, she began to discern the subtlest inklings of noise—low bass from a radio blaring out of the campground a mile away, the scraping hiss of dry brush set in motion by a wood rat or a wren.

She scrambled down the twenty-foot embankment and stood on the sandy bottom of the arroyo. It was absolutely quiet, the cooler air having settled here.

She stood for a moment, letting her eyes adjust to the meager starlight. Shapes appeared—boulders, scrubs, ten feet away, the carcass of a coyote—sharp whiff of decay.

There was movement in the sand behind her—crunch of fast footsteps.

A cottontail bounded past.

"You little shit," she called after it.

She climbed back out of the arroyo. The moon had edged above the Superstitions. The car was up ahead, a black hulk standing in the desert, the chrome glowing as the moonbeams struck it.

She walked around to the driver's side. As she touched the door handle, a bush shook behind her and she turned, saw Will.

"What the fuck is wrong with you?" she said. "I told you to stay put."

"I was afraid if he killed you, I'd be a sitting duck for him inside the car."

She lowered the gun. "Well, you don't have to worry about it now."

"You got him?"

"No, he's gone. Come on, we should go."

"Just let him walk off—"

"What would you suggest, Will? You wanna stay out here all night, walking around in the dark. 'Javier? Javier? Where are you?'"

"You said he'd warn Jonathan off if we let him go."

"I know."

"Well?"

"Well, he's gonna be concerned with finding his family, first and foremost. That's our only card, but it's a good one."

As Kalyn turned out of Lost Dutchman State Park, Will watched her face—pensive and hard in the glow of the dashboard lights.

"You know, you've been lying to me since I met you. 'Come on down to Phoenix, Will. I'm an FBI agent. We just need you to make an ID. We're just gonna *talk* to him, Will.' You had this thing planned all along. Hole already dug."

"I'm sorry. I didn't know if I could trust you."

"Anything else I don't know? Wanna drop any other bombs while we're on the subject?"

She glanced over at him, said nothing.

"From here on out, you start treating me like a partner," Will said. "I wanna know what you're thinking, what you're planning. I don't wanna be surprised again. One more lie, Kalyn, and I'm done with you. Devlin and I will take our chances on the run."

They rode on in silence, speeding west toward Phoenix now, a massive, distant glow on the horizon, like a city on fire.

Space 151

TWENTY-TWO

They walked into Kalyn's apartment at 8:30 P.M., and before he touched his daughter, Will scrubbed his hands with soap and hot water at the kitchen sink.

Kalyn went back into her bedroom and closed the door.

Will knelt by Devlin. She was snoring quietly on the couch, and he curled up on the floor beside her, the heat working on him like a sedative.

His eyes closed. Through the thin walls, he heard children playing a video game in the adjacent apartment. A jet roared overhead, shook the floor.

Someone whispered into Will's ear. He opened his eyes, saw Rachael standing by the couch.

"So this is our little Devi?" she asked.

"Yeah."

"I can't believe how perfect she is. Does she ask about me?"

"All the time, honey. All the time." A strange light shone upon Rachael, like she was backlighted, the fringes of her curly black hair laced with glow.

Will opened his eyes, the apartment silent and dark, his face wet, Rachael gone.

"You awake, Dad?" Devlin whispered.

"Yeah."

"What time is it?"

He glanced at his watch. "Midnight."

"Did you see the man who took Mom?"

"Yeah, honey, I did."

"What happened?"

"A lot happened."

"Tell me."

Will reached up, found Devlin's hand in the dark.

"We questioned him."

"Did Kalyn arrest him?"

"No."

"Why not?"

"She's not an FBI agent. She used to be, but Kalyn lost her sister to Javier Estrada, just like we lost Mom."

"So she lied to us?"

"Yeah."

"But you aren't mad?"

"Kalyn just wanted to find out what happened to her sister."

"So what happened to Mom?"

"We still don't know, just that Javier took her. But he isn't the one who killed her."

"Who did?"

"I don't know yet."

"What happened to Javier?"

"He got away."

"Are we going home tomorrow?"

"No, I think we're going to try to find out where Mom went. Would that be okay with you?"

"I don't know. I just wanna go home."

"Me, too, but I'm not sure I can walk away from a chance to know what happened." He swelled with homesickness for their farmhouse in Colorado, wished he had Rachael's sweatshirt with him now. He still slept with it on the hard nights.

"Sing to me like you used to, Dad."

She squeezed his hand.

Two verses of "Sweet Baby James" put them both back to sleep.

A light in the hallway roused Will from sleep. His watch read 4:38 A.M., and there was a woman walking toward him. He thought, *I'm dreaming again,* because she looked like Rachael—big dark eyes, curly black hair. He got up, moving toward her now, his heart thumping in his chest.

They reached each other at the entrance to the hallway.

"What do you think?" the woman asked. She'd dyed and curled her hair.

"Why'd you do that?"

"So I'd look like the missing women."

On close inspection, Will saw that Kalyn had used dark eyeliner and makeup to bring out her eyes. Colored contacts had turned them a brown so deep, it bordered on black. Excepting her height and the shape of her lips, she could have passed for Rachael.

"For a minute, I thought you were her. That I was dreaming."

"You dream about her often?"

"Yeah."

"I'm sorry."

"No, the worst are when I dream all the bad stuff didn't happen. Or that it was just a nightmare, and I wake up looking for Rachael in bed."

Kalyn touched his arm. "Sorry I blindsided you yesterday. I was afraid you wouldn't help me if I just told you what I was planning to do."

"I probably wouldn't have."

"If you want to walk away from this," she said, "I'll drive you back to Colorado."

"Tempting, but I need to know what happened to Rachael."

"I'm glad."

"One caveat. Devlin doesn't go anywhere near a dangerous situation. That's top priority." Will looked Kalyn up and down as it hit him again what this thirtysomething woman had pulled off, what she was capable of. "Javier was right about one thing," he said.

"What's that?"

"You are very good."

Kalyn let slip a little smile, and he missed her blushing in the semidark.

"So tell me," Will said, "how are we going to do this?"

TWENTY-THREE

They rented a new Land Rover from the airport, black, with a tan leather interior. Kalyn drove, Will in back, Devlin asleep against the door in front.

In the early morning, in a brown cactus-ridden neighborhood in Sun City, Kalyn pulled over to the curb.

"What are we stopping for?" Will asked.

"I have to get some things from this private investigator. He's a friend. One of the last I've got." She got out, and Will watched her walk up the driveway to the small adobe house.

A minivan passed by. Then another—people on their way to church or weekend jobs, morning coffee steaming up from the mugs in their laps.

Will envied them.

By midday, they were passing through the extravagant wastelands of Las Vegas. Then it was I-15, north through Utah, Kalyn and Will taking turns behind the wheel, even letting Devlin drive for a stretch. They made a forty-minute stop at a rest area near Zion National Park for Devlin's CPT, and played car games through the late afternoon—Punch Bug and I Spy.

They reached Salt Lake a little after 9:00 P.M. on Sunday night, road-weary, landscape-numb, tired, and hungry.

Rented a pair of rooms at a Super 8 and wandered over to the Denny's across from the string of cheap motels along the interstate.

Burgers, fries, bad salads, Mormons.

Ate at the counter, talked out, worthless, Will thinking, *All I want to do is finish this greasy meal and lie in bed in the motel room, watching something mind-less on television.*

Kalyn broke his daze. "It's a little disconcerting we haven't heard from Jav."

"I know. What if we don't before tomorrow night?"

"Things might get interesting."

Will woke in the motel, the TV still on, barely dawn outside, and the inter-state noise roaring through the thin walls. Devlin sat up in the other bed, and the first thing out of her mouth was, "Are we crazy for doing this, Dad?"

"Probably."

The call came during breakfast the next morning at a diner in Brigham City—a strong buzz emanating from Kalyn's purse.

She pulled out the BlackBerry and they all watched it vibrate across the table.

"What's the name on the caller ID?" Will asked.

"Just a number. Phoenix area code."

"Gonna answer it?"

"Yeah, I'll put it on speaker."

Kalyn pressed TALK. "Who's this?"

A few seconds of silence elapsed, followed by a sigh. "You know who this is."

Devlin mouthed "That's him?"

Will nodded.

"Javier," Kalyn said, smiling. "I was beginning to wonder if you were going to call. That was a nifty little move you pulled Saturday. What'd I miss? Handcuff key in your back pocket?"

"Where's my family?"

Will glanced at the nearest occupied table, a good fifteen feet away—young couple sharing the same side of the booth, each in the other's world.

Kalyn said, "Why do you think we would tell you that right now?"

There was an abrupt noise on Javier's end—probably a snort—which emerged as static through the speaker. "Because when I find you, I will take into consideration this moment. It's an opportunity, not for you to stop what's coming, but perhaps to make things end faster than they otherwise would. I understand this is a concept difficult to fully grasp. I'm where I am, you're where you are, and you don't think we'll ever see each other again. But I can promise you we will. And I will murder you both and take great joy and pleasure and time in doing it."

Will wrapped his arm around Devlin, caught her eyes, shook his head.

"What you must now do is anticipate that moment when I have you. What I'm offering is death. Not immediate. But considerably faster than it is currently scheduled to arrive, in light of the offense you've both given me."

Kalyn said, "Hello?"

"Yes, I'm here."

"Oh, I'm sorry, you faded out there for about fifteen seconds. Look, I'll make this very easy. Our concern is Jonathan. Have you warned him we're coming?"

Three seconds of dead air, then: "No."

"That's good, Javier. As you know, our meeting with him is set for tonight. We'll handle the finessing of why you couldn't be there, but I just need to make something clear. You listening?"

"I am."

"If it goes well, if it's obvious Jonathan has not been forewarned, someone will call you tomorrow, tell you where you can find your family."

"That's unacceptable."

Kalyn pulled the BlackBerry back from her face, pressed END, set the device on the table.

"What are you doing?" Will said.

"Let him sweat. What do we stand to lose? Our meeting. What does he stand to—" The BlackBerry buzzed. Kalyn pressed TALK, said, "I don't know what third-grade textbook you learned your negotiation skills from, but you aren't in any spot to say what is and is not acceptable. *We'll* call *you* back on this number tomorrow *if* it goes well with Jonathan. If it doesn't, you'll never hear from us again, and your wife and son will die of thirst within the next few days."

He made no reply, though Will could hear him breathing.

"Acknowledge that you heard me, Javier."

"I heard you."

Kalyn pressed END.

"We have to change the meeting place," Will said. "I'm not cool with Javier knowing where we'll be. He may not warn Jonathan, but I could see him coming after us."

"All right. I'll text Jonathan, ask him to pick another spot."

I-84 west through Idaho. Twin Falls. Gooding. Mountain Home. When they were within the Boise city limits, Kalyn spotted a shopping mall from the interstate, made the exit just in time.

It was midafternoon, and they rode under a brilliant autumn sky, leaves peaking, deep reds and blinding yellows along the riverbanks, the brown hills that rose up behind the skyline dusted with snow.

"Let's shop," Kalyn said, pulling into a parking space in front of the sprawling mall.

"For who?" Will asked.

Kalyn glanced back from the driver seat. "You. Look at yourself."

Will glanced down at his two-day-old clothes—ancient pair of jeans, tennis shoes, faded flannel shirt with the sleeves rolled up.

"She's right, Dad," Devlin said. "You need a serious makeover."

"This is a style."

Kalyn laughed. "What's it called?"

"Colorado living. Outdoor man. You could chop some serious firewood in this getup."

"That's a selling point?"

"You're telling me women don't like the chiseled, frontier man look?"

"Yeah, well, you need a new outfit for tonight. We're not out to impress the ladies, Will. We're trying to pass you off for an Alpha."

The mall was dead. They ate a late lunch in the food court, spread out on a bench beside a fountain whose bottom lay covered in green pennies and the occasional nickel.

As they rose to leave, the BlackBerry registered a new message.

Kalyn pulled it out of her purse, scanned the screen, sighed with relief. She said, "He wrote back, 'Exit 64. Café at Big Al's. OK.'"

Kalyn and Devlin were leading Will through the men's section of the Gap.

"So what look are we like going for?" Devlin asked.

"I was thinking all black," Kalyn said.

"I like these." Devlin fingered a pair of leather pants, Will thinking, *This is as happy as I've seen her in ages.* "What's your waist, Dad?"

"Thirty-four."

Devlin thumbed quickly through the pants and finally slipped a pair off the rack, handed them to her father. "Tell you what would be rad with those," Devlin said. She made for a rack of shirts, squealed with joy when she found what she was looking for, proudly holding up a black silk shirt with mother-of-pearl buttons.

"You go, girl," Kalyn said as Will sighed.

. . .

He stepped out of the dressing room and stood before his audience.

Kalyn said, "Undo the top two buttons." He did. "That's perfect, Will."

"Yeah, let's go *club*bing," he said in his best Valley Girl voice.

"With that hair?" Kalyn said. "You gotta admit, Jav has style. But you're getting there."

Will stared at himself in the mirror as the stylist ran her fingers through his light brown hair.

Kalyn said, "I'm thinking keep it kind of long, like it is, and dye it black. I want him to be able to push it back with some pomade."

"Kind of a greaser look you're going for?"

"I'm not sure how to explain what I—"

Devlin came over with a huge book of male models sporting pretentiously trendy hairstyles, and said, "I think this is what we want."

Kalyn smiled. "Yes. Good, Devi. This is it exactly."

Will said, "These are the most ridiculous things I've ever seen."

"Okay, I partly agree, but it's all we have to work with. No one will be able to tell they aren't leather at night."

He stared down at the pair of black suede, steel-tipped cowboy boots. "You guys are killing me. You know that, right?"

"It works, Dad. Trust me."

"I don't look like one of the Village People?"

TWENTY-FOUR

They sprang for one room in a motel across from Big Al's Truck Stop, caught a few winks on the pair of queen-size beds, figuring they had no way of knowing when they might have a chance to sleep again. When Will woke up, it was already dark outside and Kalyn was sitting on her bed, hunched over a laptop, the small black plastic case she'd borrowed from her PI friend in Sun City open beside her.

"What time is it?" Will whispered.

"We've got two hours."

"God, it's almost nine?" He slipped out of bed and pulled the covers back over Devlin, sighed against the first gut-prickling announcement of nerves.

He sat down beside Kalyn and stared at the computer screen.

"I'm just installing the software," she said.

"For what?"

"TrimTrac GPS. That wireless vehicle-tracking system I was telling you about."

Will lifted a black rectangular device the size of a whiteboard eraser. "Where does this go?"

"Anywhere on the truck, preferably underneath and out of sight. It's weatherproof and has enhanced sensitivity, so it doesn't have to be directly exposed to the sky."

"How's it attach?"

"There's a magnet kit. All right, look at this. You a fast learn with computers?"

"I do design Web sites for a living."

She punched in a URL on the keyboard. "I've opened a free account on

SoniyaMobile's Web site. You're gonna be able to track the truck from this computer."

"How does it work?"

"The TrimTrac device sends location updates through international SMS and GPS to a Soniya back-end server. The locations are saved and stored and you can access them on a Google map. You're gonna be operating this thing, so here, you do it." Kalyn set the computer in Will's lap. "You're in semiauto mode, and I think that's what you'll probably need to stay in. Go up here and click that. Okay, now enable the motion detector, since you only need the TrimTrac functional when the truck's moving. That'll save power. And you're gonna want real-time tracking. Click here, set update intervals at five minutes."

They spent another half hour, Will familiarizing himself with the program. While Kalyn installed the adapter, computer, and extra batteries in the Land Rover, Will mounted the magnets to the TrimTrac device.

When Kalyn returned to the motel room, her demeanor had changed. She looked pale, her eyes distracted and distant.

"Hey," Will said, "come here." She came and sat beside him on the bed. "You all right?"

She looked up, her eyes boring into his. "You up for this, Will?"

"I think so."

"I need to know for sure."

"Yes."

"I've tried to figure out some way to smuggle a gun into the trailer with me. Or that device or a cell. But it'd be too risky, so what I guess I need you to know is that my life is in your hands. Whatever truck I wind up in the back of, you cannot lose track of it."

"Look at me, Kalyn. I won't."

She nodded. "I'm sorry. I'll be fine here in a minute. Just pregame jitters, you know?"

"Yeah, I've got them, too. I keep thinking about what might happen. What if Jonathan freaks out when he sees me? What if he doesn't buy it? Demands to speak to Javier? Asks some question I can't answer? I'm guessing people in their line of work don't like last-second curveballs."

"It's a risk," she said.

"A big one."

"I've been mulling it over, and I think we may need a different approach with this guy. The whole 'Javier sent me instead and I'm sorry we didn't let you know before' is shit. I think he'd see straight through it. But you know what works with these kind of people?"

"What?"

"Fear."

"I don't understand where you're going with—"

"Remember how Javier said there were two gringo Alphas?"

TWENTY-FIVE

At 10:50 P.M., Will and Kalyn sat in the Land Rover under the seventy-foot BIG AL'S neon sign, the smell of diesel overpowering, even from inside the car. For the third time in the last minute, Will wiped his hands across his leather pants.

"You gotta quit that," Kalyn said.

"Sorry."

"You are cool and calm and in control." She handed him her Glock. "It's loaded."

"Where's the safety?"

"There isn't one, and there's a round in the chamber, but don't get all Jack Bauer on me. That's last resort right there. If you have to use it, things are seriously fucked-up."

Will closed his eyes. "He's gonna know the second he sees me that I'm—"

"It's like acting, Will, okay? Ever do any high school theater?"

"No."

"Well, you were an attorney, right? Ever represent someone you knew was guilty?"

"Sure."

"Ever get them acquitted?"

"A few times."

"Then you've acted. Convinced *twelve* people. Tonight, you only have to convince one."

"The stakes aren't even in the same league."

"You know what to say?"

"Yeah."

"Want to run through it again?"

"No, I don't wanna sound rehearsed." He held up the gun. "Where do I even put this thing?"

"Just slide it down the back of your waistband when you get out of the car. And make sure your shirt and leather jacket are pulled over it. Listen. If you have to use it, if it comes to that, you calm yourself down first. Center mass is what you aim for. That's a forty-five-cal. Thing's got plenty of stopping power."

"Jesus." Will looked at the clock: 10:54.

He opened the door, stepped outside.

"Good luck," Kalyn said. He nodded, felt like he was going to be sick. "I know you can do this," she said. "So quit doubting yourself."

But he didn't. He doubted himself as he shoved the Glock into his waistband, as he looked back across the interstate toward the motel where he'd left Devlin, as he shoved his hands into his leather jacket and started across the parking lot.

Will stepped into the convenience store that adjoined the café.

Big Al's was bustling for almost eleven, and, no surprise, 80 percent of the customers had the look of truck drivers—bearded, bulging guts, bloodshot eyes bleary with loneliness.

He walked past the drink machines, saw a black man filling what must have been a gallon-size cup from every soda dispenser—shot of Sierra Mist, Coca-Cola, orange Fanta, lemonade, Dr Pepper—a potpourri of colored, carbonated sugar water.

He headed for the rest rooms, found an empty stall, and sat for a moment on the toilet, making himself breathe, holding the Glock, turning it over, trying to settle into the weight of it. As he washed his hands, he caught his reflection in the mirror. He studied his eyes, wondered if the man named Jonathan would see the cold, callous burning that he did not.

He walked back through the convenience store, heading toward the restaurant's entrance.

A clock above the cash register read 11:02.

The hostess looked up, said, "Just one tonight, honey?"

"No, I'm meeting someone." He strode past her, made a quick scan of the tables and booths, the stools at the counter. Soft drink signs and old license plates adorned the walls. A sign over the grill read KISS A TRUCKER. *Breathe, Will. Breathe.* The place was packed. Smell of fried things, onions, old coffee, bacon, body odor, eons of accumulated cigarette smoke. *Long red hair, bushy beard, weighs over three hundred pounds. Aside from the long red hair, Javier's description matches a third of the custom—There.*

In the last booth, not far from the kitchen doors, an enormous man with braids of red hair and an unkempt beard occupied an entire bench seat. His back was to the wall, and he was staring at Will. *You aren't breathing.* Will breathed, then moved carefully across the checkered floor to the booth, the man watching him with uncertainty.

The food on the table could have fed five, breakfast, lunch, and dinner, all major fried-food groups represented.

Will slid into the booth.

"Jonathan?"

"Who the fuck are you?"

Breathe. Will's lower lip ached to tremble. He bit his tongue, glared at the man, summoning all the hate in his arsenal. *He had a hand in taking Rachael.*

"Once more. You Jonathan?" The man returned the onion ring he'd been holding to the basket and wiped the grease from his hands onto his size XXX T-shirt, which displayed three naked women engaged in some act that was indeterminate due to the stretched, faded quality of the cotton.

When he started to rise, Will pulled the Glock from his waistband, set it on the table, the barrel pointed at Jonathan, his finger on the trigger.

"You crazy?" The man's eyes cut to every corner of the restaurant, but Will didn't move. "Where's Jav?" Jonathan whispered.

"Jav went to be with the Lord." Will wiped his right hand on his pants under the table, sweat running down his sides. He tapped the Glock on the table. "Should I put this away or—"

"Yes. Nobody told me nothing about this. Who are you?"

It hadn't occurred to Will that he might be asked to give his name, and he said the first thing that popped into his head: "Never mind what my name is. We discovered that Jav had this little operation going on the side. And you know what the upsetting thing was? He never shared."

"Then why are you here?"

"Because I have the product."

Jonathan picked up an enormous hamburger and bit into it, juice and catsup running down his chin. He wiped his forearm across his mouth and spoke as he chewed.

"You think I'm gonna do business with someone I never met, never seen, never heard of? That how *you* do business?"

Will exhaled slowly through his nose. "How I conduct my business is not your affair. Just for clarification . . . you are ending your arrangement with us?"

"Us?"

"The Alphas."

Jonathan's face blanched. He swallowed. "I suspected," he said. "But I didn't know. Sure as shit didn't ask."

"Are we doing business tonight, Jonathan? I need to know right now."

Will set the Glock back on the table.

Jonathan sighed. "Yeah. Course we are. Course we are. And I apologize if I—"

"Just shut the fuck up. I'm tired, and I'd like to get some sleep. Where's your truck?"

"Space one fifty-one."

"Be there in five."

TWENTY-SIX

Will unlocked the Land Rover, climbed into the driver's seat, and shut the door. Kalyn lay silent and unmoving across the backseat, and when he glanced at her, he couldn't help seeing Rachael, and it hit him again that she'd been through all this alone, without him.

"He went for it," Will said.

Kalyn didn't move. "What now?"

"We're meeting him at his truck."

"How do you feel?"

"Like someone jammed an adrenaline shot into my heart."

"Yeah, it's a rush, huh?"

"Kalyn, it's not too late. We can still just drive away, forget this whole thing. You sure you wanna be put in the back of a trailer? God knows where it's going."

"Of course I don't, Will. I'm scared beyond shitless. But in spite of the fear, I want to know what happened to my sister. She went through exactly what I'm getting ready to experience. Nobody tracking her. Nobody watching her back."

Will cranked the engine, shifted into drive. He pulled around the side of the building that housed the restaurant and convenience store, soon found himself driving through row after row of semis, at least a hundred of them, dark and dormant, their drivers asleep for the night. Will lifted the Trim-Trac device from the passenger seat, slipped it in his pocket.

"Kalyn, I'm worried. What do I do when the next transfer is made? What if he just passes you on to another truck?"

"There's no way of knowing what'll happen, where I'll wind up. You just be close and ready to improvise. But listen, don't get yourself and your daughter killed over this, okay?"

Up ahead, just a hulking shadow in the dark, Jonathan stood waiting, the back of the trailer already open.

"I see him," Will said. "Get ready."

He parked the Land Rover behind the truck and killed the engine, then stepped out, slammed the door. He didn't like his surroundings—dark, quiet, a thousand places for someone to hide.

"Where is she?" Jonathan asked.

"Unconscious in the backseat."

Impossibly, Jonathan managed to hoist his gigantic frame up into the trailer. In the poor light, Will could just make out large cylindrical containers, wondered briefly what Jonathan's ostensible cargo was.

Will opened the door, reached under Kalyn's arms, and pulled her carefully out of the backseat. Then he slung her up so she draped over his shoulder and started toward the truck, her chest heaving against his back. *Settle down, Kalyn. Settle down.*

"Got a pretty one there?" Jonathan asked.

Will made no reply, just gave Kalyn's thigh a gentle squeeze.

At the back of the trailer, Jonathan pulled Kalyn off Will's shoulders and placed her down. He knelt beside her, ran his hands over her legs, arms, between her thighs.

"What do you think you're doing?" Will said.

"My ass is on the line now. I'll rest easier knowing it's coming into my possession with only the clothes on its body. And that you haven't done nothing to it." He continued to frisk her. "Taller than the others, ain't it?"

"You tell me. I haven't seen the others."

"Jav pick this one out?"

"Yes."

Jonathan struggled onto his feet and dragged Kalyn back into the darkness of the trailer.

Will took the TrimTrac out of his pocket as Jonathan fumbled with a set of keys. He ran his hands under the metal step beneath the Idaho license plate.

A door in back of the trailer creaked open. Kalyn slid along the floor.

Will couldn't find a surface large enough for all the magnets.

A door slammed, keys jangling. *Fuck.* Jonathan lumbered toward him as Will's hands passed over the largest flat surface he'd yet encountered. He lifted the device to the metal, felt the magnetic pull as the TrimTrac locked into place with an audible *clang.*

Will crept around the corner of the trailer, stood up, unzipped his pants.

"The fuck are you doing?" Jonathan said.

"What's it look like?" Will zipped his pants and spun around, Jonathan staring at him. "We done here?" Will said.

"Yeah. Now, in the interest of full disclosure, I'm gonna have to tell my contact that Javier is no longer selecting. Up to the buyer if he wants to use you guys again. Won't have nothing to do with me. I just wanna be clear so you don't . . . if it turns out we can't do business again, won't be me ending the relationship."

Will walked to the Land Rover and, despite his trembling hands, managed to get in and start it. He turned around between the rows of trucks and drove slowly away, watching Jonathan in the rearview mirror, and fighting against the thought that he'd seen the last he'd ever see of Kalyn Sharp.

The Last Frontier

TWENTY-SEVEN

Will and Devlin sat in the backseat of the Land Rover outside their motel room, staring at the computer screen.

"That woman has balls," Devlin said.

"Yeah, she does."

"So what are we looking at?"

"This is a Google map of the Boise area."

"The truck's not moving yet?"

"Doesn't seem to be. Maybe Jonathan's taking a nap before he hits the road. We should probably do the same." He opened the door. "Come on. I've got this thing set to fire up when the truck starts to move."

Will found it almost impossible to sleep, afraid he wouldn't hear the electronic notification that the TrimTrac had changed positions. But with the computer sitting on the bedside table, humming quietly, he finally succumbed.

His dreams came in waves, repetitive and fevered. He dreamed he woke up and the computer was gone. Dreamed it had melted into a puddle of plastic, got fried by a lightning strike. Dreamed he slept for two weeks and never heard a thing.

His eyes shot open at 4:14 A.M. He sat up in bed, instantly awake. The computer was making noise—some kind of digital alarm. He turned on the bedside table lamp and opened the laptop. As the screen sprung to life, his eyes came into focus and he saw that the icon on the Google map was no longer across the interstate at exit 64.

He shook his daughter out of sleep, and when her eyes opened, he said, "Time to go, Devi. They're on the move."

. . .

By the time Will merged southbound onto I-84, Jonathan's truck had a ten-mile head start. He'd set Devlin up in the backseat with the computer, given her a crash course, and she now knew the program as well as he did, calling out updates every couple of minutes.

At sunup, they were speeding east through Twin Falls.

As morning swung into full gear, they were heading northbound on I-15, climbing steadily into the high country of southwest Montana.

They gave Jonathan's truck a solid five-mile berth, and what had been pure exhilaration at the outset soon deteriorated into mind-numbing monotony.

There was no stopping.

Dillon. Butte. Helena. Big Sky Country.

On the plains, ten miles north of Great Falls, it occurred to Will where Jonathan was heading, and Devlin must've heard him sigh, because she said, "What's wrong, Dad?"

"He's going to Canada."

"Cool, I've never—"

"No, not cool, Devi. We have a gun in the car and we're fugitives."

"That gun's illegal?"

"It is in Canada."

"But we have identification for Joe and Samantha Foster, right?"

It was true. Will carried Social Security cards, a driver's license, passports, and certified copies of their birth certificates at all times, though he'd had only one interaction with law enforcement—a city cop at a DUI checkpoint near their home in Colorado.

They stopped in the town of Shelby, Montana, thirty miles south of the border, and after thirteen straight hours of driving, Will's legs cramped as he stepped out of the Land Rover and swiped his credit card at the pump. While the tank filled with gas, he stashed the small Glock in his leather jacket and approached a pair of Dumpsters behind the convenience store.

The gun clanged inside the empty bin.

In the store, Will used the rest room, and he and Devlin loaded up on junk food, soft drinks, coffee, packs of NoDoz.

By the time they were back on the road, it was evening, and the little icon representing Jonathan's truck on the Google map stood motionless for the first time all day on the Montana-Alberta border.

"I need you to listen to me, baby girl. What's your name?"

"Samantha Foster."

"Where do you live?"

"Mancos, Colorado."

"What's my name?"

"Joseph Foster."

"Why are we going to Canada?"

"To follow a renegade FBI agent in the back of a transfer—"

"Not funny. The Canadian border agents won't have a sense of humor. What they do have is the power to detain us—on any old whim. Something goes wrong? That's it for Kalyn. So you be respectful, give the information requested, but nothing more. The story is, that you and I are going to visit a friend in Calgary."

"Shouldn't I be in school?"

"You're home-schooled."

"What's our friend's name?"

"Nathan Banks."

"How long are we staying?"

"A week."

"You're a really good liar, Dad."

The man who knocked on Will's window was young and garbed in dark clothes.

Will lowered his window. It was already night and bitterly cold.

The customs officer said, "Both of you step out of the car, please."

Will had their Social Security cards and birth certificates in the sleeve of a notebook.

"Our documents and my driver's license," he said.

The man took the notebook and began to examine their papers as another customs officer emerged from the small Canada Border Agency shack, a long Maglite in his hand.

As he climbed under the Land Rover to inspect it, the first officer asked why they were coming into Canada. Where were they going? Coming from? Did they have any firearms? Alcohol? Tobacco? Pets? Plants? Anything to declare?

"Just my watch and a computer."

The officer helped them fill out a B4 form while the other man opened a door and shone the flashlight inside the car. After a moment, he came over and joined them.

"All in order?" his partner asked.

"Almost."

Almost?

The man who'd searched the Land Rover asked, "How long are you two planning to stay in Canada?"

"A week," Will said.

"So where's your luggage?"

Shit. Shit. Shit.

Devlin said, "We had an accident in Montana."

"What kind of accident?"

"We came over a mountain pass and I guess the air pressure blew two corks out of the bottles of wine in our suitcase. Ruined everything. We threw the suitcase away. We'll buy new clothes and stuff in Calgary."

The customs officers glanced at each other, gave a brief nod, then the man with the Maglite said, "Have a safe trip."

They stopped in Lethbridge, four miles from where the Google map said Jonathan's truck had been for the last fifty minutes.

Stayed at an inn outside of town, ate takeout in their room, and slept hard and without dreams until the computer woke them at three in the morning with notification that the truck was on the move again.

The next twenty-four hours were murder. They followed Alberta Provincial Highway 2 for three hundred miles, north through Calgary, Red Deer, all the way to Edmonton, where they picked up the Alaska Highway, spent the afternoon blasting northwest through Alberta, taking turns driving.

Whitecourt. Valleyview. Grande Prairie.

Near Dawson Creek, they came within a mile of Jonathan's truck as it stopped in town to gas up.

Evening approached and they prayed, hoped, begged the truck would stop, both starving, their eyes burning after a second full day on the road.

But Jonathan didn't stop. He continued on that northwest trajectory, driving right on into the night through the uncitied wilds of northern British Columbia, on the most desolate two-lane stretch of highway they'd ever seen, Will driving, popping NoDoz with a chaser of flat Mountain Dew or cold coffee, the computer now in the front passenger seat, angled toward him, Devlin having long since fallen asleep.

It wasn't his mind that was the problem, but his vision. With the exception of a gas stop in Fort St. John, Will had been on the road for twenty-four hours, and there was nothing NoDoz could do to recharge his eyes.

They passed into Yukon as the sun breathed its first shot of warmth into the sky.

Devlin stirred, sat up suddenly in the backseat. "Dad? You okay?"

"I don't even know how to describe how tired I feel right now. Worse than cramming for the bar."

Devlin reached forward and lifted the computer into the backseat.

"He's just ahead in a town called Whitehorse, Yukon," she said. "I think he stopped."

"Are you serious?"

"The icon hasn't moved in the last ten minutes."

"Thank God. You were about to pull driving duty."

They stopped at the first gas station they came to, just past the small airport in Yukon's capital city.

Will turned off the car and shut his eyes.

"Wake me when he's on the move again."

TWENTY-EIGHT

Will had just begun to dream, when his daughter's voice broke through.
"He's moving, Dad."

"You are fucking kidding me." Will rubbed his eyes, felt like he'd been asleep less than ten minutes, but the sun was above the horizon now, early rays glittering on the waters of the Yukon River. *Pretty country up here,* he thought, looking out at rolling foothills covered with fir trees.

According to the dashboard clock, he'd slept for almost two hours, though the brief reprieve had barely made a dent in his exhaustion. He turned the ignition, drove the Land Rover slowly through town, letting the truck put a few more miles of distance between them.

"You need to talk to me," he said. "I'll nod off, end up running us off the road."

"I can drive."

"Not yet."

"What do you wanna talk about?"

"I don't care. Just engage me. Take my mind off how tired I am."

Devlin was quiet for a moment, staring out the tinted glass as they passed through downtown Whitehorse.

"Okay," she said finally, "do you think Kalyn's pretty?"

Will straightened in his seat. "Well," he said, "I think that did the trick."

"No, you have to answer my question."

Whitehorse was fading away in the side mirrors, and they had the Alaska Highway all to themselves, a corridor of pavement through a forest of black spruce.

"Sure, she's pretty."

"You like her?"

"Excuse me?"

"In school, we have this rating system. You can like someone. You can *like* like them. Or you can *like like* like them."

Will laughed. "So what was your rating with little Ben over the summer?"

"We're not talking about me right now, Dad."

"I don't know, Devi. What do you think? That these last few days have been one big date? This is an incredibly stressful time, and I—"

"That doesn't mean you can't like her."

He caught her eyes in the rearview mirror. "Look, I'm not saying this to judge or be mean, but Kalyn's a damaged person, Dev. Nothing against her. I'm just saying I think she's had a really hard time since her sister disappeared."

"Harder than us with Mom?"

"Yeah. Why are you asking me all this? You *want* me to like her?"

"I guess it'd be all right. I mean, you haven't dated anyone since Mom. Aren't you, like, lonely?"

"You don't like it, just the two of us?"

"No, I do, it's just—Dad!"

Will's eyes cut from the rearview mirror back to the windshield.

An enormous bull moose stood straddling the dotted white line of the Alaska Highway, thirty yards ahead.

Will slammed down on the brake pedal, lunging forward, something shooting through the space between the front seats, smashing into the dashboard.

"Devlin!"

The Land Rover skidded to a stop, the front bumper five feet from the moose, which just stood there staring dully at will through the windshield. He looked in the backseat, confirmed that Devlin was buckled in, safe but rattled, tears streaming down her face.

"No, honey, don't cry. It's okay. We're all right."

She shook her head, and Will's stomach fell. He glanced down. Near the gearshift, in the front passenger seat, on both floorboards, and on his lap lay pieces of the computer, and the portion of the screen still attached to the shattered keyboard was black.

"Oh God," he said.

"We can still find her, right?"

"Oh God."

"Dad?"

He drove around the giant moose and floored the accelerator.

It was midday before Will finally spotted Jonathan's truck, pulling away from the border station into the state of Alaska.

He and Devlin spent fifteen agonizing minutes talking with the American customs official, Will thinking the officer had probably sensed his impatience and decided to ask more questions than he otherwise would have. By the time they were on the road again and passing a sign welcoming them to the "Last Frontier State," Will figured Jonathan had at least a twenty-mile head start.

He pushed the Land Rover to eighty-five, speeding along the Alaska Highway, passing RVs at the rate of one every couple of miles. In the nowhere town of Tok, Alaska, ninety-three miles west of the border, Will came to what he'd dreaded more than anything—a fork in the road. Stay straight on Alaska 1, head west to Fairbanks. Or make a left onto Alaska 2 and head south toward Anchorage.

"Which way, Dad?"

Will pulled onto the shoulder, shifted the car into park.

"Fairbanks is two hundred miles that way," he said. "Kind of in the middle of the state. I don't know much about it. Anchorage is in the south, on the coast."

"How close do you think we are to the truck?"

"I don't know."

"Dad—"

"Just give me a minute here, Dev!"

After thirty seconds of the most excruciating deliberation he'd ever put himself through, he finally shifted into drive and stomped the gas.

"Anchorage?" Devlin asked as the Land Rover accelerated to ninety miles per hour.

"It's a shipping city. Lots of ports. I have a feeling they're putting Kalyn on a boat."

"Are you sure?"

"No, baby girl. Nowhere close to sure."

TWENTY-NINE

When Kalyn woke, the truck was still and silent. She hadn't intended to fall asleep, but the boredom and emotional heft of recent days had overtaken her again. She had no idea how long she'd been inside the trailer, though it felt like weeks. She sat up from the thick yellow foam, stared at the shiny metal ceiling, the two remaining jugs of water, the dwindling box of food. The metal pail in the farthest corner reeked of her piss and shit.

Strangely enough, she felt closer to her sister than she had in years, just knowing Lucy had spent time cramped in this little space.

Lucy was four years younger, and Kalyn had often lied to herself, insisted her sister was a brave, fearless person, that whatever had happened to her, she'd handled it with grace and courage. But locked in the trailer of this eighteen-wheeler, Kalyn knew that wasn't the case. Lucy had awakened here confused, disoriented, and more terrified than she'd ever been in her life.

Kalyn heard something beyond the walls—impossible to tell what through the soundproofing.

A piece of yellow foam turned back, the door to her cage opening. She stood up, her feet bare, the rest of the trailer dark and the flickering lightbulb above her head doing nothing to illuminate whoever was out there.

A pair of handcuffs flew through the door and dropped on the yellow foam.

"Put 'em on."

Flat voice, white male, no accent.

She picked up the handcuffs and closed them around her wrists.

"Come on out."

Cold air swept through the trailer.

"Where am—"

Someone reached in, dragged her out, and then she was being lifted, hands gripping her arms above the elbows. She smelled day-old cologne and remnants of cigarette smoke.

They came to the end of the trailer and she was lowered into the arms of a tall man with blond hair, eyes the color of sea ice, but with less warmth.

THIRTY

In the late afternoon, Will pulled the Land Rover onto the shoulder at the junction of Alaska 1 and Alaska 4, yet another split in the highway.

Devlin read the mileage sign: "Anchorage, one eighty-seven. Valdez, one seventeen."

Will let out a deep sigh, his head resting on the steering wheel. "We've lost her," he said.

"Maybe the truck's up ahead."

He couldn't bear the hope in his daughter's voice. "I've been doing ninety for the last hour and a half. If he'd come this way, we would've caught up to him by now."

"Where else could the truck have gone?"

"Where? Maybe he stopped in Tok and we didn't see him. Probably he went on to Fairbanks." He lifted what was left of the computer out of the front passenger seat and stared at the destroyed screen.

"Is Kalyn going to die?"

"I don't know, Devi."

"But probably she is?" Will punched the gas, spun the car around. "What are you doing, Dad?"

"Only thing left to do."

THIRTY-ONE

They were passing through a city big enough to boast a pathetic skyline—meager collection of ten- and twelve-story buildings—the tall blond driving, a man on either side of Kalyn in the backseat of the new Suburban. The man to her right was young, twenty at most, and he kept eyeing her, fidgeting with his hands, his hair long and black, drawn back into a greasy ponytail. *He's nervous.* The man to her left was perhaps ten years older—buzz cut, light brown hair, heavily freckled. They both wore black jeans and long-sleeved button-ups with down vests over the top, fat with pocket bulges—knives perhaps, or cell phones. She fought the urge to glance back, dying to know if the Land Rover was tailing them.

"Where are you taking me?" she asked.

The driver turned up the radio—NPR, "Talk of the Nation."

It was 2:46 P.M., and they soon left the city, passing now along quiet residential streets, then stretches of forest, the houses more scattered, only a few per mile, then no homes or power lines and the road gone to gravel, narrowed into one lane, with tall spruce trees on either side. The Suburban was kicking up substantial clouds of dust, so she couldn't see in the side mirrors if Will was following them.

Another five miles and the dirt road ended on the shore of a long, skinny lake.

The tall blond turned off the car. They waited, parked parallel to the lakeshore, affording Kalyn a view of the road as it disappeared into the trees. The dust of their passage had settled. *Something's happened. He isn't coming.*

"Would you please tell me where I am?" Kalyn asked.

The man behind the wheel looked in the rearview mirror, said, "Shut up."

"I have to pee."

"Hold it."

"Seriously, my bladder's about to rupture. I don't know if I can hold it much longer, and I don't want to pee all over your seat."

The blond said, "Take her, Marcus." She hoped he meant the younger of the two, but the freckled man opened his door instead and helped her out of the car.

He walked her twenty feet from the Suburban to a cluster of saplings, and Kalyn pulled her panties down, lifted her skirt, and squatted.

As her piss hit the ground and steamed, Marcus did exactly what she'd hoped for—looked away.

Kalyn came quietly to her feet, stepped out of her panties, and slipped her hands over Marcus's head, squeezing them back into his neck for all she was worth. He was a few inches taller, much stronger, but that didn't matter, because Kalyn had the edge of the metal cuff digging into his carotid artery, the bone of her forearm crushing his windpipe, and it only took five seconds for his knees to go.

She dragged him behind the saplings, ripped open his vest, calculating that she had maybe ten or fifteen seconds before the other men started to wonder where they were.

She found a .357, broke open the cylinder—six rounds—snapped it closed and started toward the Suburban, her bare feet freezing as she moved low and fast across the grass and rocks. She crouched behind the Suburban and peeked around the left rear taillight, spotted the side mirror on the driver's side, the tall blond in the reflection, his head turned, talking.

She glanced back toward the cluster of saplings, Marcus already sitting up, trying to climb to his feet.

Kalyn crawled past the gas tank, the rear passenger door, stopping finally at the driver's door.

You can do this. You have to do this. For Lucy.

She thumbed back the hammer, stood up, Marcus shouting in the distance, the whine of another car coming up the road.

Will?

Though the side window was deeply tinted, she could see the profile of the man's head.

Glass shattered. Blood sprayed.

She jerked open the door behind the driver's seat, the young man wide-eyed, shaking his head and mouthing "No" as he reached into his vest.

Two squeezes, center mass, gurgling, pieces of down floating between them.

The sound of the engine getting louder.

Three bullets left. Be judicious.

Marcus was coming toward the Suburban now, knife in hand, moving awkwardly, zombielike, his brain still reeling after the lapse in blood flow.

Kalyn ran toward him, ears ringing, stopped ten feet away, feeling comfortable enough with the .357 to draw a bead on the man's face, yelled, "Drop the knife and stop right there!"

But he didn't do either, just kept staggering toward her.

"I've shot your friends. I will shoot you. Do you want to die today, Marcus?"

He kept coming, Kalyn thinking, *Maybe he doesn't believe he's capable of dying at the hands of a woman.*

The shot took the top of his head off and he collapsed to his knees, toppled over in the moist, spongy soil.

Two bullets left. Not enough.

Kalyn ran back to the Suburban, opened the driver's door. Sea Ice Eyes had slumped over into the passenger seat, and she hauled him out of the car, searched him, found the handcuff key and a handgun—.45 Smith.

The car engine had become deafening, and then she realized it couldn't be a car, because the sound was coming from the lake.

A single-prop floatplane had just landed, its engine screaming as it sped shoreward.

Kalyn unlocked the handcuffs and crawled behind the Suburban, ducked down, watching through the rear tinted glass as the plane sidled up to the pier. The propeller had stopped. She heard the pontoons bump into the wooden posts. The plane's door swung open, and a man climbed out. Impossible to see any detail in his face or even determine his height, since he was still thirty yards away and dimmed by the smoked glass.

As he walked down the pier, the Suburban's rear passenger door opened. *Shit.* The young man with the ponytail fell out, struggled to his feet, and stumbled toward the plane, Kalyn watching him go.

Now the pilot had stopped. He stared at the injured man coming toward him, yelled something Kalyn couldn't understand, then ran back toward the plane, scrambling up into the cockpit, the propeller sputtering to life.

She stepped out from behind the Suburban as the plane pulled away from the dock, saw the young man lying facedown in the grass. She sprinted the length of the pier as the engine roared, the plane gliding away from her, skimming the surface of the lake with increasing speed. It was already a hundred yards away. Two hundred.

The high-pitched whine sounded like a buzz saw as the plane lifted from the lake, climbing into the sky. It banked left and screamed west over the forest, disappearing after ten seconds, its engine no louder than the mosquito behind Kalyn's ear.

She ran back to the young man and rolled him over. Lines of blood trailed from the corners of his mouth into the grass, his glassy eyes reduced to slits. She propped him up against a spruce tree, slapped his face.

"Where's that plane going?"

He shook his head and ripped open his vest, looked down at the two dark stains on his shirt merging and spreading across his stomach. He began to cry.

"I can help you," Kalyn told him, lying. "Get you to a hospital. You could survive this. But I need to know where that plane's heading."

His voice came ragged and wet: "I'm cold."

"You wanna live?"

He nodded.

"Then tell me."

He whispered something.

"What?"

"Hills."

"What does that mean?"

"—ine Hills."

"The ing hills?"

"Wolverine Hills."

"Wolverine Hills?"

He nodded.

"Where's that?"

The young man coughed up a mouthful of blood, moaned, "Please."

"What's his name? The guy who got out of the plane."

His eyes grew more distant, like someone had pulled down the shades.

"Was this the last exchange, or was that man going to deliver me to someone else? I need to—"

He let out a long exhalation and the muscles in his neck and back relaxed. He drooped forward. Kalyn touched the side of his neck. She came to her feet, surveyed the scene—three bodies in the wilderness and darkness falling.

THIRTY-TWO

Will and Devlin walked into the rich-smelling coffee shop that doubled as an Internet café, waited impatiently for a computer, staring at the bizarre series of photographs that adorned the walls—black-and-white images of mating caribou. A college kid was setting up on the stage against the back wall, adjusting the levels on his amp and tuning an acoustic guitar. It was already dark outside, and Will was on the verge of ordering someone off a computer when one opened up.

He and Devlin shared a chair at one of the Macs. The connection was maddeningly slow, and it took five minutes for SoniyaMobile's Web site to load. It had been three days since Kalyn had made him memorize her log-in ID and password. He remembered her ID immediately, but her password was alphanumeric, and it took him five tries to get it right.

When the Google map finally loaded, he said "Fuck" loudly enough for the patrons seated at adjacent computers and nearby tables to glance over and shoot him dirty stares.

Devlin said, "Oh no."

The little icon representing Jonathan's truck was already in northern British Columbia.

"He's going home," Will said. "Already delivered her to the buyer."

"Is she dead?" Devlin whispered.

"Stop asking me that," he replied, his words sharper than he intended.

The acoustic guitarist was now crowding a mic stand, strumming his guitar, and introducing what he described as experimental–hip-hop–folk.

"Trace it, Dad."

"What?"

"You can see where all Jonathan's truck has been. Here, I'll do it." She grabbed the mouse and moved the cursor up to the command menu. As she clicked on VIEW TRACKING HISTORY, Will's cell phone rang. He pulled it out of his pocket, stared incredulously at the display screen.

"Who is it?" Devlin asked.

"I don't recognize the number."

He hit TALK. "Hello?"

"Will?"

"Shit, Kalyn, are you okay?"

"Where are you?"

"Fairbanks, Alaska."

"Where in Fairbanks?"

"This coffee shop near the university. The Last Drop."

"I'm ten minutes away. Stay put."

Will closed the phone and stared at his daughter in disbelief.

Devlin began to cry.

Scars

THIRTY-THREE

Will and Devlin stood shivering outside the coffee shop, preferring the cold of the Alaskan night to the earnest warbling of the guitarist inside. At last, a black Suburban pulled into the parking lot, Kalyn grinning at them through what remained of the driver's side window—tinted jags of glass.

She got out, and Will and Devlin walked over, embraced her.

"I'm so sorry," Will whispered in her ear.

"Hey." Kalyn framed his face with her hands. "I'm all right. Let it go."

"What happened to you?"

"Let's swap stories later. Right now, I want you to follow me. I have to ditch this car. It's full of glass and blood."

Will followed the Suburban for several miles through the heart of Fairbanks, coming at last to a Safeway. Kalyn parked in a far corner, spent five minutes wiping everything down—the steering wheel, doors, gearshift—anyplace she might have left fingerprints or sweat, skin cells or hair.

Then she climbed into the front passenger seat beside Will, said, "I've got a room at the Best Western. Head back the way we came."

As Will pulled onto the Alaska Highway, Kalyn noticed the remains of the computer on the floorboard. She lifted a piece of the shattered keyboard, turned it over in her hand.

"That happened this morning outside of Whitehorse, Yukon," Will said. "A moose was standing in the middle of the highway. I had to slam on the brakes to avoid hitting him, and the computer launched into the dashboard. We were trying to track Jonathan's truck at the coffee shop when you called."

"It was my fault," Devlin said. "I was talking to Dad to keep him awake. I should have been holding on to the computer tighter than I was."

Kalyn glanced into the backseat, reached out for Devlin's hand. "Not your fault, baby," she said. "Some things—they just happen. Nothing we can do."

"So what happened to you?" Devlin asked.

"Jonathan turned me over to three men this afternoon at a warehouse, somewhere in Fairbanks. They drove me out into the countryside, to this lake. I was able to get away."

By the way she said it, Will knew. "You mean you killed them."

"Yeah."

"Three men? How?"

"They made a mistake. Cuffed my hands in front of me instead of behind my back. If they'd done that, it would've made it impossible for me to do what I did. Or at least much more difficult. Also, they underestimated what I was capable of."

"Who were they?"

"I've been trying to work that out. Seemed like muscle for organized crime."

"There's an Alaskan mob?"

"Probably an offshoot of an Anchorage syndicate. Turn up here."

Will took the next exit onto S. Cushman, saw motel, hotel, and restaurant signs glowing in the distance.

"They were definitely delivering me to someone," Kalyn said. "While I was dealing with them, a floatplane landed on the lake, came up to the pier. This man got out, saw that something had obviously gone wrong, and hauled ass out of there."

"You find out where he was going?"

"I questioned one of the men before he died, but the only piece of information I got was a place called the Wolverine Hills. You heard of it?"

"No."

"Me, neither. Hey, there's the Best Western."

As Will pulled into the hotel's driveway, Devlin said, "Dad, your backpack's buzzing."

Will and Kalyn looked at each other, said, "Javier" at the same time.

"Hand it up here, Dev," Will said, and then to Kalyn: "Jesus, how long's it been since we put his wife and son in that mall?"

"Five days."

He pulled into a parking space. "Five?"

"I know. Long time, but they had plenty of food and water. I'd anticipated this possibility, Will. It's why I left some books in there, extra flashlights. What number is the caller ID showing?"

Will glanced at the BlackBerry. "Same as before." He pressed TALK, then SPEAKER. "Hello?"

"It's been three days since your meeting with Jonathan. I have not interfered. You will tell me where my family is now?"

Kalyn snatched the BlackBerry out of Will's hand.

"Hi, Javier. Really sorry we haven't gotten back to you yet, but it's been a crazy few days. I'm sure you understand."

"No, I do—"

"Well, look, here's the thing. As it turns out, I'm not going to tell you where Misty and Raphael are, because it wouldn't matter. I killed them both last Saturday."

Kalyn pressed END and immediately began to dial again.

Will said, "What are you—"

She waved him off, then waited through several rings before a voice answered.

"Yes, I'd like to report something. There's a woman and a boy locked up in one of the dressing rooms in the children's department of Belk. . . . That burned-out mall in Scottsdale . . . Desert Gardens Shopping Center . . . No, that's all the information I have. . . . No, you can't have my name."

She ended the call and opened her door as the BlackBerry vibrated again.

Will said, "Come on, Kalyn—"

"Guess who's calling back." She powered off the BlackBerry, put it in her pocket.

"Are you crazy, Kalyn?"

She stood grinning by the open door.

Will turned off the engine, and he and Devlin opened their doors, got out.

"Too far," he said as they walked toward the entrance. "Telling a man, even a bad one, you killed his wife and son? Too far."

Kalyn stopped under the entrance overhang and faced him. "Why?"

"There's a line."

"Where?"

"Separates us from people like—"

"Fuck him, Will. Let that piece of shit taste what it feels like to lose your family."

They showered at the hotel, then went out and bought new clothes at a Kmart to replace the filthy, road-shabby apparel they'd worn since Idaho. At a nearby steak house, they had supper, and after days of living on convenience-store food, they splurged and ate like gluttons, just glad to be

together again, relishing the company, filling one another in on every detail of their respective journeys from Boise to Fairbanks.

They returned to the hotel, Will as tired as he'd ever been.

While waiting for the elevator, Kalyn spotted the unoccupied business
center.

"No, let's look in the morning," Will said. "I'm worthless now."

"Come on, only take a minute."

They gathered around the computer, Kalyn at the keyboard, Will and
Devlin looking over her shoulder.

She pulled up the Google home page and typed "Wolverine Hills" and
"Alaska" into the query box.

The search results were unimpressive, not a single Web site devoted to
the Wolverine Hills, and they were mentioned just two times in passing:
under a place-name listing titled "Minor Ranges of the Alaskan Interior"
and in a three-year-old forum posting—an outdoorsman inquiring if anyone had ever hunted caribou in the Wolverines.

"Okay, here's something," Kalyn said. "Says they're a small grouping of
hills ranging between two and four thousand feet. Oriented east to west.
Thirty miles long, ten wide. Two hundred miles north of Denali National
Park. Two hundred west of Fairbanks."

"I'm guessing you can't drive there," Will said.

Kalyn had already accessed MapQuest and was executing a search of
the area west of Fairbanks.

"Alaska Three goes south to Anchorage. Looks like there are some un-
paved roads that head north and west, but none of those come within a
hundred and fifty miles of the Wolverines."

"Hence the floatplane."

Devlin said, "So this guy is flying women out there, into those hills?"

"Looks that way," Kalyn said.

"Why would he do that?"

"I don't know, baby. Part of me doesn't want to know."

THIRTY-FOUR

Will gave Devlin her physical therapy and left her half-asleep in front of the TV. He took the stairs up to the next floor, knocked softly on the door of room 617. Kalyn answered in a tank top and running shorts that accentuated her long-muscled arms and legs.

"Can we talk?" Will asked.

They sat on the king-size bed, everything quiet save for the whisper of the central-heating unit blowing warm air out from under the window. Kalyn's curls were uncurling and the shower had nearly stripped the black dye from her hair, returning it to its natural brown, now pinned up off her shoulders.

"What are you thinking of doing?" he asked.

"Same thing you are."

"There's no telling what we'll find out there, and Devi's been through a lot already."

"I can protect you both," Kalyn said.

Will smiled. "Aren't I supposed to say that? You're challenging my fragile ego."

"Look, you don't have to go. Head home if you want."

"But you're going to the Wolverine Hills."

"There's nothing else for me to do."

"What if that guy was lying? He was dying, Kalyn. What'd he have to lose?"

"Guess I'll find out."

"Or we could call the police now. Let them take it from here."

"Same sort of folks who never found Rachael to begin with, but accused you of her death? No thanks, Will. I've sacrificed too much to hand them the ball on first and goal. Watch them fuck it up."

Will leaned back against the headboard, glanced toward the window at the lights of downtown Fairbanks.

"Suppose we do find out what happened to my wife. Your sister. Then what? They'll still be gone. We'll still be missing them."

"Won't it help you move on?"

"I don't know. Rachael's been gone five years, but you know, I still remember the night she didn't come home, and the following day, when everyone came to my house to hold vigil, like it just happened. I feel stuck in that moment."

"I'm well acquainted with that feeling."

"What do you want, Kalyn? What do you expect to gain from all this?"

"Peace. I think. And to know exactly what happened to my sister. You don't understand. Before Lucy disappeared, my life was on this perfect trajectory. I'd made special agent. I was doing well, advancing at the Bureau. Doing exactly what I wanted to do. Making the friends and the connections I wanted to make. I loved my place in the world, but I was also thinking ten years down the road, fifteen. Had it all planned out. Stint with the FBI, then prosecutor. Maybe a run for office. But after Lucy . . ."

"You derailed."

"Yeah."

"You can still do anything you want. You know that, right?"

"Actually, I can't. I was fired from the FBI. A Bureau psychologist wrote terrible things in my file that'll always be there. 'Emotionally unstable.' 'Clinical depression.' That part of my life, those dreams . . . they're dead." She said it with no emotion, no resentment. For the first time, Will noticed the long blanched lines down Kalyn's wrists.

He touched them, traced a finger along the scars.

"Last year," she said, her voice just a whisper, "was rough. I was just so tired, you know? I couldn't breathe. You ever think about doing something like that?" He nodded. "But you had Devlin."

"Without her, I don't know that I'd still be here."

"You ever feel just . . . broken?"

Will looked up from the bedspread into Kalyn's eyes, realized he'd never really seen her before. "You're one of the most extraordinary people I've ever met," he said. "That's the truth."

Kalyn scooted toward him.

It was a soft and effortless melding of energies, long pent-up electrical currents with someplace finally to go. They came apart breathless and a little stunned, Will's heart going like mad, the cool smoothness of Kalyn's leg against his arm practically unbearable and the taste of her humming in the corners of his mouth.

"I can't do this," he said, and he climbed off the bed and left the room.

THIRTY-FIVE

The next morning, Will was shaving in the bathroom when Devlin knocked on the door. She walked in, climbed up on the sink, stared at her father, shaving cream smeared across his chin.

"Morning," Will said, and went back to shaving. "Sleep well?"

"Yeah. You?"

"Too well. I could still use a few more hours."

Devlin smeared paste on a toothbrush, started brushing her tongue. "What are we doing today?"

"Well, you get to hang out here, do whatever you want."

"You're leaving?"

"Kalyn and I are gonna see if we can find someone to fly us into the Wolverine Hills." Will drew the razor carefully over the curve of his chin.

"And if you find someone to do it?"

"Then we're gonna go."

"Without me?"

"Yeah."

Devlin spit into the sink and slammed her toothbrush down.

Will turned on the tap, rinsed the shaving cream and the severed bristles off the blades.

"Honey, I have no idea what, if anything, we'll find out there. I've already put you in enough danger, and you are way too precious to be dragged—"

"You wouldn't be dragging me, Dad."

Will picked up a hand towel, dabbed his face. "It's just gonna be for a day, Devi."

She'd gone short of breath, her eyes welling.

"Calm down, baby girl. I want you to—"

"Stop calling me that! I'm not a kid!" Her eyes were burning.

"You're right. You're not a kid, but you are sixteen, and I feel rotten enough having brought you along. I'm not making that mistake—"

Devlin wrapped her arms around him, shaking, crying. "Please take me with you. I don't wanna be left. She's *my* mother, you know. I wanna find out what happened just as bad as you."

"Look at me. No, look at me." He held his daughter by the arms. "I'm not putting you in danger."

"You're all I have, Dad. You know that?"

"Of course I do."

"So we stay together, no matter what."

The office for Arctic Skies was tucked into a strip mall along a river that snaked through the middle of Fairbanks. Devlin, Will, and Kalyn walked in at 10:00 A.M.—when the phone book said the business opened—found a man leaning back in a swivel chair, his feet propped up on a desk, smoking a cigar, perusing the *Daily News-Miner*. The office was small and spare, just a desk, computer, couple of chairs, artificial tree. Framed posters hung on the walls—photos of snowy mountains, grizzly bears catching salmon, the northern lights.

"Buck Young?" Will asked.

The man glanced over the top of his newspaper, blew a puff of smoke out the side of his mouth.

"One and the same."

He looked trail-worn—red, watery eyes, weathered skin, salt-and-pepper beard. A Yankees baseball cap that might have been twenty years old rested on a mop of shoulder-length graying hair, unwashed for God knew how long.

Will said, "We're looking for someone to fly us out to the Wolverine Hills."

"Wolverines? Really?"

"Yeah. You familiar with the area?"

"Sure. Flew a hunter out there couple years back. Here, ya'll sit down."

There were just two chairs on their side of the desk. Devlin sat on the arm of Kalyn's.

"Anybody live out there?" Will asked.

"Oh no. You'd be hard-pressed to find a more remote piece of country in all of Alaska."

"So it's public land?"

"If I recall, some of it's public-owned, but most belongs to the Athabascan Indians. Look, if you're paying customers, I'll fly you anywhere you wanna go. But I have to ask, why the Wolverines? Next to the Brooks Range,

McKinley, the Wrangells, they ain't much to look at. And it's an awful long flight for such dinky mountains."

"I'm afraid we have our hearts set on it," Kalyn said.

Buck swung his boots off the desk and leaned forward in his chair. "What exactly you wanna do out there?"

Will said, "We'd like to spend two nights. Do some camping and hiking."

"You have gear?"

"No."

"I can outfit you with everything you'll need." Buck took a pocket calculator out of a drawer and began punching in numbers and mumbling to himself. "Four hundred miles round trip. Gear rental for two nights. Three people. Guided? Unguided?"

"Just the three of us."

"You're looking at around three thousand."

Kalyn glanced at Will. He nodded, mouthed "I can cover it," then turned back to Buck. "We'd like to leave as soon as possible. Today would be ideal."

They went to meet the bush pilot at 1:00 P.M. at the Chena Marina, a floatplane pond on the outskirts of Fairbanks, found Buck loading supplies into a cargo pod under the fuselage of a high-winged single-engine Cessna 185. The exterior of the Skywagon did not inspire peace of mind, the green-and-yellow design scheme chipped and faded, dents in the amphibious floats.

"I think I've got you all set," Buck said. "There's supposed to be some weather coming in this evening, so we should get in the air straight away."

It was a four-seater, with plenty of storage space in back, the interior upholstered in light gray carpeting, the leather seats covered in sheepskin. Devlin begged to sit next to Buck, and she was awarded copilot status. They got themselves buckled in, and soon the engine was firing up, Buck taxiing away from the docks toward the end of the pond, his voice blaring through the headsets that everyone wore: "Should be up about ninety minutes."

"How fast and high will we go?" Devlin asked.

"Hundred and twenty knots at forty-five hundred feet."

"Cool."

They'd reached the far end of the lake.

The three-hundred-horsepower engine wound up, the prop disappeared, and the Cessna accelerated on the water.

Will stared out the window as the shore raced by, the plane skipping across little waves, and he was thinking about their conversation on the drive over from the hotel. He and Kalyn had agreed on the ground rules

of this expedition. They were going to look. Not get involved in anything, with anyone. If they found something, they'd wait for Buck to come
get them, notify the authorities on their return to Fairbanks. Safety, protecting Devlin—that was their top priority.

The bumps soon turned into smooth forward motion, Buck easing back
on the stick, Devlin watching his feet work the rudder pedals.

They soared over the trees. Will swallowed, his ears popping, the pond,
the city of Fairbanks falling away beneath him, and he could see at once
how small and insignificant it seemed, surrounded on every side by miles
and miles of muskeg bogs and untouched boreal forest, marred only by an
occasional road and the braids of the Chena and Tanana rivers. He reached
forward, patted Devlin's shoulder, felt Kalyn squeeze his hand.

THIRTY-SIX

For fifteen minutes, they followed the westward track of Alaska 3, climbing steadily toward cruising altitude. That gray thread of pavement hooked south toward Anchorage, but they flew on, due west into the Alaskan bush.

Not even the brown, unpeopled waste of northern Arizona rivaled this level of desolation. No sign of human habitation. Endless spruce forests interspersed with patches of turning paper birch—veins of gold from Will's vantage point.

They flew over foothills, expanses of high tundra. Buck pointed out herds of caribou and a massive white bulk far to the south—McKinley, highest mountain in North America.

An hour into the flight, Devlin asked, "Are there grizzly bears where we're going?"

"You bet," Buck said. "Bears live everywhere out here. And you want to avoid them, especially now. It's late season and they're trying to fatten up in advance of hibernation."

"What about wolves?"

"Plenty of those, too."

"Are they dangerous?"

"Oh, no. You're lucky if you see one. Also keep an eye out for caribou, moose, fox. One good thing about coming to a little-known place like the Wolverines—the wildlife will be abundant. Hey, I think I see our destination way, way off on the horizon. Samantha, why don't you take the controls for a little while?"

Will felt nauseous and he had a crushing headache from the noise.

"We'll be in the Wolverines in just a minute here," Buck said.

"Could you do a quick flyover?" Kalyn asked. "Just so we can get a sense of the area."

"Sure." He pushed the stick and the Cessna dipped earthward, Will's stomach lifting, Devlin squealing.

"It's like a roller coaster," she said.

The plane banked left.

"That's them?" Kalyn asked.

"There're your hills."

They were only a thousand feet above the ground now, and the Wolverines lay beneath them like a succession of low earthen waves. It was undisputedly a minor range, a rippling uplift amid a vast, otherwise-unbroken forest. They could see the whole of the chain in one glimpse—wooded hills rising toward the biggest mountain of the bunch, a four-thousand-foot unnamed peak, most of it above timberline and blanketed in scarlet and yellow from the turning underbrush. A valley cut through the middle of the range, and it was here that they spotted two lakes, one in the middle, one on the eastern edge.

"You could land on either of those lakes?" Kalyn asked.

"Yep. I'll set down on whichever one you prefer."

"Joe, do you see that?"

It took Will a moment to realize that Kalyn was speaking to him. "What?"

She was pointing out her window. "Oh, now I've lost it."

"What was it?"

"Looked like a structure of some sort on the shore of the interior lake."

"Could very well be," Buck said. "I called a friend of mine after ya'll left my office this morning, just hunting for a little information about the Wolverines. He said there was a gold strike out here, turn of the century, along the Ice River, which flows south out of these hills. Apparently, nothing much ever came of it, but it wouldn't surprise me if there were still some old structures down there."

"This thing was big," Kalyn said. "But it was in the trees. Hard to see."

"Well, there you go. Be a great day hike for you three to undertake. Look, this cloud deck's starting to come down on us. Where do you want me to land?"

They touched down on the outer lake, a turbulent landing, water spraying up onto the windshield, the plane listing on its floats.

When Buck killed the engine, it was 2:30 P.M. The prop sputtered to a stop, and the Cessna drifted up onto a sandy shore.

They climbed down one at a time onto the pontoons.

It was cold, a raw, steady wind pushing small waves onto the beach, the sky a uniform, textureless gray, mist falling out of it.

Will and Buck opened the cargo pod and carried the three backpacks up onto the beach.

Buck said, "You know a little something about camping, Mr. Foster?"

"A very little. Why?"

"Think you can figure out setting up the tent on your own? And how to use the water filter and the propane stove?"

"Sure, I can do that."

"I'd stay and give you the rundown, but this weather's coming in faster than I expected, and I'd like to get back to Fairbanks."

"No, that's fine. We really appreciate your flying us out here on such short notice."

"My pleasure." Buck waded back over to the plane, climbed up onto the pontoons. "I'll be back Sunday, three P.M., to pick you up. There's no cell phone service out here, so just be aware of that. Don't get hurt. You'll be here?"

"Sunday, three P.M. We'll be here," Will said.

"I hope ya'll enjoy your time out here, and I hope the weather holds for you."

Buck climbed into the plane and shut the door.

The Cessna roared, and Kalyn, Will, and Devlin stood watching it from the sandy beach.

The engine screamed as the Skywagon sped away from them.

After thirty seconds, it lifted into the gray sky, eastbound.

They watched it dwindle, then vanish into the clouds, the drone of its engine fading.

Soon there was no sound but the lake lapping at their feet.

The Loneliest Sound

THIRTY-SEVEN

K alyn knelt down, dipped her fingers into the clear lake water.

"Weird, how quiet it is."

"I'm cold," Devlin said.

"You've got gloves in the pocket of your fleece. Put them on, baby girl."

Will sat down in the sand, pulled a folded sheet of paper out of his back pocket—a map he'd printed off from TopoZone.com.

"All right, look here." Kalyn and Devlin flanked him, peering over his shoulder. "Obviously, the plane Kalyn saw yesterday didn't land on this lake. Now the interior lake is the only other body of water in the Wolverines large enough to accommodate a floatplane."

"You think that's where that plane landed, Dad?"

"I don't know. Part of me thinks there's no one here but us and that we're wasting time."

"What was the alternative?" Kalyn asked. "Walk up to the Alaskan mob, ask them who they're delivering kidnapped women to? We'd be buried in the tundra, pushing up glacier lilies."

Will touched a point on the map. "We're here." He traced his finger over the paper. "The inner lake is here. That's about six miles away."

"Here's what I propose," Kalyn said.

"What?"

"We've got a few hours of light left. Let's see how much ground we can cover. We'll find a safe place to camp, close to the inner lake, so we can explore from there without having to drag these monster packs around with us."

"Okay. I like that."

. . .

There was no trail marked on Will's map of the Wolverine Hills, but a stream connected the inner and outer lakes, and this is what they followed, progressing slowly for the first hour, taking their time navigating the mossy bank where they could, bushwhacking through underbrush where they couldn't, the air so clean, redolent of white spruce.

They stopped midafternoon at the base of a waterfall, a set of smaller cascades above it. Will searched his pack and found the Ziploc bags containing nuts and dried fruit that Buck had packed for them. While he distributed the snacks and water bottles, Kalyn studied the map, tracing their path from the outer lake up into the hills.

"How far have we come?" Devlin asked.

"That's what I'm trying to figure out here." She finally located the tight contour lines that crossed the blue line on the map, denoting the series of waterfalls.

"Looks like we've covered about . . . three miles."

"Look!" Devlin whispered.

A pair of caribou were working their way carefully above the lower waterfall, stopping every few feet to look and listen.

They pushed on, the stream narrowing, becoming steeper, rockier, with fewer stretches of flat water and more cascades.

Devlin was leading the way, and she stopped suddenly, said, "Listen."

Will heard only the babbling of the stream. "Devi, I don't . . ." No, there it was—a man-made sound, possibly two of them, in the middle of nowhere, engines barely audible over the rushing water.

"That what I think it is?" Kalyn asked.

The sound of the planes grew louder. They couldn't see them through the overstory of spruce trees, but they seemed to fly right over them before fading away, leaving only the whisper of the stream.

"No way one of those could be Buck, right?" Will said.

"I don't think so."

Devlin said, "Maybe one of them is the plane you saw yesterday, Kalyn."

"No way to know, baby."

It was getting colder and darker, the mist that landed and clung to Will's black fleece jacket freezing into flecks of ice.

"We should probably start looking for a campsite," he said.

It was another hour before they crossed a piece of ground level enough to pitch a tent on. They'd climbed more than a thousand feet from the outer lake, and the character of the forest had changed—the spruce trees more withered-looking, more space between them, the underbrush a violent red.

"Let's camp here for the night," Will said. "Pretty little meadow, close to the stream."

They found their sleeping quarters in Devlin's pack—a roomy four-person, four-season domed tent. Will hadn't set one up in years; Kalyn never had. It took them the better part of thirty minutes to assemble the poles and finally run them through the corresponding sleeves, another fifteen to stake out the guylines and get the rain fly fitted. When the tent was finally erected, they tossed their packs and sleeping bags inside and climbed in out of the deteriorating weather.

"It'll be dark soon," Will said. "Wish I could say that I'm a master outdoorsman and will have a fire ready momentarily, but that's not gonna happen with everything soaked."

"Just fire up the stove and you'll be my hero," Kalyn said.

While the women inflated the Therm-a-Rest pads and unrolled the sleeping bags, Will took the kitchen set outside. He vaguely remembered the bush pilot warning them against cooking near the tent, so he found a grouping of rocks fifty yards away.

Pockets of mist had begun to form around the edges of the meadow, drifting between the poplar and spruce, and he thought about the previous night with Kalyn as he scanned the directions for the camp stove. It hadn't been as strange with her as he'd feared it might be. Maybe they'd take a walk later tonight, talk about what had happened—the kiss, the obvious attraction they both felt for each other.

By the time Devlin and Kalyn walked over, he had a pot of water coming to a boil over a blue propane-fueled flame, bubbles rising to the surface, steam swirling into the air.

They drank hot chocolate and ate surprisingly delicious rehydrated suppers, standing in the meadow as the snow began to fall—big downy flakes melting on the rocks and trees.

No one spoke, and it was cold, wet, and nearly dark as they stumbled back toward the tent, the ground now frosted, their breath clouds pluming in the dusk.

"This sucks," Devlin said.

THIRTY-EIGHT

They sat bundled in sleeping bags, their faces illuminated by a flashlight Will had rigged to hang down from the tent ceiling. In the poor light, they could barely make out one another's faces.

Kalyn held the map under the flashlight. "I think I see where we are," she said. "The contour lines stay together for a while after the waterfall, and then they spread out again. If so, we're only about a half mile or so from the inner lake."

"We made good time today, didn't we?" Devlin said.

"We sure did. And you did great."

Will said, "Well, we should probably get your therapy over with. Being at this altitude has got to be stressing your lungs." Devlin sighed, climbed out of her sleeping bag, and stretched out on her stomach across the Therm-a-Rest.

As Will moved into position, Kalyn said, "Can I do it?"

"Um, I guess, if that's okay with Devi."

"I wouldn't mind," Devlin said.

"Okay, show me how."

Will unzipped the tent and poked his head outside. Snow danced through the beam of the flashlight, a few inches having already accumulated. He ducked into the tent and zipped the door back. Kalyn and Devlin were revving up for the final game in a three-set match of Rock Paper Scissors. Will would face the winner.

He said, "All right, Devi, all comes down to—"

The high register of a howl erupted in the dark—long, sad, and beautiful.

Devlin looked up from the game. "Was that a wolf, Dad?"

"I think so."

"That's the loneliest sound I've ever heard."

Devlin lay in her sleeping bag, snuggled between Kalyn and her father. They'd turned the flashlight off, and it was black and soundless except for the pattering of snowflakes falling on the rain fly.

"Dad?" Devlin said.

"Yeah, honey."

"Kalyn?"

"What?"

"Just wanted to see if you two were still awake."

"Not for much longer. What's wrong? You scared?"

"No. Well, a little."

Kalyn said, "We aren't going to let anything happen to you, all right?" Devlin felt Kalyn kiss her cheek, savoring the warmth of this kind woman beside her.

Devlin woke to the familiar noise of her father's quiet snoring. Both he and Kalyn had slung their arms over her. The darkness was complete, without the slightest trace of light. She thought about the wolf, wondered if it was sleeping in a warm den or still tramping somewhere out there in the snow. She hoped it wasn't lonely.

Her nose was cold, but the rest of her body felt comfortable and snug in the sleeping bag. Even her toes were warm. She wiggled them and shut her eyes, fell quickly back to sleep.

Devlin's eyes opened. Still in the tent, buried in the warm sleeping bag.

She heard whispering, and it took her a moment to recognize Kalyn's voice.

Devlin sat up. It wasn't as dark as before, and she thought perhaps it was dawn already, until she saw the spill of light on her father's sleeping bag.

"What's wrong?" she asked.

"Nothing, I just have to pee," Kalyn said. "Will, I can't find my boots." He shone the light into the corner of the tent, spotlighted the muddy pair they'd borrowed from Buck. Kalyn laced them up, and in the semidarkness, Devlin heard the soft rip of a zipper.

"Do you need to go, Dev?" her father asked.

"No." A waft of bitter cold swept into the tent.

Kalyn took the flashlight from Will and climbed outside, zipped the tent back up. Devlin heard her say, "Man, it's snowing out here." Devlin listened to Kalyn's footsteps trail away—muffled squeaks in the snow. When all was silent again, she lay back down and closed her eyes.

She woke some time later to movement inside the tent, asked, "What's happening?" A headlamp blinded her, and when her eyes adjusted, she saw her father lacing up his boots. She glanced at the sleeping bag on her left, back at her father, said, "Where's Kalyn?"

"She hasn't come back yet."

"How long's she been gone?"

"I don't know. Longer than she should have. I fell asleep." She saw that he held a gun in his trembling hands. "I have to go out there, see what's keeping her."

"Why are you taking a gun?"

"Just to be on the safe side. I'll only be gone a—"

"No!"

"Devi. You remember our talk in the hotel? Now is not the time to argue with me. Do not leave this tent no matter what."

THIRTY-NINE

The beam of Will's headlamp cut through the onslaught of snow, and aside from the wind, it was stone-silent. He followed Kalyn's footprints away from the tent. Her tracks headed down through the meadow, and as he walked, his headlamp seemed slowly but steadily to dim, until he could barely see anything but the ankle-deep snow at his feet.

The headlamp winked out. He reached up, tapped the bulb. It flickered on and off, then on again. He went on in the snow, the coldness of the flakes nicking his face like shaving cuts.

As he came to the collection of boulders where he'd cooked supper, his light winked out again. He tapped it. Nothing. Just darkness, cold, and snow.

He called Kalyn's name and waited, kept thinking his eyes would adjust, begin to pick out things in the dark, but they didn't. Though he knew the general direction of the tent, he hated the prospect of having to stumble back to it, sightless in the storm.

The snow let up.

A fingernail moon glanced over a cloud, and the world appeared before him out of the void.

The snowpack glowed. Will could see his breath in the eerie light, the profile of trees, the tent forty yards away at the opposite end of the meadow.

He looked into the woods—mostly dark there, save for where beams of moonlight slanted through the spruce, lighting random patches of snow.

Kalyn's tracks veered into those woods.

Everything began to darken. It snowed again. The moon vanished and the world returned to black. He fiddled with the headlamp, but it was dead.

In the dark, arms outstretched, he started back for the tent.

. . .

Devlin had pulled the sleeping bag over her head, and she was trying to return to a beautiful dream—back at her home in Colorado, a cool summer night, crickets chirping, purr of the river coming across the pasture and no moon, but a million stars. She was walking toward the farmhouse, where her father and Kalyn sat on the back porch, drinking wine, laughing. She opened her mouth to speak, to tell them how happy she was.

Will was working his way through profound darkness, trying to find the tent, confident he was headed in the right direction, but soon his hands were touching the snow-glazed bark of spruce trees, and he realized he'd wandered out of the meadow, back into the woods.

He should have stopped right there, but he kept plodding forward, no sense of sight, everything else in overdrive, his ears picking up the steady thudding of his heart, the dry-grass scrape of snow falling on the hood of his parka, his nose detecting the sterilized odor of snow-rinsed air.

The world blinked—a strange electric blue. He saw trees, his footprints.

Darkness again.

It thundered.

He imagined where the tent stood, saw it in his mind's eye, assured himself he hadn't veered that far off track.

He started to call out for Devlin, let her voice guide him back to the meadow. But what if she couldn't hear his words, just heard him yelling? She might leave the tent, strike out into this darkness by herself, lose her way.

The forest lighted up again. He corrected his bearing and kept going, fighting off the first needling tinge of panic as he stumbled along in the dark.

FORTY

Will stopped walking. As far as he could tell, he was still in the trees. It was snowing and moonless and he might as well have been blind. He decided there was no point in going on in these conditions. He'd been on the move for at least ten minutes, and if he went any farther, he might not be able to find the tent again, whenever the hell the moon decided to reappear.

He sat down against the trunk of a large birch and waited.

Within a minute, he was shivering. He'd left the tent without gloves—a stupid fucking thing to do—and the gun was freezing to the touch, so he set it beside him in the snow and pulled the sleeves of his parka and fleece jacket over his hands.

Ten excruciating minutes passed, his face growing numb, the snow still falling.

The darkness held.

He stood up and brushed the snow off his pants, his parka, having decided to walk around the tree several times in an effort to get warm.

Something moved in the vicinity.

He held his breath, straining to listen.

Whispered, "Kalyn?" The sound repeated, closer now, ten or fifteen feet dead ahead, and he'd started to back away from it, when he heard another noise behind him, close enough to recognize—careful footsteps sinking in the snow.

"Kalyn, that you?" He was picking up noise on his left. Now his right. He squatted down, digging through the snow until he grasped the Smith & Wesson. "I have a gun," he said in full voice, panic rising in his chest, constricting his throat.

The snow dissipated. He looked up, saw the moon again, or at least a piece of it. A handful of stars. Ragged black clouds.

He scanned the woods—slim black tree trunks, his footprints leading up a gentle slope. *The meadow's just over the top, I think. I haven't come that far. I'd have heard Devi scream if anything had happened.*

At first, he thought it was a person crouched down twenty feet ahead, and he raised the .45. But as it skulked toward him, he recognized his mistake, took several steps toward it, waving his hands wildly in the air.

The wolf was pure white, and the moon made its pink eyes appear to glow. It loped back through the trees. After thirty feet, it stopped, turned, and faced him again, head cocked. "You're endangered," he said, "so don't make me shoot your ass."

Will began to follow his own footprints back toward the hill, the moon shining down into the forest now.

He sensed movement to his right and left and behind him, though he hadn't heard a thing.

Will spun around, looking back toward the tree he'd been hunkered down against. The three black wolves that were tracking him stopped.

He ran at them and waved his arms.

They dispersed among the spruce but didn't go far. He glanced back toward the hill, caught the white wolf creeping toward him again. It stopped when it saw that Will had noticed.

He heard the three black wolves coming from behind, turned and faced them.

As they stopped in their tracks, the lead wolf moved toward him again. "I don't have time for this stupid game," he said.

He began following his footprints back up the hill, that white wolf backpedaling in the snow as Will moved toward him, its head low, muzzle pointed toward the ground, long tail flicking back and forth. Will could hear the others coming behind him.

He reached the top of the small hill, but instead of seeing the meadow and the tent as he'd expected, he saw only more forest, his footprints winding aimlessly through the trees.

I've come farther than I thought.

He turned slowly around so he could see the wolves, noticed for the first time that they wore collars. They were closer than before, all within fifteen feet, and the black wolf on his left had arched its back, its ears now erect, hackles raised, lips curled back. Will could see the long incisors.

And he felt pure old-fashioned terror—primitive fears, eons of old programming firing in the synapses. He lunged at them and waved his arms, but they backed only a few feet away, and the largest of the black wolves, a 150-pound male, didn't move at all, just stared him down through focused yellow eyes. For the first time, Will noticed the pair of gray wolves lurking thirty feet behind the others.

Jesus. Six of them.

He jogged up through the trees.

It was snowing again, and he thought he heard thunder, but he wasn't sure with his heart banging relentlessly in his chest.

The wolves loped along beside him as Will tried to retrace his own footprints, and something snapped near the back of his left leg, the click of teeth clamping shut.

He stopped, spun around, leveled the .45 between the big black wolf's eyes, and fired.

The report filled the woods, and the wolves scattered.

The one he'd killed lay crumpled in the snow, a mound of black fur. "Go find an elk or something!" Will yelled.

He pushed on through the trees, now moving at a solid clip through the snow.

He kept expecting to emerge from the forest, and at last he did, but it wasn't into the meadow they'd camped in.

He came out of the trees, and the ground sloped for two hundred yards down to the shore of a narrow lake whose water appeared black as blood. *The inner lake.* He looked to the near end, saw where a ribbon of water flowed out of it, knew that was the stream they'd followed earlier in the day, hoped it would guide him back to the meadow, to Devlin.

As he started for it, he heard something moving in the woods, and not creeping or sneaking, but the full-on noise of something, *somethings*, running toward him.

He ran for the end of the lake, glancing over his shoulder every few steps, trying to keep his footing in the snow. The third time he looked back, he saw five shadows break out of the trees, racing toward him in tight formation, kicking up powder clouds in their wake.

It was snowing hard again, and the moon disappeared, the world now gone cavern black. He could see nothing, but he heard them coming, and as he looked back, the sky flickered with lightning and he saw them—*Oh God, so close*—aimed the .45, firing at the lead wolf, the big white one with pink eyes. It was panting, its huge blue tongue swinging out of its mouth.

Lights-out. No way to know if I hit—

Something rammed him from behind, a wolf throwing the full weight of its muscled frame into his back.

Will went down, toppled over several times in the snow, jaws snapping all around him, as he smelled the sharp odor of their scent glands, then on his feet again, somehow untouched.

Lightning offered a fleeting glimpse of where he stood, forty feet from the lake's edge, the mouth of the stream, and the wolves surrounding him, snarling, growling, the ones behind him lunging at the back of his legs.

Darkness again. He'd dropped the gun when he'd fallen up the slope, had nothing but his bare, freezing hands. *This is not happening.*

Something ripped a piece out of his leg and he screamed—more out of fear than pain, too charged with adrenaline to feel a thing—kept spinning around in the merciless dark, his hands outstretched, getting shredded as he fended off bites.

The sky lighted up, the wolves right there, five sets of bared teeth and eyes mad with the ravenous rage of the hunt, crouched down, on the verge of lunging.

Will spotted a stand of spruce trees at the mouth of the stream, thought, *You get to those trees and you climb them.* He pushed on through the dark as thunder echoed across the lake, struggling against the mounting pain in his legs.

Electricity raked the sky. He was just five yards from the trees, saw that the branches were low, thought, *I can climb that.*

The Lodge That Doesn't Exist

FORTY-ONE

Devlin crawled out of her sleeping bag and unzipped the tent, caught a draft of bitter, choking cold that ran down into her lungs like battery acid. The moon shone upon the meadow. The snow had let up. She didn't know how long she'd hidden in her sleeping bag—an hour, perhaps two—and though, up until this moment, she'd done exactly what her father had said, not leaving the tent, she still felt like a coward.

It had been some time since she'd heard the gunshots, and the Wolverine Hills stood silent now. She laced her boots and zipped up her oversize parka, dug the pair of gloves and hat out of her father's backpack. In Kalyn's, she found the .357. She'd never held a gun in her life, but she picked it up and put it in her pocket.

The snow came halfway to her knees, having partially buried the tracks around the tent. She followed them down through the meadow to the point where they split, one set veering into the woods, the other crossing the meadow, back toward the tent, missing it by less than ten feet.

She was seized with a sudden coughing fit, her eyes watering as her lungs strained against the cold. When it passed, she turned and followed the tracks that went by the tent, her legs sore from yesterday's hike, her lungs raw, her body reeling with every breath.

She pushed on through woods, down small hills and up them again, through glades of drifted snow, thinking the tracks seemed strange. They didn't go in any one direction, but wound erratically through the spruce, crisscrossing over themselves, and, at one point, even circling the same tree three times.

Her legs were killing her when she came out of the trees at last. She stopped to let her racing heart slow down. A long lake stretched out below her, and the way the moonlight fell upon it, the surface resembled black ice, though it had yet to freeze. Her eyes followed the course of what she hoped were her father's tracks. They beelined downslope toward the lake's end, and she smiled, spotted movement by the water, just a few hundred yards away.

Dad. She almost shouted the word as she started down the slope.

Thirty yards out from the trees, she stopped. From the woods, she had seen only movement by the lake. On closer inspection, she saw with more clarity what she was heading toward, and it didn't appear to be her father. It looked like several people, children perhaps, on their hands and knees, crawling around in the snow in some sort of game. In the windless silence, she could hear them, but they weren't speaking any language she understood. They were growling and snarling, fighting over something. *Wolves. Why do Dad's tracks go down there?*

She turned around, and quietly, carefully started back up the slope.

Halfway to the woods, she felt it coming—an insuppressible itch in her lungs, growing exponentially with every passing second. *Hold it, Devi. You have to hold it.* The cough jumped out of her, then another, a series of violent spasms that shook her body and burned her throat.

When the coughing spell had passed, she looked downslope, saw the wolves already coming—five of them bounding toward her through the snow.

She ran for the woods, only fifteen yards away, but her legs felt leaden and stiff, barely capable of pushing her up the hill. She lost traction and fell facedown in the snow. By the time she'd regained her footing, she heard the wolves panting, close enough for her to see their eyes gleaming, big tongues lolling out of their smiling, bloody mouths.

She reached the edge of the woods. The first three spruce trees she passed didn't have a branch below ten feet. The fourth did. Weak, sluggish, and out of breath, she reached up, grabbed a snowy branch, and hoisted herself up as the first two wolves entered the forest. The next branch above her head was barely the width of her thumb, but she took hold where it joined the trunk, climbed another two feet.

Teeth snapped down on her right boot. She screamed, kicked the wolf's muzzle with her other foot, now dangling five feet above the ground. She barely hung on to the branch, her wool gloves ripping.

The wolf fell onto its back, and she scrambled up another two feet, found a solid branch to stand on, her arms wrapped around the trunk of the spruce as if clinging to life itself.

She peered down. Five wolves—two black, two gray, one white. The white one was the biggest of the bunch, bigger than any dog she'd ever seen, and it stared up at her, its pink eyes brimming with intelligence and cunning, its mouth stained black. The wolves were leaping toward her now, some coming within two feet of the branch she occupied.

She climbed higher.

After awhile, the wolves gave up. The black ones and the white one lay in the snow, while the gray ones circled the tree and growled.

Devlin found a big branch to sit down on.

In five minutes, she was shivering. She considered taking out the gun, but she was trembling to the point where she didn't think she would hit a thing. It had begun to snow again, and now all the wolves lay around the base of the tree, looking up from time to time, whimpering for her to come down.

Devlin was colder than she'd ever been, and every few breaths, her lungs clogged and she coughed until her throat burned.

The sky dumped snow.

She wept.

The blizzard had obscured her view of the lakeshore, and she wondered where her father's tracks went, where they stopped, refusing to even contemplate the worst. Instead, she closed her eyes and tried to imagine her birthplace in the desert waste of Ajo, Arizona—the bone-dry air, how the heat radiated off the pavement, making it feel like you'd stuck your face in a furnace, the desert at sunset, the warm nights, beautiful cacti. She never wanted to see snow again, not even on Christmas.

FORTY-TWO

When she opened her eyes, the wolves were gone. She'd dozed off, her face flattened against the tree trunk, her cheek bark-scraped and numb from the cold. She felt the congestion in her lungs, thought, *I shouldn't be out in this weather. I need my therapy. This could turn into pneumonia.* The snow fell even harder than before, but now she could see.

Dawn had come, the sky a few shades shy of black, and the muscles in her arms were strained from clinging to the tree.

Devlin took her time climbing down, and when her boots finally touched the ground, the powder rose above her knees. She walked to the edge of the woods and looked down toward the lake, the world all snow and wind, the utter silence terrible. She wanted to follow her father's tracks to the lake's edge, but they'd been covered in snow. Besides, that would put her out in the open, and for all she knew, the wolves were lying in wait for just such an opportunity. She'd have to stay in the trees.

Devlin walked along the forest's edge, paralleling the lake, her coughing fits coming more frequently. Every few minutes, she'd stop to listen for the wolves or her father calling her name. Often, she thought she heard him, but it was only wind and her own longing.

She walked for an hour, the open space between the lake and the woods narrowing, the sky lightening toward morning and the snow still falling, harder than before, if that were possible. She realized there must be a leak in her boots, because her feet were wet and she couldn't feel her toes. She was hungry, thirsty, more afraid and unsure with every passing moment.

Devlin was contemplating turning around, trying to find her way back to the tent, when she broke out of the trees and saw it. For a moment, she forgot the pain in her legs and lungs, the fear of being alone in the wilderness. *Oh, thank you.* She'd seen something like this before, and it took her a moment to recall where. The summer after her mother's disappearance, she and her father had taken a road trip. One of their stops in the Pacific Northwest had been Crater Lake, and there was a lodge on the rim of that caldera that bore a striking resemblance to what stood a half mile in the distance, on the shore of this unnamed Alaskan lake.

It was a sprawling five-story tower with projecting four-story north and south wings, some of the windows glowing with what appeared to be candlelight.

She took shelter under a massive spruce tree, weighing her options. She didn't remember for sure, but she thought the pilot was flying back to pick them up sometime tomorrow afternoon. In the face of wolves and the blizzard and the cold, her choice was easy. *Just check it out. I'll die if I stay out here. Besides, maybe Dad and Kalyn are inside.*

She didn't like leaving the cover of the forest, but with the snow coming down so hard and all visibility shot, she figured it hardly made a difference.

She was wading through the snow now, up to her thighs, and she was as close to the inner lake as she'd yet come.

Two floatplanes were tethered to a nearby pier, so blanketed in snow, the only parts showing were slivers of their amphibious floats just above the surface of the water.

The facade of the lodge loomed ahead—an ornate porch of fir pillars, a huge wooden door, those eerie candlelit windows, behind which she thought she saw shapes moving.

A howl rose up from the other end of the lake, and in light of her recent encounter, it was the most horrifying thing she'd ever heard.

Devlin worked her way through the snow toward the lodge, but instead of heading directly for the porch, she made for the south wing, close enough now to see the construction. The first floor had been built of stone, and the top three stories shingled, a handful of which had peeled away. Long, steep eaves sagged down from the roof, occasionally sloughing off enormous blocks of snow.

She smelled wood smoke as she worked her way around the chimney to the back side of the south wing. There were few windows cut into the stone of the first floor, and she ran her hand along the rock as she moved toward the veranda that extended from the back of the central building.

The steps leading up were buried, and she didn't want to climb them.

Another howl split the silence, much closer now. She glanced over her shoulder, half-expecting to see the wolves emerge from the storm.

She saw an opening beneath the veranda. Struggling thirty more feet through drifts, she finally stepped under the veranda, out of the snow. On bare ground again, she took a moment to brush the powder from her parka and pants and to shake it out of her hair.

She approached the opening.

A set of stone steps descended underground to a wooden door, and she followed them down, put her gloved hand on the door handle, turned it slowly, but not slowly enough to prevent the horrendous squeaking from the accumulation of rust. She pushed and the door swung open, creaking on hinges that should have been replaced decades ago.

The smell of stale air overwhelmed her. She had no flashlight, so she opened the door as far as it would go, now smelling other things, including the acrid, sharp stench of urine. What light fell through the open doorway did little to illuminate the cellar. There were old tools hanging on one of the walls—scythes and machetes, a pitchfork—and cracked leather saddles, grinning bear traps with giant metal teeth. A wrought-iron staircase spiraled up out of the center, disappearing into the darkness above. Glancing at the far left corner, Devlin spotted something that gave her pause—large metal cages, their doors thrown open, water bowls inside, and pieces of bone lying on the moldy straw.

Devlin proceeded into the cellar, still trembling with cold as she stopped at the foot of the spiral staircase, put her hands on the railing, and gave it a little shake. Seemed sturdy enough.

She took the steps one at a time, ascending out of the cold, rank filth of the cellar. Soon she was climbing in total darkness, enveloped in a silence beyond anything she'd known, the humming in her head like transformers in the middle of nowhere.

The stairs spiraled up and up, farther than she'd anticipated. Then she walked into something, reached out, ran her hands along the rough surface of a door. She groped around, finally got her hands on the doorknob.

That it wasn't locked surprised her.

FORTY-THREE

Devlin stepped into a study, let the cellar door close softly behind her. The room was gloriously warm, a fire burning in the hearth. The ceiling must've been fifteen feet high, and there were bookshelves built into the walls and filled with leather-bound volumes, the spines lettered in small gold calligraphy. Leather chairs and ottomans stood grouped around the fireplace. An Elie Bleu Medaille humidor occupied an end table.

The fire was low, only a few logs remaining. Devlin sat on the hearth, removed her gloves, and held her hands to the heat. Her heartbeat had finally slowed.

She glanced around the room. A door led out of the study, presumably into the rest of the lodge. French doors lined the back wall, and looking through the glass, she glimpsed the veranda, its surface buried in snow.

Her snow pants and parka made too much noise, so she stood up and took them off, left them in a pile beside the cellar door. She was finally warm, and the urge to cough seemed to have dissipated.

Devlin walked to the door leading out of the study, stood for a moment with her ear against it, listening. There was only silence, and the occasional snap as sap boiled off in the fire. She put her hand on the doorknob, turned it quietly, pulled the door open.

The room she stepped into was an enormous lobby, fifty feet high from floor to ceiling, with a freestanding fireplace rising up the middle of it. Its floor was made of polished stone, and open staircases ascended on either side, giving access to the north and south wings.

Her footsteps echoed as she crossed to the other end and stood gazing up the staircase, then down the first-floor corridor of the north wing, which glowed with points of candlelight. Something echoed above and behind her on the third or fourth level of the south wing—footfalls perhaps.

She walked around to the stairs and started to climb, the creak of the steps reverberating through the cavernous lobby.

The fourth-floor corridor was empty and quiet as death, two dozen globes of firelight dancing through the tops of iron sconces. She walked into the corridor, its floor plushly carpeted, passed closed doors with brass numbers.

Halfway down the corridor, she noticed a peephole below the number designation on each door, and one in particular drew her attention, because she could see light coming through it. She stopped walking, crept up to the door of 413, and put her ear to the wood. She could hear something coming from inside, but it was soft, indiscernible. She was at the level of the peephole, and when she looked through it, she gasped.

It was installed backward, the room all shadowy blue save for the orange coils of a kerosene heater and the candle sitting on the windowsill, its flame restless, flickering. Shapes and details came into focus—a bed and dresser, a desk by the window. As her eyes adjusted to the low light, she realized there was someone lying under the bedcovers. The body was turned away from her, but she could see the person's breath pluming in the cold.

Something crackled above Devlin's head, and the entire lodge seemed to rumble.

Up and down the corridor, recessed ceiling lights flickered to life, one after another, and the warm breath of central heating pushed up into her face through a large vent in the floor.

She proceeded to the end of the corridor, just an empty alcove with a big window and a doorway leading to a set of stairs.

Starting down the stairs, she heard a noise coming from the lobby. It sounded like footsteps creaking on wood. She continued down, emerged from the stairwell into the third-floor alcove, and peered around the corner.

Something was moving toward her down the corridor, and as it passed under the illumination of a ceiling light, she saw it was a man in a black jumpsuit. He had a red bandanna tied around his left bicep and held a pump-action shotgun, its strap dangling from his shoulder. He was tall and blade-thin, wore a Stetson, and had long hair flowing down over his shoulders.

She ducked back into the stairwell, went down to the first floor, and ran up the corridor and back into the lobby.

Beside the library was an archway she hadn't noticed before. She headed toward it, and as she went through it, she passed an opening on her right that led to another staircase.

Thirty feet on, the passage terminated at a thick wooden door, and just ahead, it opened to the left.

She stopped, glanced around the corner into a high-ceilinged dining room, in the center of which stood a table expansive enough to seat ten comfortably on each side and two at each end. Its centerpiece was an exploding bouquet of greenery—native flora. An immense candelabra stood near each end, the candles burning. The set of chairs looked terribly expensive, and a chandelier hung down from high above, fifteen feet above the table.

At the far end of the dining room was another massive fireplace, big logs roasting within.

Light filtered in from windows twenty feet up, the wall below adorned with numerous trophy mounts—moose and caribou with cartoonishly huge racks, a pair of wolverines, Dall sheep, a grizzly bear.

Out in the lobby, a bell tolled—the light, rapid announcement of a meal.

She retreated from the dining room and entered the passage just in time to hear footsteps on the nearby staircase, accompanied by the voices of men.

Devlin turned and slipped back into the dining room, realizing as she did that sound was now emanating from the double doors to the left of the fireplace.

Running water, dishes clanking—kitchen noise.

She scanned the dining room, saw no place to hide. A long dry sink was pushed flush against the west wall, the kitchen was occupied, and there was nothing larger than a potted spruce tree behind which to take cover.

People were coming, and her legs had begun to weaken. She felt a deep shuddering behind her knees.

Devlin did the only thing she could.

FORTY-FOUR

Through the forest of chair legs, she watched them come—disembodied feet and legs, at least half a dozen pairs, strolling into the dining room. They didn't immediately take seats at the table, congregating instead at the dry sink, beckoned by the constellation of exotic glass bottles.

"Bloody Mary, Sean?"

"Absolutely."

"Looks like we've got Diaka, Grey Goose, some Russian shit."

"Gotta go with Diaka."

Crouched under the table, she watched a man in khaki slacks standing at the dry sink, carving up a lime and twigs of celery.

"Want one, Zig?"

"No, I'm gonna sip on this Pasión Azteca. Can't believe they scored a bottle of this tequila."

"I didn't even see that."

"I'll pour you one."

Breakfast smells had begun to waft in from the kitchen—bacon, brewing coffee, eggs, frying pancake batter.

Someone said, "Boys, to decadence."

Glasses banged into one another.

"Damn, that's smooth."

"Fuckin' A."

"You believe how much snow fell overnight?"

Footsteps could be heard from the passage, and Devlin glanced through the chair legs just in time to see a pair of boots and blue-jeaned legs stroll into the dining hall, followed by a voice that boomed over the others.

"Gentlemen! Welcome! Glad you all made it here ahead of the storm!"

The man stopped at the end of the table, his legs so close, Devlin could have reached out and touched them.

The other men drifted over from the dry sink, said their greetings—slap of hard handshakes, small talk of the raging blizzard.

"My brother, Paul, is working on a busted generator, so we probably won't see him until lunch. But meantime, everybody have a seat, please."

Devlin crawled toward the fireplace as the chair legs squeaked across the marble, legs swinging under the table, one boot nearly striking her face.

She settled just out of range of the nearest leg as that voice boomed again: "Everybody good on drinks?"

Grunts of affirmation.

"Breakfast will be out shortly, so let me officially welcome each of you to the Lodge That Doesn't Exist."

The men laughed conspiratorially.

"I'm Ethan, and a couple of you have been here before, but there're a few things I need to discuss up front with the newbies. We run on generators here, and they shut down automatically from midnight to six-thirty A.M. We'll probably shut them down quite a bit earlier tonight. When we go dark, feel free to use candles and lanterns. You should have a stash in your room. You wanna hunt, fish? Gonna be colder than fuck, but either Paul or I will be more than happy to take you out. However, something tells me no one came here to hunt."

More laughter.

Someone said, "Damn right."

"We run a sensitive operation, to say the least. Maybe you've heard things. We had another group from Presidian over the summer."

A gruff male voice: "Them boys had fun."

"Well, now we come to the tough-love portion of my welcome, and after this, I promise it's all about fun and meeting your *every* need. But we need to be clear on this point. You've all been to Vegas, I imagine. We've co-opted a famous Sin City saying for our little lodge. What happens in the middle of nowhere *stays* in the middle of nowhere."

The men began to laugh.

"That's not a fucking joke."

Everyone shut up. The only sounds now were the quiet roar of the fire and melting ice clinking in drink glasses. Devlin's eyes began to water as she fought back a cough.

"Maybe you noticed Gerald and Donald strolling the halls with Mossberg 590 combat shotguns. They're here for your protection. But if for a second we think letting you go home might jeopardize our operation? If you strike us as the type who might grow a conscience, or blab to his buddies back home about all the fun he had in Alaska? We will put you in the pan of one of the grizzly traps in the cellar, spring it, and sink you to the bottom of the lake. Let you join our garden of guests who couldn't be trusted. We also have other ways of discouraging you from discussing this place after you leave. I'm talking about photographs, videotapes. Pure, ugly blackmail.

"But you each paid two mil for five days here, so I'm assuming everyone's *enthusiastically* on board."

"Course."

"Yeah."

"Hundred percent."

"Absolutely."

"We know the deal."

"Just thrilled to be here."

Devlin heard something jingle, metal sliding across the surface of the table.

"Master keys, gentlemen. The south wing is your playground, and these open every door. Fourteen rooms on each floor. They're not all occupied—we're working on that—but many are. Peepholes are reversed, so feel free to browse. Redheads, blondes, brunettes. We have something for all tastes. We've even got a preggy on the fourth, if that's your thing. Check the closets in your rooms. Should have a kimono hanging up, pair of sandals. I encourage you all to wear them for warmth and ease of access. Now, I've gotten blood work back from everyone, so you're all good to go. Our women are healthy. Pristine. Protection's not necessary is what I'm saying, but, of course, that's entirely your call."

"What if we want—"

"Why don't you let me finish my spiel, Zig, as it'll probably address any questions you have."

"Sorry, of course."

"Here's our policy when it comes to your conduct with the women. You break it, you buy it. You injure someone so they have to be moved to the north wing to convalesce, we're gonna assess you with appropriate damages. Now don't misunderstand me. Follow your fancy, you twisted motherfuckers. No one's telling you you *can't* do anything you want. Seriously, go crazy. Just understand that on your last day here, there will be an accounting, and each of these women represents an investment of about one point five million. That's our replacement cost.

"Other things, other things . . . Ah, yes, the wolves. They roam the grounds, and occasionally, particularly at night, we let them in. You're probably all wondering why you were instructed to wear a red bandanna on your left arm. That's to let our wolves know whose team you're on. They see that, they'll leave you alone. This does not mean you should go outside by yourself, or that you should approach a wolf and try to make a new friend. Ignore them if they come around, and don't make eye contact. They are trained, vicious murderers, and they work in tandem, and if you don't follow protocol with them, they will tear you apart. Okay?"

Devlin heard the kitchen doors swing open.

"Perfect timing. Breakfast is served."

She turned, saw two pairs of miniskirted legs in fence-net stockings moving toward the table.

"Gentlemen, meet Alena and Jill. They're on kitchen duty this week for some exceptional behavior over the last year."

Devlin heard what she guessed were platters of food being set on the table.

"Now, I believe that plate in the middle is reindeer sausage," Ethan said. "You should all try it. Little gamey, but very good."

FORTY-FIVE

Devlin huddled under the table for forty minutes, her legs cramping, listening to the six oilmen devour what sounded like an all-out feast, based on the intermittent stretches of blissful silence as they chewed, and the ferocity of their consumption.

Though little was said, she committed every detail to memory. They were executives from a company called Presidian Oil, and all spoke with great familiarity and affinity of Houston. An older-sounding gentleman named Reynolds gave a heartfelt, if drunken, toast to the "astronomical third quarter." Sean was apparently the son of Ken, and there was frequent lamentation that a "first-rate son of a bitch" named Bobby couldn't be with them to partake.

Then, as quickly as they'd come, the chairs scooted back from the table, and the oilmen departed en masse with Ethan.

Devlin crawled between two chairs and struggled to her feet, staring at the table, which resembled the aftermath of some epic battle—dishes and silverware strewn with haphazard abandon, plentiful portions of meat, eggs, and fruit still occupying china.

Her stomach ached with hunger, and she was reaching for a strip of bacon when voices erupted from the kitchen.

She rushed out of the dining room, up the passage, and, upon nearing the lobby, remembered leaving her parka and snow pants in the library, her gut telling her it would be a disaster if they were found.

The lobby stood empty.

She crossed the stone floor.

The door to the library was closed, and she put her ear to it, detecting the noise of the fire, nothing else.

It was empty inside, and her clothes lay exactly where she'd left them on the floor beside the cellar door.

As she picked them up, fast-approaching footsteps drove an electric shock of adrenaline down her spine.

She spun around, taking stock of available exits, anyplace she might hide, but there was just the furniture and the French doors, straining against all the snow that had piled up on the veranda.

With the footsteps seconds from the library, she lunged for the cellar door, palming the doorknob, turning it, praying the hinges wouldn't squeak.

She slipped through into darkness, had it almost closed when two men strolled into the library, the door slamming after them. They stopped before the fireplace, just five feet away, Devlin watching through the four-millimeter crack between the door and the door frame.

"Goddamn it, Sean," said the older of the two, a silver-haired man, tall, wide-shouldered, dressed in exquisite navy slacks and a plaid shirt rolled up to his elbows.

"Dad, I feel sick—"

"Lighten up."

"This isn't right. You know it." Sean looked very much like his father facially, subtracting the wrinkles and the gray, adding some baby fat, though he wasn't as tall, or as powerfully built.

The older man put both of his hands on his son's shoulders.

"*Don't* embarrass me, Sean."

"Dad, there are women—"

"Lower your fucking voice. Nobody's *making* you do anything. Go sit in your room the whole time, for all I—"

"What are you gonna do?"

"Me?" Devlin remembered the older man's name—Ken. "I don't know." Ken walked out of Devlin's line of site and Sean followed, the two just voices now, operating at scarcely more than a whisper. "Listen to me. You heard what Ethan said at breakfast, didn't you?"

"Yeah."

"So deal with it."

"I can't be here for five days, Dad."

"Hey, I twisted some major arms to get you on this trip. You know how many of my guys would kill—"

"Yeah, thanks so much for that."

"Now wait just a doggone minute. I didn't know it was gonna be, you know. . . ."

"What'd you think when they loaded us into floatplanes with blacked-out windows? Wouldn't tell us where we were going?"

"Look, Sean, you're here. You aren't leaving early. So make the best of it."

"How?"

"I don't care, just . . . don't embarrass me."

"Fuck you."

Footsteps tracked across the library, and Devlin heard the door open.

"Sean, come back. Sean!"

His father went after him, the library quiet again, just the fire crackling.

Devlin waited two minutes, straining to pick out the slightest patter of returning footsteps, but the men were gone.

She eased the cellar door open, moving carefully through the library, then into the lobby, where she stood holding her parka and snow pants, listening to distant voices, the clatter of door slams traveling up and down the corridors above.

She wandered into the south wing, quiet here and empty, just the ceiling lights humming above her.

There were peepholes in these doors as well, and she stopped at each to look inside, saw women behind three of the doors, sitting up in bed in skimpy lingerie, waiting.

At the end of the corridor, she turned the doorknob of an empty room, 119.

The door opened. She stepped inside, shut it.

She stashed her pants and parka in a chest of drawers across from the bed, then, taking out the .357, crouched under the peephole for five long minutes, willing back the fear, the tears.

FORTY-SIX

She slipped back into the corridor, then into the alcove and up the stairwell to the second floor. She hadn't gone five steps before she heard voices up ahead. Devlin slowed, inching her way into the alcove, glancing around the corner. The corridor was empty.

She looked back through the alcove window, saw that it was still snowing, spruce trees loaded with powder. Even from inside, she could hear branches creaking, snapping under the weight.

She eased out into the corridor, stopping at each door she passed to glance through the peephole—more women, half-naked, lying in bed and staring absently into space.

Ten steps into the corridor, someone groaned behind the door of 215.

Devlin stopped, felt a knot in her stomach, thought she might be sick.

She stepped forward, put her ear to the door.

Zig's voice: "You like that, don't you, you naughty girl?"

"Yes."

"Convince me."

Through the door, Devlin heard the woman moan.

Zig: "Yeah, that's . . . oh . . . that's better, oh God."

Footsteps were ascending the stairs at the lobby end of the corridor.

She turned back, hurried into the alcove, ducked around the corner, and glanced back in time to see someone emerge into the corridor.

As the person drew closer, she saw it was a man—short, wide, pit-bull jaw, cropped blond hair, shotgun hanging from a strap around his neck.

Every few doors, he'd stop to look through a peephole, lingering a little longer at 215.

Devlin turned and started up the steps.

The fifth cracked under her weight, footsteps audible now in the corridor below, the man definitely coming.

She moved quickly into the third-floor corridor, passing the brass-numbered doors: 314, 312, 310. She tried 308, but it was locked.

The man with the shotgun must have hit the noisy step, because a loud crack resounded through the corridor.

The doorknob to 306 turned. She slipped inside, her heart pounding in her chest. Out of instinct, she peered through the peephole, realized instantly that she was staring through it backward, the view long and distorted, like looking through the strong prescription lenses of her father's reading glasses. She could hear the man's footsteps coming down the corridor, wondered if he'd actually seen or heard her. She turned away from the door, squatted down out of sight in a corner beside the bed, the gun quivering in her hands as the footsteps passed by the door.

She stayed in the room for a long time. When she finally built up the nerve to leave, she got to her feet and moved over to the door, listened. Silence. She glanced through the peephole, and what she could see of the corridor was empty.

She pulled the door open, poked her head outside. It took her a moment to remember where she was. Third floor, south wing. She crept out into the corridor, the lodge momentarily quiet.

When she reached the stairs, she glanced down into the lobby, saw a kimonoed man thirty feet below disappearing into the first-floor corridor.

Devlin took the stairs up to the only corridor she'd yet to search—the south wing's fourth floor. As she climbed, she spotted that longhaired man in the cowboy hat, strolling the third floor of the north wing with his shotgun, his back to her, walking away.

The fourth floor was empty.

She crept up to each door, peered through the peephole, taking note of which rooms were occupied, which vacant and unlocked.

At the end of the corridor, she came to 429, the last room on the left-hand side before the alcove and the stairwell. She stood on her tiptoes, leaned in to look through the peephole. Inside, a woman was sitting in bed. She was wearing a yellow chemise, her hair long and dark, the color indistinguishable in the poor light. Her face was turned toward the window and she was watching the snow fall. Devlin could tell by looking through the thin fabric of her nightgown that the woman was with child, perhaps half term, her face a little swollen from the pregnancy, and pale, with dark bags under her eyes.

By the light from the lamp on the table, Devlin saw that the woman's hair was a deep black, and then she drew in a sharp breath and her eyes welled up and ran over and her throat closed.

She was looking at her mother.

Scalding

FORTY-SEVEN

At first, she didn't believe it, thinking, *This must be some kind of nightmare or hallucination. No way she could still be alive. That's what Dad said.* But it was her. As she stood there breathless, watching Rachael Innis in bed, Devlin recognized the big-black eyes, the shape of the mouth. Her mother didn't look angry or sad or anything like what Devlin might have expected. Just older, tired, worn-out.

Devlin wiped her eyes, looked up and down the corridor, then back through the peephole as she knocked at the door.

Her mother glanced up but didn't move, sat motionless in bed, as if waiting.

Devlin knocked again, then cupped her mouth and spoke through the door, "Mom."

Rachael showed no sign she'd heard a thing.

Devlin knocked once more, and finally, Rachael stepped tentatively down onto the floor and moved slowly toward the door.

Devlin tapped the peephole and stepped back several feet into the corridor, praying her mother would look.

Ten seconds elapsed, and then she heard a sound come through the door like a gasp for breath or a stifled sob, followed by something hitting the floor.

Devlin ran to the peephole, peered through, saw her mother crumpled down into a pile, her back heaving, weeping.

She ran up the corridor, trying doors until she found an unlocked, unoccupied room, tore through the drawers, the bedside table, saw at last what she was after. Ripping a page from the notebook, she had to wait for her hand to stop trembling so she could write.

Mom, I came to Alaska with Dad and an FBI agent to look for you. Can't find them. Are they here? Will get you out somehow. I love you. We never forgot.

Devlin ran back into the corridor, dropped to the floor at room 429, and slid the sheet of notebook paper under the door. Through the peephole, she watched her mother take the paper over to a desk.

Rachael kept wiping her eyes, shoulders bobbing. She sat down, spent thirty seconds scribbling on the sheet of paper. Then she got up, hurried back to the door, knelt down, and shoved the paper underneath.

Devlin had to stand under a light to read what her mother had scrawled, the handwriting wobbly, as if she hadn't held a pen in years.

Get out of this place. Don't try to do anything. Just get out back to safety and find help. I love you so much.

Devlin set the paper on the floor and scribbled under her mother's handwriting:

Wolves outside and blizzard. Our pilot not coming back until tomorrow.

Devlin slid the paper through. Rachael picked it up, holding it flat against the door while she wrote.

It came back quickly, and as Devlin grabbed it, she heard footsteps.

Terrible people here. You cannot let them find you. Go to an empty room and hide there until you can leave. You have to listen to me. I love you. Now go.

The footsteps were coming up from the lobby stairs. Devlin took the sheet of paper, wrote "I love you," and held the message up to the peephole, then moved quickly into the alcove and down three steps before stopping.

Now there were footsteps climbing this stairwell, too, these faster, with a kind of clicking, like a dog's toenails on a hardwood floor.

She backtracked to the fourth floor, glanced around the corner from the stairwell, the footsteps getting louder on the lobby staircase, at the other end, the faster ones rushing up beneath her.

She ran into the fourth-floor corridor, searching for that unlocked door, finally finding it four down and across the hall from her mother's room. She slipped inside just as someone's head emerged into view from the lobby stairs.

She eased the door shut, stared through the peephole.

A long black shape loped by.

Five seconds later, it returned, stood staring at the door, whining and sniffing the floor.

A man walked into view—the tall, cowboy-hatted guard with long hair. He patted the wolf's head, knelt down, let the animal nuzzle into his neck.

Another man drew everyone's attention—short and round, wearing a green kimono, sandals, with a red bandanna tied onto his left arm, pursuant to Ethan's instructions.

The great black wolf sat at attention beside the guard, hackles raised, eyeing the guest.

"Hey, Reynolds," the guard said. "Good to see you again."

"Likewise, Gerald, likewise. Say, would you be so kind as to point me in the direction of the pregnant woman Ethan mentioned this morning?"

"Sure, right this way."

The men and the wolf started back toward the alcove, and just before their voices diminished entirely, Devlin heard the guard say, "She's in four twenty-nine. I think you're going to enjoy yourself, my friend."

FORTY-EIGHT

Devlin stood outside room 429, the corridor empty, her right arm sagging with the weight of the gun.

The high twang of Reynolds's voice passed easily through the door: "I want you to take that off right now and sit down. You know how much money I've made this year?"

"How much?"

There was a sound like a hand clap. "Don't you fucking say one word to me. Eighty-four million. One year. That moisten you up?"

Devlin thought she heard footsteps coming up the staircase at the other end, hustled into the alcove for a moment to wait, but no one came.

When she returned to the door, she could hear the bed creaking, Reynolds making noise.

Winded, he said, "Feel free to moan or whatever the fuck."

Her mother moaned.

"You know I could kill you if I wanted?" he said, breathless.

Devlin wiped the tears out of her eyes so she could see, tried but couldn't stop herself from glancing through the peephole, saw it happening, knew instantly she never should have looked, that the sight of the small, fat man riding her mother was an image she would never expunge, and a deep seed of rage sprouted up in the pit of her stomach, swelling her throat, flooding her eyes.

She put her hand on the doorknob, turned it, the bolt retracting, the room unlocked.

A hairsbreadth from pushing it open and walking inside, she stopped, willing back the rage. She could shoot this man right now, but the gunshot would summon everyone to the fourth floor. There'd be no hiding out until nighttime, then slipping back to the tent to await the return of their bush pilot. It might save her mother in the short term, but it would kill them all in the long.

The bolt slid back into the door frame and Devlin leaned against the wall beside the door.

She wept soundlessly, praying her mother wasn't present, that she'd managed to transport herself to another place and time—a childhood memory, her wedding day, perhaps a family holiday, like the Christmas they'd spent eight years ago in Tahiti, opening presents at sunrise on the beach.

FORTY-NINE

When Reynolds had finished with her mother, Devlin crept back to room 420, and shut herself inside.

She waited for hours, huddled in a corner, out of eyesight from the peephole, watching the gray sky fade up, plateau, and begin its short return to darkness. She was hungry, thirsty. She prayed for Kalyn, her father and mother, and despite everything, just knowing that Rachael was four doors down brought her a comfort she hadn't felt in years.

Dusk had come when Devlin decided it was time to leave the lodge and head back to the tent.

She got up and walked to the window, saw it was still snowing, the landscape gray and bleak. The long inner lake was wind-stirred, small waves lapping at the snowy shore, and the snow-bowed spruce trees stood completely white as she looked down on them from four floors above.

Devlin went to the door, glanced out the peephole, the corridor empty from her vantage. She slipped outside and ran down to 429, peeked through the peephole, saw her mother asleep in bed.

Devlin moved quietly toward the stairwell, descended to the first floor, and crept down the corridor, stopping along the way in 119 to retrieve her parka and snow pants.

She finally emerged into the lobby. It smelled of wood smoke, a fire burning in the freestanding hearth, and someone had placed candles on the newels of the staircase. Lanterns, mounted to the walls, glowed with firelight, casting strange shadows on the stone floor. Noise and more light emanated from the archway at the other end of the lobby, adjacent to the library.

She stole up to it, light and sound filling the passage, wonderful smells wafting out from the dining hall, accompanied by the voices of fucked-out, happy Texans.

Supper. Her stomach ached, but the thought of eating snow outside, that she might at least quench her thirst, spurred her on.

Devlin glanced at the front entrance but decided it would be safer to depart the way she'd come, down through the cellar, out the door under the veranda.

She walked into the library, which was empty and warm.

As she reached to open the cellar door, someone raced in, and a hand covered her mouth before she even had a chance to turn around.

"Don't scream, baby. It's just me."

Kalyn let her go, and the girl and the woman embraced, Devlin flushing with relief.

Kalyn quietly closed the library door and knelt down with Devlin by the hearth, said, "I've been looking all over for you."

"I've been hiding. Have you seen my dad?"

"No, honey."

Devlin tried to reassure herself. *Doesn't mean he's dead,* she thought. She said, "My mom's here. She's alive, so maybe your sister is—"

"I know, I already found her."

"Where?"

"She's in a room on the second floor of the north wing, where they keep most of the pregnant women."

"What happened to you last night?"

"The wolves came after me when I went outside to pee. I got myself treed. Stayed up there until first light, then finally found my way here a few hours ago."

"You know what this place is?"

"I'd like to burn it to the fucking ground."

"I was heading back to the tent, Kalyn. I thought I'd spend the night there, hike down to the outer lake in the morning, wait for our pilot to come so I could get help."

"Yeah, that's probably our best course of action."

Devlin got up, opened the cellar door. "I came in from here. I think it's the safest—"

Kalyn shook her head. "That's where they keep the wolves. Come on. I know a better way."

Kalyn led her out of the library, into the adjacent passage, and up a stairwell that branched off to the right.

Climbing, Devlin noticed blood spatters across the hem of Kalyn's pink down jacket.

After two flights of stairs, they emerged into a short corridor lined with several unmarked doors. Kalyn glanced back, put a finger to her lips. Devlin nodded.

They proceeded to the last door on the corridor, stopping just shy of it.

Kalyn turned and whispered, "Wait here for a minute."

"What are you doing?"

"You'll see."

Kalyn stepped forward, palmed the doorknob, turned it, and went inside, the door closing softly after her.

Devlin waited, the ceiling lights humming above her. Then the building rumbled again and the overhead lights cut out, a vacuum of silence filled only by the hiss of the lanterns mounted to the corridor walls.

The door opened and Kalyn poked her head out.

"All right, come on," she whispered.

Kalyn took her by the hand, pulled her inside, and closed the door.

Devlin found herself standing in an expansive bedroom suite with a low fire burning in the hearth.

She didn't notice the man until he spoke.

"How old are you, Devlin?" His voice was soft, almost a falsetto, tinged with a slight accent that Devlin couldn't place due to the confusion and the sudden banging racket of her heart.

He set down a book and rose from the recliner beside the fireplace, removed his wire-rim glasses so he could look Devlin up and down.

"Did you not hear my question?" he asked.

Devlin looked at Kalyn, who just said, "Answer him."

"What's happening?"

"*Answer* him."

"Sixteen."

The man nodded. "You favor your mother."

Kalyn said, "So, Paul? We good?"

Devlin ripped her hand out of Kalyn's grasp and backpedaled into the wall beside the door. She stared at Paul. His vest, wire-rim glasses, and banker's haircut struck her as incongruous, given his apparent station in the lodge.

"What are you doing, Kalyn?" she asked.

"Are we all set, Paul?"

"We still have the matter of Gerald. He was a good man. Had been with me for—"

"You can't hire another guard?"

"What are you doing, Kalyn?" Devlin asked again.

Kalyn looked at her, just shook her head. "I don't have a choice here, okay?"

"A choice? About what?"

Paul said, "Okay, we'll call it good as soon as you find Rachael's husband and bring him to me."

"And then you'll fly Lucy and me out of here first thing tomorrow?"

"Weather permitting."

"How do I know?"

"What?"

"That you'll keep your end."

Paul shrugged. "Guess I'll have to earn your trust."

Devlin reached into the pocket of her parka, fingers grazing the .357, thinking, *I should've taken it out, made sure it was loaded earlier today. I don't even know how to use this thing.*

Devlin ran her thumb over the hammer. In the movies, she'd seen people pull on it. She tried, and the cylinder made a clicking sound, the hammer locked back.

"You gonna kill him?" Kalyn asked.

"You really wanna know?"

Before anyone had noticed, she was bringing up the .357 and aiming it at the center of Paul's chest. She could barely see the revolver, the metal dull in the low light. It felt so heavy, smelled of oil.

Paul was the first to notice, and he said, "You stupid cunt, you didn't frisk her."

Devlin said, "Go stand beside him, Kalyn."

"Devlin—"

Devlin swung the gun toward Kalyn.

"All right."

As Kalyn approached him, Paul said, "Your first time holding a gun, Ms. Innis?"

"Why are you doing this to us, Kalyn?"

"The way your hands are trembling, I would assume the answer is yes."

Devlin began to cry, glancing between Paul and Kalyn, a knot tightening in her stomach. "I don't understand." She barely got the words out.

"Give him the gun, baby." Kalyn seemed harder than she remembered, something different, changed about her. Devlin blinked through the sheet of tears.

"Devlin." Paul found Devlin's eyes, locked her in with a gaze that seemed to hum. "You come here and lay that big gun down in my hand like Kalyn just told you. What? You think I'm going to hurt you?"

"Stop moving."

"I'm not moving. I don't know—"

"You think I won't pull the trigger, but I swear to God I will." The initial shock was waning, making room for the rage. "Why'd you do this, Kalyn?"

Kalyn was crying now. "They caught me. Three hours ago, after I'd killed one of the guards. It wasn't like I had planned all this. I told them about you, said I could find you. If I did, he was going to let my sister go. Fly me and Lucy out of here tomorrow. If I didn't, he was gonna let one of the oil-men kill her tonight. You see? I didn't have a—"

"You were gonna trade me for your sister."

"I'm sorry," Kalyn said. "Wouldn't you trade me for your mother? To get her back?"

"I wouldn't sell anyone out."

"Well, congratulations on being a better person. Now come here and put the gun in my hand."

"Fuck you."

Devlin noticed Paul inching toward her, the subtlest of movements. He said, "You aren't gonna hurt anybody. Fact, you've got the safety on right now."

Devlin knew if she averted her eyes even for a second, it would be over. "Guess we'll find out," she said.

Kalyn said, "Dev, no—"

Devlin winced as the recoil pushed her back against the wall, her ears ringing, temporarily blinded from the flash.

Paul's brow furrowed up and he looked down at the black hole in the upper left quadrant of his sweater vest, darkness blossoming below his heart.

The room smelled sweetly bitter, the cordite burning in Devlin's nose.

Paul said, "You didn't shoot me. You didn't." He sat back down in the chair, paling. Devlin could hear the fading suck of his punctured lung, the man emitting soft, drowning gurgles. She pulled the hammer back once more and aimed at Kalyn.

"If you move," Devlin said, "I'll kill you, too."

FIFTY

Devlin rushed back into the corridor, ran down the stairwell and into the passage. She heard voices in the dining hall, but she kept going, back into the lobby. It was much darker here, now illuminated only by candles and lanterns. As she entered the first-floor corridor, she heard it—rapid footfalls on stone, people running through the lobby, a man yelling. Devlin glanced back, saw a group of shadows appear at the far end. She rushed into the alcove, started up the stairwell, came out onto the second floor. The wolf loped down the corridor toward her, its head low, sniffing the hardwood floor. Devlin fired off three shots, then turned, ran back into the stairwell, sprinting up two more flights, emerging finally onto the last floor.

There were footsteps below her now and more coming up the stairs from the lobby. *You have to find a room and hide.* She ran through the corridor, trying doorknobs on both sides of the hall—locked, locked. She could hear the wolf running up the stairwell, growling. Locked. Locked. Shouting resounded in the lobby. Locked. Room 403 opened.

She stepped inside, shut the door, out of breath, on the verge of tears. It was completely dark in the room. She ran to the window, looked through it, light from the veranda glittering on the billions of snowflakes loading the fir trees with tons of powder, burying saplings, boulders, swirling madly as the wind blew drifts to the second floor.

She heard doors opening, shutting out in the corridor, the slams getting closer. A wardrobe stood to the left of the door. She set the gun on the bed, got behind the wardrobe, put all her weight against it, straining to shove the enormous piece of furniture across the floor. It inched. They were coming, just a few doors down now.

The wardrobe finally slid. She pushed it behind the door, then went to the desk, pulled it away from the window, braced it against the wardrobe.

Outside, someone said, "I can't see through this peephole."

"Unlock it."

"It is unlocked."

The door shook. "There's something blocking it."

Another man's voice came very quietly and very evenly through the barricade. "Can you hear me?" Devlin made no response. She picked up the gun. "Open the door right now." She didn't move. After a moment, the footsteps trailed away, and she stood trembling in the darkness of the bedroom, the only sound the whisper of snow striking the glass. Another minute passed. *Could they have left? Oh, please God, please.* She thought she heard the echo of footsteps, but the sound was soft and she couldn't be sure.

There was a knock, and his voice passed through the door.

"Gonna let me in, do this easy?"

Devlin looked at the wardrobe braced against the door, realized with a horrifying pressure between her eyes that this was it. End of the line.

"I will break it fucking down."

The knock was explosive this time. She thought he'd destroyed his hand, until the second and third and fourth blows came and the door began to splinter. She squeezed back the hammer, pulled the trigger twice, shot a pair of holes through the wardrobe and the door, the gun nearly jumping out of her hands. After her ears quit ringing, it was quiet, and she thought for a moment she'd hit him.

Soon he started up again. The wardrobe began to shudder, the ceiling rained plaster dust and paint chips, and the chandelier was tinkling. Her legs quaked so violently, they barely kept her upright. Tears streamed down her face.

As he broke through the back of the wardrobe, she backpedaled toward the closet.

Now she could hear him thrashing around inside. The wardrobe doors were flung open. He stood amid the old dresses, and she could see his face only by the faint illumination of the lantern that he held. The ax thudded blade-first onto the hardwood floor and he climbed out, set the lantern by the ax. He drove his shoulder into the side of the wardrobe and inched it back into the corner. The ravaged door stood exposed, wrenched from its hinges and leaning back against the door frame.

He picked up the flashlight and the ax and came toward her, the dome of his bald head shining with sweat in the firelight. She recognized his blue jeans and boots—Ethan, from breakfast this morning.

He stopped when he saw the revolver in her hand, the weapon twitching with each heartbeat. Devlin put both fingers on the hammer, pulled it back, squeezed the trigger. *Click.*

He lunged forward, slapped the gun out of her hand. As it slid across the floor, he pressed her up against the window, their hearts heaving into each other. She could feel the cold of the storm through the glass, the cold of the ax blade against her leg. He gazed down at her, their breath pluming in the lantern light. His smelled of wine.

Thunder resounded, porcelain figurines rattling on a nearby bureau.

He ground his teeth together. "He was my brother, and now he's dead."

"He was going to—"

"He was my brother. Now he's dead."

He let go of the ax and his fingers glided through her black curls, his fist closing on a handful of hair.

"That hurts," she cried.

"You have no idea." And he dragged her screaming toward the smashed door, which he kicked aside. She clung to his arm as he hauled her out into the corridor and past the rooms on the fourth floor, the wolf trotting alongside, snapping at her face. It was just the two of them now, the others gone, firelight glinting off the brass numbers.

405.

407.

409.

Devlin screamed, dug her fingernails into his arm. He shrieked and she tore herself away, ran back down the corridor. On the fifth stride, she tripped, fell, glanced back toward the lantern and the shape of Ethan and the wolf, fast approaching.

The moment she regained her footing, he was upon her.

FIFTY-ONE

When she opened her eyes again, the first thing she saw was the blurry image of her feet sliding across the stone floor of the lobby and past the hulking tower of the freestanding hearth, its blaze burned down to the embers, the only light coming from Ethan's lantern.

Devlin was being dragged by her hair. Her right eye throbbed and she could see only a slit of the world through it. The Texans who stood in their kimonos at the far end of the lobby resembled a collection of phantoms in the dark.

One of them yelled, "What you got there, Ethan?"

"Not your fucking concern!"

Ethan produced a knife from his pocket, grabbed her jacket, and sliced the blade through it, cleaving two layers of fabric—her fleece and the long underwear shirt. He ripped them off, then unbuttoned her jeans, slid them down her legs, and threw her to the floor. He tore off her pants, stripped away her long underwear bottoms, her panties, then set her back on her feet.

She stood dazed, embarrassed, and numb with shock as he shoved open the heavy iron doors to the storm.

"No, please, I'll—"

He pushed her outside, and she stumbled back into one of the pillars. Ethan lifted a long, thin whistle to his lips and blew, the frequency too high to register with her ears. Then the doors slammed shut, Ethan ramming home the three bolts on the other side.

Her feet ached. She looked down at them, but they were submerged in the snow the wind had blown against the pillar. She ran at the door and beat her fists against it and screamed. On a summer evening, her voice would've carried across the lake and up the mountain slopes. This night, the blizzard destroyed the echo and her voice went wherever the wind took it. She turned away from the doors, looked down toward the lake. She stamped her feet, snow continuing to fall onto the porch.

She turned back to the doors, put her lips to the snow-glazed iron: "It hurts. Please." She registered the desperation in her voice. It scared her like nothing else had.

Devlin shut her eyes. *I'm going to die out here.* She ran out naked into the snow. It was waist-deep, numbing. She collapsed, sank into a drift. Above the chattering of her teeth there was only the hush of the storm, until a howl erupted across the lake.

She looked up, her head nodding with cold. The howl came again, closer this time. She struggled to her ice-burned feet. In the nearby woods, more howls answered. *Not the wolves, please God, not the wolves.*

Now she glimpsed something—a shape bounding through deep powder. There were tears and snowmelt in her eyes, and when she blinked them away, she saw the wolf. She looked back up the corridor of spruce leading to the lodge. The five-story tower, the projecting four-story north and south wings, stood black against the storm.

A series of explosions shattered the silence. She felt the vibration in her chest. Somewhere in the distance, an avalanche thundered down a mountainside.

An idea struck her—she envisioned climbing up to the veranda. She would break a window, slip into the library.

Now the wolf was coming toward her through the snow.

By the time she reached the end of the south wing, she was moaning from the pain. Her hair hung in her eyes and when she tried to brush it away, it broke off. To stay above the snow, she held on to the cold rock of the first level, making her way around the chimney to the back side of the south wing, coughing now in painful, choking fits.

Thirty yards from the veranda, her left foot stepped on something. She bent down, brushed away the snow. Screamed. A woman sat against the stone wall, naked, half-eaten. While new snow blanketed the dead girl's face, Devlin pushed on toward the veranda, swimming through snowdrifts as deep as she was tall.

Now the burning had begun to subside in her feet and hands, her extremities assuming a clumsiness that made it impossible to grip the stone wall. She looked down at the deadweight hanging at the ends of her arms, imagined the flesh and the bone and the blood freezing solid in her fingers, wondered if she'd already lost them.

The steps to the veranda were buried, the balustrade covered. She fought her way through the snow, her cheeks going numb, the dull intoxication of hypothermia beginning to cloud her brain. From below she could see the

French doors leading into the library, the glass panes fogged, firelight rico-
cheting off a wall of books.

Devlin heard something behind her, turned, saw three wolves emerge
around the corner of the south wing, only their heads visible, rising and
falling in the deepening snow.

She backed up to the foot of the stone steps, nothing to do now but
watch them come, steel herself to die. She closed her eyes, felt the snow col-
lecting on her face, her eyelids, the tip of her nose. Possessed by a strange,
sudden warmth, she sensed the delusional euphoria lurking, and she wel-
comed it. Her lips moved in rhythm with her thoughts. She was thinking
that she would have a little nap to gather her strength and when she woke
she would climb out of the snow and go inside and sit by the fire.

But there was no great urgency. She could last the night if she had to.
She could last until spring, until the thaw. She was finally comfortable and
getting warmer by the minute.

Devlin heard the wolves coming now, tramping toward her through the
snow, snarling, the sound of their great jaws snapping closed all around
her like gunshots in the night.

What They Lost

FIFTY-TWO

Twenty minutes had passed since he'd thrown the teenager out into the storm, and in the dining room, the oblivious Texans were still playing Hold 'Em for foolish stakes, trashed beyond all reason.

He'd lived in this lodge and run its business going on ten years, with nothing approaching this level of catastrophe—Gerald dead, now Paul, and that woman, Kalyn, still unaccounted for, though Donald, that imminently capable sociopath, would surely find her before dawn, as he had so many others.

Ethan reclined in one of the brown leather chairs in the vicinity of the library's hearth, his legs stretched across the matching ottoman. He'd left his brother in his bedroom in that chair by the fireplace, Gerald in the south-wing alcove, where Kalyn had slit his throat. He'd deal with it all in the morning—the cleanup, public relations with the Texans, if they even remembered—and think of nothing more tonight but how monumentally fucked up he was about to get.

He filled his lungs with a hefty intake of smoke.

When it finally hit him, Ethan let the long bamboo pipe slip from his fingers and eased back into the chair, grinning stupidly at the ceiling, blowing smoke rings at the fire.

Through the opium fog, he heard a banging sound, thought for a moment it was his heart, since frequently, after a big hit, it raced and thumped in his chest like a blacksmith shaping out a piece of iron. But this wasn't that. He could feel his heartbeat, which was soft and slow; there was something comforting about its methodically steady pace.

He rarely hauled himself out of the chair on nights he smoked, preferring to pass out before the warmth of the fire, letting the twisting flames and the coals and the sounds they made occupy his mind.

It took considerable effort to maneuver out of the chair. At last, he did, looked down at his feet when finally standing, puzzled at the strange sensation, as if he was watching appendages that didn't belong to him. He certainly couldn't feel them, even as he walked onto the freezing stone of the lobby, where Donald was already waiting in the vicinity of the door with his shotgun.

Ethan said, "Tenacious little thing, isn't she? Give me that." He swiped the shotgun out of Donald's hand. "Wanna watch her go airborne?" he asked.

The guard chuckled as Ethan slid back the three iron bolts and pulled open the doors.

From Don's perspective, it appeared as if the back of Ethan's head exploded, his knees buckling, his body dropping like an inanimate sack of bones to the stone, a razor shard of Ethan's skull lodged in Don's eye.

A figure stood in the threshold, shadowy and formless in the candlelight. Don was backpedaling, reaching for the Glock in his jacket as a second muzzle flash blinded him, followed by a fragment of white-hot pain that was the end.

FIFTY-THREE

W ill Innis, frostbitten, mauled, half-delirious with cold and exhaustion, limped through the open doors into the lodge, glancing down at the two men he'd shot, both undoubtedly gone, great pools of blood like black lacquer in the light of a nearby lantern.

Footsteps resonated through a passage at the other end of the lobby, and uncomfortable with the .45, the way it had seemed to spring out of his hand when he'd pulled the trigger, he traded it for the shotgun of the first man he'd killed.

Pumping it, he aimed down the passage as three shadows emerged into the lobby, silhouetted by candlelight.

One of them shouted, "Ethan, you having a little target practice without us?"

The first blast filled the lobby.

Will pumped again, fired again, the men running now, chased by two more thunderous booms that put everything quiet.

Will hurried across the lobby into the dimly lighted passage, glimpsed three men in kimonos on the floor, one sprawled and unmoving, two whimpering like puppies as they dragged themselves across the stone, leaving dark, sluglike trails in their wake.

Devlin lay on the porch in several inches of snow, shaking violently, naked. Will's eyes flooded at the sight of his daughter like this.

He lifted her out of the snow, carried her into the lodge, and as he pulled the doors closed and shot home the bolts, a wolf howled somewhere out in that snowy dark. He hadn't managed to kill any of them.

On the other side of the lobby, through an open door, what appeared to be fire shadows moved along the walls. Will carried Devlin past the free-standing fireplace into the library, where a fire raged in the hearth.

He placed his daughter down in the chair, stretched her legs across the ottoman, and pushed her close to the flames. In light of her disease, he couldn't bring himself to even consider what her time in the snow had exposed her body to. She'd be going straight to a hospital the moment they left this place.

Pulling a stack of blankets off a shelf above the hearth, he wrapped Devlin in them, her body still cold to the touch, shivering.

He knelt on the floor, ran his hand over her thawing hair.

"Dad's here," he said. "You're safe, baby girl."

Footsteps echoed in the lobby.

He turned, stood looking through the open door at darkness and candle flames. Unlacing his boots and slipping them off so they wouldn't squeak, Will hustled out of the library, softly shutting the door behind him.

He didn't hear the footsteps as he ran across the stone back toward the entrance, waited there, listening to the moan of wind pushing on the doors, his face burning with frostbite, his legs sore from yesterday's wolf bites.

Someone appeared in the passage beside the library—from his vantage point, just a silhouette-shaped black hole in the darkness. Will, who wasn't standing in the illumination of any lantern or candle, wondered if whoever it was could see him, then wondered if the person standing there had the same thought.

He pumped the shotgun, held at waist level, aimed at the opening of the passage. When he spoke, he tried to make his voice sound bigger, more unfazed than he felt.

"That lantern mounted to the staircase . . . walk into its light so I can see you. I'm holding a shotgun, I've just killed five men, and I won't hesitate to do the same to you."

The dark spot in the passage moved forward, entering the illumination of a lantern, firelight giving texture and depth to the troubled face of Kalyn Sharp.

She said, "Will?"

FIFTY-FOUR

Will lowered the shotgun and moved quickly across the lobby, feeling the cold of the stone through his socks. Drawing near, he let the shotgun drop to the floor.

They embraced, Will burying his face in the soft, warm side of her neck, just breathing her in. "You in one piece?" he whispered.

"Yeah. Where's Devi?"

"In the library. They threw her out in the storm."

"Oh God. Is she okay? She talking?"

"Not yet. She's still unconscious."

They came apart and Kalyn said, "What's wrong with your face?"

Will touched the cut across his cheek, the blackened skin. "I had a run-in with some mean-ass wolves. Spent last night outside, all of today trying to find you and Devlin. Between the wolves and the cold, I'm in pretty rough shape."

She glanced over her shoulder into the passage. "I see you took out a few of the guests."

"Guests?"

"Don't worry, they had it coming. But there're three more of them, probably unarmed. They were playing cards in the dining room before you rolled in."

"You okay? You seem—"

"No, I'm not okay. Look, Will, I have to—"

The library door opened. Devlin stood on the threshold, a blanket draped over her shoulders, hair hanging down in her face.

"Dad?"

Will smiled. "Hey, baby girl. How are—"

"Who's that with you?"

"It's all right. Just Kalyn."

"No, it's not all right."

"Honey—"

"She was gonna leave us both here."

Will looked at Kalyn, felt her beginning to pull away from him. He stared into her eyes, said, "What are you talking about, Devi?"

"Do you have a gun?"

"On the floor behind me."

"Get it."

"I think she's confused from the cold," Kalyn whispered. "Let's go reassure her." Kalyn started past him, moving toward the shotgun. Will grabbed her arm.

"Dad!"

"Where are you going?" Will asked. "Devlin's over there."

"You trust me or not, Will?"

He smiled weakly. "Of course. You take the gun. You're better with it than I am."

Kalyn smiled, said, "You gonna let go of my arm?"

"Oh, yeah. Sorry."

"No, Dad." Devlin was crying now.

"It's all right, honey. I think you're just a little confused."

"I am *not* confused!" Will started toward his daughter, Kalyn toward the shotgun.

He suddenly spun around, saw Kalyn bending down, then lunged and shoved her across the floor.

As she fell hard on the stone, he picked up the shotgun.

"What the fuck is wrong with you?"

"If I'm wrong," Will said, "I apologize. Get up slowly, hands where I can see them."

"Will, I can explain—"

"Maybe so. Maybe we'll all have a big laugh about this in a little while. Walk toward the library. Devlin, we're heading your way."

Devlin stepped back into the library.

"Why don't you trust me?" Kalyn asked.

"I'm not saying I don't. We're just gonna sort this out."

They entered the library and Will closed the door behind them.

"She might have a gun or something, Dad."

"Kalyn, sit in that corner and keep your hands on top of your knees."

Devlin sat bundled in covers by the fire, glaring at Kalyn as she took a seat against the base of the bookshelves.

Will stood several feet away, the shotgun trained on Kalyn's chest.

"Devlin," he said, "tell me what's going on here."

"I've been in this lodge since early this morning, trying to keep from getting caught, looking for you. Then a little while ago, Kalyn found me. She took me upstairs. I thought we were sneaking out. Instead, she took me to this man named Paul. She was gonna trade me."

Kalyn said, "Will, please—"

"Shut up. Trade you for what, Devlin?"

"Her sister, Lucy. They keep women here."

"Why?"

"For the guests. So they can have sex with them, even kill them if they want."

"Where's Paul now? Was he one of the men I—"

"I shot him."

"Oh, honey."

"He was gonna hurt me. I didn't have a choice."

Will stared at Kalyn.

"You know me, Will."

"No, I know my daughter. You're a big fucking question mark right now." Will stepped toward her, raised the shotgun, trying to spurn the blood lust he felt. Not even with Javier had he wanted to hurt something this bad.

Kalyn's eyes ran over, and she wiped her face.

Will said, "Did you have this planned from the start?"

"No."

"To use us to help you get here, then trade my daughter for your sister? Was that the deal?"

"No, I just got caught. I never would've let them keep you or her. I would've—"

"I should kill you right now," Will said.

"Let's lock her up, Dad. In one of the rooms."

"Do we have a key?"

"I know where you can get one."

"All right, but meanwhile . . ."

He swung the Mossberg's composite stock into the side of Kalyn's head.

FIFTY-FIVE

Will and Devlin walked together out of the library, leaving Kalyn unconscious on the floor. They turned the corner into the candlelit passage, the three bodies lying up ahead, thankfully obscured in the low light.

"Why don't you hang back, Dev," Will said. "No sense taking in what you don't have to."

"Okay, Dad. I think each of the guests has a master key that opens all the rooms."

"And the dining hall is up ahead on the left?"

"Yeah."

"Yell if you need me."

Will went on, stepping carefully between lakes of blood as he negotiated his way past the men he'd killed, marveling at the merciful numbness.

Three torches had been ignited in the great dining hall, the walls aglow and the far end of the table littered with cards, poker chips, wads of cash, wineglasses, shot glasses, highballs, martini glasses, cocktail shakers, bottles of wine, liquor, and two enormous bongs, all shimmering in the firelight.

"Anybody in here? I won't hurt you if you come on out."

He walked to the near end of the table, the room reeking of cigars and marijuana smoke, soured with spilled alcohol and the licorice stench of absinthe.

Ten feet away, he spotted a dark shape lying down against the wall beside a potted spruce tree. Will's finger moved onto the trigger.

He heard the sputtering of a drunken snore, and his eyes pulled detail out of the dark: an older silver-haired man having partied out of his league.

Something clanged in the kitchen.

"Come out of there!" Will hollered. "Your chance to do this without getting hurt is slipping away."

The kitchen doors swung open and two men staggered out—a man in his late twenties, naked except for his boxer shorts, looking disoriented and sheepish, and a shorter, much rounder kimonoed man, balding and more sober.

"Tell him it's cool, Reynolds."

"Keep your mouth shut, Sean." To Will: "What's going on here?"

"Come closer."

The men stepped forward into the full illumination of a torch.

"Who are you?" Will asked.

"Guests of this lodge. Who the fuck are you?"

Footsteps sounded outside in the passage. Will glanced over his shoulder.

"Just me, Dad."

"I told you wait out there."

Reynolds said, "Where's everybody else?"

"They're dead, sir."

Sean said, "Oh shit."

"Are you law enforcement?" Reynolds asked.

"No."

Devlin sidled up to her father.

"Then what gives you the right to—" The racket of a pumping shotgun stopped him cold. Will turned, to see his daughter leveling a Mossberg on both men.

She said, "You with no shirt on, step out of the way, please."

Sean staggered around the table and sat down unsteadily against the wall beside his father. Reynolds looked confused and terribly put upon.

"Honey, what are you doing?" Will said.

She shouldered the shotgun.

"I'm gonna kill that fat man."

"No, Devlin—"

"Trust me, Dad, he has it coming."

"In cold blood?"

"Yep."

"Wait just a second."

"Why are you so angry with me?" Reynolds asked.

"Remember that pregnant woman you raped this morning?"

"I don't know what you're—"

"You told her you'd made eighty-four million dollars this year? That you could kill her if you wanted?"

"I think you're mistaking me for—"

"I'm not mistaking you for anybody."

Will said, "Devlin, this isn't the way to handle this. You didn't have a choice with Paul, but you do now." He reached for the shotgun, saying,

"Here, give me that," but his voice was lost in the shattering report. Will watched, stunned, as his daughter struggled to pump the Mossberg again.

Reynolds was sitting on the floor in a puddle of himself, not making a peep, just staring at the shredded kimono and all that was leaking through it.

Devlin approached him with the Mossberg already shouldered, said, "I hope you go to hell," and shot him in the face.

When her ears quit ringing, the only sound in the room was Sean's whimpering.

Devlin looked back at her father, saw something like disappointment or disgust.

"Please don't look at me like that, Dad."

Will just shook his head, and for a moment Devlin thought he might cry.

"You wanna know why I'm never going to lose a wink of sleep over that?"

"Why?"

Devlin reached into her pocket and pulled out a key.

"Come with me. I'll show you who I watched him rape."

FIFTY-SIX

They locked Kalyn, Sean, and his father into separate rooms on the first
floor of the south wing, and Will followed Devlin up the staircase to the
fourth, where they stopped in front of the door to room 429.

"Here." She handed her father the master key.

"What do you want me to do with this?"

"Just open it."

Will slipped the key into the lock.

"I'm gonna wait out here," Devlin said. "You'll need this." She handed
him a lantern, and Will turned the key, pushed the door open.

The room was dark. Someone lay crying in bed. He set the lantern on
the table, assumed it was a woman under the covers, one of the captives.

Will said, "Everything's okay now. The people who've kept you here
and the man who hurt you today are dead."

The covers turned back.

Will's wife sat up, and he lost his breath.

"Rachael?"

Firelit tears trailed down her cheeks.

He had dreamed of this a thousand times—what it would be like to hold
his wife again, to wrap his arms around her. None of them had approached
the sweetness or the pain of this moment, and he was crying because of her
smell. "You smell like you," he whispered.

"Is this real?" Rachael asked.

"I promise it is."

"Where's Devlin?"

"Outside in the hallway."

"Tell her to come in."

Will called their daughter, and Devlin came, climbed into bed between them. They sat in the low light of room 429, huddled together under the covers, Devlin rubbing her mother's round belly and doing most of the talking, answering an endless stream of questions about school, boyfriends, her disease, their new life in Colorado, both parents in tears half the time, laughing the rest.

It had been over five years since they'd last been together. They talked and held one another and cried, all knowing in the back of their minds that they could sit on this bed for twenty years, for fifty, but it wouldn't matter. There would be no real catching up, no recovery of lost time, no understanding of the damage the separation had caused. They were different people now—haunted, ridden with scars and nightmares. There was no going back to that stormy July night in Ajo, Arizona. That Innis family was gone, and they would have to find themselves and one another again, start over, and pray that somehow the pieces fit back together.

Despite the joy and the overriding hope, it wasn't until this moment, sitting in this bed together on the fourth floor of this old lodge, that they each understood how much had been stolen from them, the incomprehensible arithmetic of what they had lost.

The Innises didn't sleep that night. They walked together up and down the corridors, looking for the rooms where the rest of the women were kept.

It was the most gut-wrenching, emotional two hours of Will's life, setting these prisoners free, telling them that the people who'd held them here and destroyed their lives were dead, incapable of ever hurting them again. Most of the women broke down, hysterical with relief. A handful had gone mad. One laughed at the news. One just sat on her bed and stared out the window, comatose. Kalyn's sister, Lucy Dahl, didn't say anything when they unlocked her door, just walked out without a word, and Will couldn't yet bring himself to broach the topic of her sister. In the north wing, they found two women emaciated from starvation, so weak that Will had to carry them down into the library, each weighing less than eighty pounds, their hair thinned, their teeth falling out. A woman on the third floor had died in her sleep at least a month ago, and after seeing her, Will stepped into the alcove and knelt down in a corner and wept. So much pain here, so much ruin.

FIFTY-SEVEN

They pushed all the furniture into the lobby and brought in mattresses and blankets from the nearest rooms. Twenty-two women, half of them pregnant, crowded into the library as Will added logs to the fire and stoked up the blaze, the room of books warming, the fire shadows moving in endless patterns across the walls as the blizzard shrieked and snow piled up against the French doors. A woman who'd given birth that morning sat in a corner nursing her infant, mother and child wrapped in blankets.

Will stood in the open doorway, looking across the library, wall-to-wall with mattresses. Some of the women were already sleeping, wrapped in each other's arms, others crying softly to themselves and rocking back and forth, as if not quite ready to give themselves over to this reality, afraid it would vanish from under their feet as it had so often before.

Will said, "Could I have your attention for a minute, please? My daughter and I are going to get some food from the kitchen, since we haven't eaten all day. Is anyone hungry?" No one spoke or raised a hand. "Tomorrow, if this storm has let up, a bush pilot is supposed to land on a nearby lake at three in the afternoon. I'm going to head out early and try to reach him, fly back to Fairbanks and get help. Try to find a big seaplane to fly to this inner lake. Hopefully, come tomorrow evening, you'll all be back in civilization, with your families en route."

A half hour later, Devlin sat on the hearth before the fire, eating beef stew and buttered biscuits.

When she finished her late supper, she crawled under the covers next to her mother. She could feel the warmth of the fire through the blanket, the room dark, quiet, filled with the respirations of women sleeping, the crack and hiss of the flames devouring the wood, a slumber party like Devlin could never have imagined. She was asleep within a minute.

Rachael lay on her side, facing her husband, his face awash in firelight. She thought for sure he'd aged more than five years, his features harder, leaner, not a hint of the baby fat that had once smoothed his jawline, given him those boyish good looks she'd fallen for in college. She even thought she saw strands of silver.

Will opened his eyes. Rachael smiled.

"Are you warm?" he whispered. She nodded, the child in her belly active. She wanted to take Will's hand, let him feel the tiny thrusts of the baby's knees and elbow. "You've got that deep-thinking look on your face," he said.

"It's going to be difficult."

"What?"

"Reintegrating, coming together again. I'm not sure how I'll make it on the outside. I feel like I'm being released after a twenty-year prison sentence. Like I won't know what to do with myself. How to be a mother again. A wife."

"We'll make it work, Rachael."

"You say that, but . . . you don't realize—"

"I don't care how hard it is."

"You say that now."

"I mean it now. I'll mean it later."

"I want you to feel something." She took his wrist and pressed the palm of his hand against the side of her stomach.

"Kicking," Will said.

"Yeah. It's his busy time. Usually wakes me up doing this in the middle of the night."

"You know it's a he?"

"Not for certain, but I've gotten good at telling. Feels like boy energy."

"How many have you had since you've been here?"

"This is my fourth."

"What happened to the others?"

"They sold them."

"Jesus. How far along are you?"

"Six and a half months. I'm going to keep him."

"Why would you—"

"I've had three of my babies taken away from me—a week after birth. I think they must sell them. I tried not to get attached, fought it. But it didn't matter. They didn't know what they came from. All they knew was that I was their mother, and I loved every one of them, and I still do. I want to keep this one. Raise him. Might be the only good thing about any of this. I know this is difficult for you. I've been damaged beyond repair in your eyes."

"I don't feel that way, Rach."

"Well, if you do—"

"I don't."

"*If* you do . . . just understand that I don't expect you to do something you aren't capable of. You know, this almost would've been easier if you'd met someone, remarried. At least you wouldn't have a choice then."

Will put his hands on Rachael's face. "You're still my wife. Devlin's mother. I have no illusions about how hard it's gonna be. But we are going to try. I want to."

"How do you feel about keeping this baby?"

"Puts my stomach in knots, but maybe that'll change. You can help me. Look, you were a psychologist, so keep in mind all you've been through. You're in no shape to try to think about your life when you leave this place. Just try to stay in the moment for now. I am."

"Why didn't you remarry?"

"Because I'm in love with you."

"You didn't meet anyone who—"

"I never opened myself up to it."

"Why?"

"Because I still loved my wife. Even when I thought you were dead." He reached out and wiped her face, touched the tiny white scar under her bottom lip that he used to kiss religiously. "Now close your eyes and think only about the fact that you're lying between your husband and daughter. We both love you, and you're safe. That's it. Now sleep."

FIFTY-EIGHT

The sunlight passed clear and sharp through the glass panes of the library windows.

A perfect silence. No wind. No snow driving against the doors.

Devlin sat up and pushed off the covers, squinting in the brilliant light. Her father was already up. Her mother, too. She rubbed her eyes and yawned and went to find them.

They were standing at the entrance to the lodge, holding steaming mugs of coffee, the doors pulled open, surface hoarfrost glittering outside under the midmorning sun, several feet of snow piled up on the porch. The lake water was still and deep green, rimmed with a layer of thin ice that smoked beneath the sun. The bodies of Ethan and the guards had been dragged away, their blood frozen on the stone. Rachael and Will turned as Devlin approached.

"Morning, honey," her mother said. Devlin stood between them, noticed for the first time that she was a few inches taller than her mother. "So how long will you be gone?" Rachael was asking.

"Hope to be back tonight," Will said, "but if we don't reach Fairbanks until after dark, I don't know. Can you keep things under control if we don't come back until tomorrow?"

"Yeah. But I worry about you going out there with the wolves loose."

"I'll have the shotgun, plenty of shells."

"You have to take Devlin?"

"Yeah, Buck and I will fly back here to the inner lake and pick her up. I want to get her into a hospital tonight. I worry all this is going to get her sick."

. . .

In a supply room, four doors down from where Paul sat dead in a chair beside a cold fireplace, Will found snowshoes, a parka, and an extra box of twelve-gauge buckshot.

He ate an early lunch of beef stew, and Will said good-bye to the women in the library, explained that he would try to return that evening, but if it wasn't possible, first thing tomorrow morning at the latest.

Rachael and Devlin walked Will to the front door, where he cinched the straps of his snowshoes down across the tops of his boots.

Rachael hugged her husband.

"I'll see you soon," she said, and watched him step outside and climb up onto the snowpack.

She stood in the warm, direct sun, watching Will go, his snowshoes sinking into a foot and a half of powder with every step, her eyes burning from the harsh reflection off the ice crystals.

Seconds before retreating back into the lodge, she and Devlin registered a distant droning, which grew exponentially louder with every passing second, until a floatplane buzzed the lodge's roof, its engine screaming as it descended toward the water, the pontoons catching sun, glimmering like mirrors.

Her heart leaped as the plane touched down midway across the lake, Will stopping just fifty yards out from the lodge—he wouldn't have to make the long haul to the outer lake.

The engine had cut off. Devlin was squinting, trying to make out the details of the plane, though it had almost reached the far end of the lake, more than a mile away.

Her smile faded.

Will had turned around, tracking back toward the lodge as fast as his snowshoes allowed.

Something was wrong. Will was wearing that same worried expression he used to get just prior to opening arguments for a big trial.

He reached them breathless and sweating.

"What's wrong?" Rachael asked.

Will leaned over with his hands on his knees, drawing in lungfuls of cold air.

He shook his head, gasping between ragged breaths. "That isn't our plane."

The Lesser of the Evils

FIFTY-NINE

From the porch, Will and Rachael had an unobstructed view of the entire lake, the floatplane clearly visible at the far end—a piece of red amid all that blinding white.

Will lifted the binoculars to his face as sunlight and frigid air streamed in, adjusting the knobs, bringing the plane into focus.

"Okay, here we go. There are one . . . two, three . . . people standing in a foot of water, unloading the cargo pod, throwing duffel bags up onto the bank. They're all wearing big white parkas, definitely dressed for the weather."

"Hunters?" Rachael asked.

"They don't look like hunters." He drew in a quick shot of air.

"What?"

Will noted the sudden pressure in his chest, behind his eyes, strength flooding out of his legs as approaching footsteps echoed in the lobby.

"*What?*"

"I recognize one of them," he said.

"Who?"

"Oh God."

"*Will? Who?*"

He lowered the binoculars and stared at his wife. "Javier Estrada just climbed down out of the pilot's seat."

"That man you and Kalyn—"

"Yeah."

"What's he doing here?"

"What do you think? We took his family, left them for days in a burned-out mall."

Devlin walked up, stopped between her parents, said, "So did you find out who they are?"

"Bad men," Rachael said. "Very bad men."

Will put his arm around Devlin, kissed the top of her head.

"Who is it, Dad?"

"Javier. But we're gonna be all right, honey," he said, wondering if the words rang as hollow for Devlin as they felt tumbling out of his mouth. "I need to talk to Mom. Stay here for a minute, okay?" He handed her the binoculars. "Keep an eye on that plane at the end of the lake, and the four men who just climbed out of it."

"No, Will. No fucking way. Absolutely not."

Will and Rachael stood in the corridor, twenty feet down from Kalyn's room.

"Rachael, we can't do this on our own."

"She betrayed you. Tried to trade our *daughter*."

"I know, but we need her, and we're running out of time standing here fighting about it."

Rachael flashed her eyes at the ceiling, her most vehement eye roll.

"Wow, five years since I've seen that one," Will said.

She smiled. "Missed it, huh?"

"I need you to trust me. As bad as Kalyn is and what she did, the man who's coming here is ten times worse. We're going to need her."

"The lesser of the evils. That's where we're at?"

"Afraid so."

Will looked through the peephole, saw Kalyn under the covers, asleep in bed.

"All right."

Rachael slipped the master key into the lock. It turned, and Will nudged the door open with the barrel of the shotgun.

Kalyn sat up, her face swollen from a night of steady crying.

"We're in trouble," Will said.

Kalyn stared back, eyes darkened with shame. "I wanna see my sister. Is she okay?"

"Yes, she's fine. A plane has landed on the inner lake." He hesitated, as if by not speaking his name, it might undercut the reality that the man had actually, impossibly, found them, that he was here, less than a mile away. "Javier and three men."

Kalyn's face paled, the shame deferring to a crisp alertness, tinged with fear.

"Where are they now? Right out front?"

"No, far end of the lake."

"And you're sure it's him?"

"I took a pair of binoculars from the supply room. There's no question."

"Who are the other men?"

"I don't know. One is Hispanic, maybe another Alpha. Other two are white."

"Well, we know why they're here—for what we did to Javier's family, to him, possibly those men I killed in Fairbanks three days ago." She threw back the blankets.

"The Alaskan mob?"

"They're probably cocounsel with the Alphas on this."

"Aren't you really the one they—"

"Oh sure. Walk out and explain the situation to them, Will. I dragged you into this. It's all my fault. I bet they give you a pass, probably even fly you and your family out of here before the shit starts to fly."

SIXTY

Rachael, Will, and Devlin were following Kalyn down the first-floor corridor.

"All right," she said. "So here's how I see it. What do they want?"

"To kill us."

"No, you're rushing ahead. Think of a more concrete motivation."

"I don't know."

"First, they want to get inside this lodge. We want to keep them out, or at least know if they make it in and be ready to deal with that."

"Okay."

"So we start thinking about all the points of entry."

"How many are there?"

"Right now? Probably more than forty."

"How's that possible?"

Kalyn stopped, opened the door of room 111, pointed to the window. "First priority is locking every room on every corridor." She knocked on the wood. "These doors are thick, and the locks look damn near indestructible. That's not to say they won't be able to get through, but they'll make a hell of a lot of noise doing it. You have a master key, Will?"

"Yes."

"Give it to Devlin, let her go and do that right now."

"I don't feel comfortable with her running around by her—"

"I think we have some time to work with here."

Will pulled one of the master keys out of his pocket, handed it to his daughter. "Go," he said. "Be careful, and remember to check every door after you lock it."

As Devlin took off back toward the lobby, they reached the alcove.

"Here's our first trouble spot," Kalyn said. "I'll bet they try to come in through a window either here or at the north-wing alcove. Or both. We should station someone, maybe even two people, a little ways back in the corridor with shotguns."

"Who? There's just me, Rachael, and—"

"We'll need help from Sean and Ken, maybe even some of the women. Come on."

They jogged back down the corridor, emerging finally into the lobby.

Kalyn pointed to the entrance.

"I'm not terribly worried about those doors. We'll lock them, but no one storms the castle through the front door. With those iron bolts, they'd literally need to blow it off the hinges. I'm not sure they're going to announce their presence like that, since they won't know what they're facing."

She led them through the passage, past the dining hall, to a door that opened onto the veranda. "We'll need someone here."

They backtracked into the lobby, now approaching the library.

Devlin was already to the end of the first floor of the south wing. Will could hear the doors slamming, locks turning.

They entered the library.

"No one can be in here, since they could pick us off through the windows. We'll station someone in the lobby to watch this door and the front entrance and back up the corridors." She opened the small door to the right of the fireplace. "This would be another great point of entry."

They started down the spiral staircase, their footfalls echoing on the metal, causing it to vibrate, Will gliding his hand along the railing.

"Move very slowly," he said.

"I'm not going anywhere, Will. Don't know if you've realized, but we need each other."

They reached the floor of the cellar. Peering just ahead, Will could see a door outlined by seams of light where the sun passed between the cracks.

Kalyn opened it. Light poured in. He saw the empty cages.

"They won't all enter the same way, but this is where I'd come in."

Kalyn's eyes fell upon something that made her smile.

She approached a wall adorned with ancient tools—saddles, scythes, machetes. Kalyn tapped one of two enormous bear traps.

"This thing's made to catch grizzlies," she said. "Break a man's leg like it was nothing."

"You think they still work? Looks pretty rusted out to me."

"We'll see. Come on, let's head back up. I want to take a look through the binoculars."

SIXTY-ONE

don't see them," she said. "It's just the plane."

Kalyn stepped back inside, and Rachael shut the doors and locked them.

"How much time you think we have?" Will asked. "That's deep snow. Might take them what? An hour? Hour and a half to get here? And we've burned thirty minutes already."

Kalyn shook her head. "I actually think we've got time on our side. They flew right over the lodge, ballsy fuckers, set down in plain site, so they have to realize we're aware of them. For all they know, we've got a small army in this lodge."

"What are you getting at?"

"I'm fairly certain they won't make their move until dark."

Rachael said, "I felt better when I thought this was going to happen in daylight."

"No, it's good. Gives us time to prepare. We should meet with Sean and Ken and the women, tell them the good news, sign up a few recruits. But I'd like a moment with my sister first. I only saw her through a peephole yesterday. I don't even think she knows I'm here."

"She doesn't," Will said.

"Well?"

"You really think we have time for a family reunion?"

"Please, Will."

"Five minutes."

Will unlocked the door and walked inside, caught him rising out of bed, puffy-eyed from dehydration and looking very afraid.

"Sit down, Sean."

Sean complied as Will closed the door and dragged a chair away from the desk. He sat facing the young man, the shotgun lying across his lap.

"Are you going to kill me?" Sean asked.

Will shook his head. "My daughter overheard a conversation between you and your father yesterday morning. You know what I'm talking about?"

Sean stared at his bare feet for a moment. "You mean in the library? After breakfast?"

Will nodded. "You didn't want to be here, did you, Sean?"

"I didn't know what this lodge was. I swear to you."

"Did your father?"

"No. I mean, he'd heard it was a wild place, but we didn't have any idea. Would you have believed it without seeing it?"

"My wife has been here for five years."

"I'm sorry, man. Really."

"I need to know something."

"What?"

Will locked his gaze on Sean.

"Did you help yourself to any of the women here?"

"No."

"You can tell me the truth."

"I swear to you. This place makes me sick."

"Then what did you do yesterday?"

"I stayed in my room."

"All day?"

"Until dinner."

"What about your father?"

"I don't know. I don't think he would have hurt anyone. That's not like him."

Will stood. "Did you grow up with firearms around the house?"

"My dad and I go elk hunting in Montana every fall."

"Good."

"Why is that good?"

Will walked to the door, pulled it open, cold air from the corridor sweeping in.

"Let's go talk to your father. I've got some bad news."

Lucy Dahl sat in a chair by a fireplace in one of the guest rooms, a book in her lap, her legs propped on a footstool, basking in the heat.

Kalyn closed the door and moved quietly across the room toward her sister, no sound but the shift of smoldering logs and the paper scrape as Lucy turned the pages of her book.

It had been three years since Kalyn had laid eyes on her sister, and their last words had been angry ones, a stupid fight that Kalyn had started—big sis telling little sis what was best for her life.

Two steps from the chair, Kalyn's eyes welled up. She couldn't see Lucy look up from her book through the lens of salt water shivering on the surface of her eyes.

"Kalyn? Oh my God."

They sat on the floor by the fire, Lucy crying, Kalyn whispering, "I'm here, honey. I'm here." Wanting to tell her she was safe now, that they had a plane waiting on the lake to take her home, back to her husband, away from this nightmare.

Lucy must have sensed her holding back, because she said, "What's wrong, K? What is it?"

Kalyn shook her head, footsteps entering the boondocks of her perception, Will already coming back, the five minutes gone faster than it seemed possible.

"We're together," she said. "Just that we aren't home yet."

Will stood in front of the hearth in what had been Ethan's room, facing twenty-two women (most of whom watched him with the desperate blankness of refugees) and Sean and Ken (still massively hungover from the previous night and looking more than a little uncertain about their demoted stations under the new management).

"As Rachael mentioned to you all, four men have landed on the inner lake. While Kalyn and I are the primary targets, you're all in danger here, and we have to prepare. Kalyn and I can't defend everyone on our own, and I know you've been through so much hell, and I'm sorry we have to deal with this, but we need your help. Sean and Ken have come on board, along with Kalyn's sister, but we need one more volunteer."

The women glanced at one another. A few began to cry.

It was thirty seconds before a hand went up—raised by a dark-haired woman who appeared to be in the first trimester of her pregnancy.

Will said, "Yeah? What's your name?"

"Suzanne Tyrpak. I'll fight. I've never even touched a gun before, but if you show me how, I'll do it. I mean, if this is what we gotta do to get back to our families."

There were no other volunteers, the rest too weak or pregnant or broken, some still whispering to themselves—incoherent, devastated babblings.

He looked at Kalyn. "That makes eight of us. Can we pull this off?"

. . .

"The beautiful thing about a twelve-gauge," Kalyn said, "is you can be a terrible shot, and it doesn't matter." They all stood outside the supply room—the Innises, Kalyn, her sister, Suzanne Tyrpak, and the oilmen—shouldering pump-action Mossbergs.

Kalyn said, "I think these guys may come wearing bulletproof vests, which is why I want you to aim either below the waist or at the head. You have to pump it after every shot." She pumped her shotgun. "The kick is strong, so remember to lean into it."

"Is it loud?" Suzanne asked. "When you pull the trigger?"

"Loud as hell. All right, let me show you how to load."

It took both Kalyn and Will to pull the grizzly traps off the wall, the monstrous contraptions weighing in at forty-eight pounds of rusted cast iron apiece, with jaw spreads of seventeen inches. Will stepped on the release, and they strained to force the jaws open.

Although barely legible, *American Fur and Trade Company, HBC No. 6* had been engraved into the iron of the pan. When Kalyn popped it with one of the pitchforks, the snare jumped, the giant teeth chomping together, snapping the wooden handle in two.

The sun hung low in the sky, sitting just over the horizon at the end of the lake, turning clouds and snow pink, the water scarlet. Devlin watched from a window on the third floor, thought it was the most striking end of day she'd ever seen, the sky at war with itself.

Kalyn stood at the window in Rachael's old room on the fourth floor, glassing what she could see of the surrounding grounds and forest behind the lodge.

"Light's getting bad," she said. "I thought maybe I'd see tracks or something."

"You think they're out in the woods somewhere?" Will asked.

"I would imagine, but the trees are too loaded with snow to see that far into them."

"What if we went ahead and cut the power? Might give us an advantage, since we know the lodge better than they do."

"Not if they have night-vision goggles. One of the things the Alphas are known for is using state-of-the-art equipment. I mean, we might as well have a Force Recon team coming after us." She lowered the binoculars. "What's my role from here on out? I've helped you prepare. Will you trust me? Let me fight when the time comes?"

"You mean am I going to give you a gun?"

"Will, no one here is as proficient as—"

"I understand that, but what you need to know is that part of me is more afraid of you than of what's coming."

"Will, you don't under—"

"I understand plenty. Come on. Let's go check the other side."

Will found Rachael and Devlin eating leftovers with the others in the kitchen.

He asked them to walk with him, and they followed, going back up the passage, then out into the lobby, where he finally pulled them into the library and shut the door.

"Come here, guys."

The Innises sat down in a corner by the French doors, protected from the view of anyone who might be watching from outside.

Above the skyline of firs, evening faded from pink into purple.

"It's gonna be dark soon," Will said, and already he could feel the sadness rising in his throat. He looked at his long-lost wife. His teenage daughter. "It's gonna be a long, long night, and the truth is, we don't know what's going to happen. If we're gonna be together in the morning. Or if this is the last . . ." He ground his molars together, fighting the surge of emotion. *Be strong for them.* He reached out, touched his daughter's face. "I'm so proud of you, Devlin. The courage, the nerve you've shown."

"But I'm afraid, Dad."

"I know. We all are, and that's okay. What matters is how you handle it. That you don't let it handle you." They all embraced, held on to one another for nearly a minute.

When they came apart, Will grabbed Rachael's hands. "I want you to see the little farmhouse we have in Colorado. There are mountains, aspen trees. There's a river nearby, and sometimes you can hear it from our bedroom. I want to be there with you and Devi and this little guy." He touched Rachael's rounded belly. "I'm gonna do everything I can tonight to make that possible. You both know what you have to do?" His girls nodded. "No matter what happens, I love you, Rachael. I love you, Devlin." Rachael was crying, Devlin's chin quivering. "All right," Will said. "I guess it's time."

SIXTY-TWO

Ethan's old room was already stocked with food and water and plenty of blankets, since they couldn't risk the light or smell of a fire. Will and Kalyn had set the weakest women on the mattress and swaddled them in covers, left Devlin in charge of protecting the women who couldn't fight.

"This is your room now, Devi," her father said, "and these women are your responsibility. You kill anyone who comes through that door to hurt you."

"I will."

"There're two more shotguns, fully loaded, and three boxes of shells on the bedside table. I don't care what you hear out there, stay put."

"Yes, sir."

Through the glass, the sky deepened from purple to navy.

"Keep them quiet, away from the windows, and use no light." Will tapped the walkie-talkie in the pocket of her parka. "Emergencies only. You remember the channel?"

Outside in the corridor, Will closed and locked the door. He looked at Kalyn, said, "Come with me," and led her down to the supply room, which he unlocked. "Go on, pick out whatever you think you'll need."

Kalyn stepped inside, pulled a shotgun from one of the glass cases, then broke open a box of shells. She loaded it and crammed the pockets of her fleece jacket with as many shells of buckshot as they would hold. Then she opened a drawer, took out a Browning 9-mm.

"Will?" she said while loading a magazine with hollow-point rounds.

"What?"

"Thank you for not telling my sister about what I—"

"It's not the time to deal with that."

Kalyn lifted the shotgun strap over her head, slammed a magazine into the Browning.

Suzanne and Lucy sat side by side near the end of the south-wing corridor, twenty feet back from the alcove, the shotguns lying across their laps.

It was perfectly silent—just the steady pulse of their heartbeats and the humming of a ceiling lamp above their heads.

Sean and Ken waited twenty feet back in the passage, their shotguns trained on the thick wooden door that led to the veranda.

Their only light was a lantern mounted on the passage wall.

"Dad?" Sean said.

"Yeah."

"We're in trouble here."

Ken glanced at his son in the lantern light. "Your old man's working on something."

"What?"

"A way to get us out of this."

Kalyn sat on the stone of the freestanding hearth. With a quick turn of her head, she could keep an eye on either the front entrance or the library door, now closed and locked. She could also look down the first-floor corridor of both wings, see Suzanne and Lucy camped near the end of the south, Will walking toward the end of the north. She kept replaying the afternoon and evening and all the preparations they'd made, haunted with the fear she'd overlooked something.

Will approached the end of the corridor, spotted Rachael twenty feet back from the north-wing alcove, out of sight from the east- and west-facing windows. He eased down beside her, set the shotgun on the floor. She glanced over, tried to smile.

"It's just not fair," she whispered, "to get you and Devi back, only to have to go through this."

"I know, but we haven't experienced much fairness in the last five years, have we?"

She shook her head. "How do you think Devi's handling this?"

"She's scared but dealing. Our daughter is an amazing human being, Rachael."

"She is, isn't she? Felt so good just to be able to give her therapy this morning."

They were quiet for a while, sat there holding the shotguns, listening.

On his way to Rachael and their post, Will had stopped in one of the rooms to look out the window. He'd seen a starry, windless night, the lake serene, a model of absolute stillness.

Nearby, wood creaked. Rachael looked at Will, but he shook his head, whispered, "An old place like this makes all kinds of noise. Probably just wood settling."

"I'm glad we have these gloves. It's freezing in here."

They waited, evening assenting to night.

An hour slipped by, then two.

"My legs are cramping," Rachael whispered. "I'm gonna stretch them, just to the lobby and back."

As his wife walked away, Will took out his radio, asked for everyone to check in.

When Kalyn's voice came over the channel, she said, "You probably just heard the front doors close."

"No, I didn't actually. What's going on?"

"I stepped outside with Ethan's whistle, called in the wolves. Figured maybe if they find our bad guys, we'll hear them, get a sense of where they are."

"Good deal."

The radio went quiet.

Rachael returned. She leaned against Will and closed her eyes for a little while, then let him do the same.

Two minutes shy of midnight, Will glanced over his shoulder, saw Kalyn right where she'd been all night, sitting on the base of the freestanding hearth.

"I'm gonna go talk to her," Will said.

"Why?"

"Something's not right. I mean, why haven't they come yet?"

"I don't know."

Will sighed. "You'll be all right on your own for a minute?"

"I'll be fine."

He struggled up, legs sore, feet numb from two hours of sitting in one spot, immobile. "If you see anything, hear anything strange, radio me immediately."

Will started down the corridor toward the lobby, and it had just crossed his mind that maybe Javier and his men weren't coming tonight after all, that maybe they'd decided to let them sit it out until morning, until everyone was nerve-frayed and psychotic with exhaustion. Just then, the lodge rumbled and all the lights winked out.

Flashbang

SIXTY-THREE

Will froze in his tracks, Suzanne's voice squeaking over the radio in his pocket. "What just happened?"

Kalyn responded, her voice a whisper: "They cut the power. This means they're close, wearing night-vision goggles, and getting ready to make their move. I know it's pitch-black at the end of those corridors, but your eyes will adjust, so everyone stay calm. You all have flashlights, and if you shine the beam in their eyes, you'll screw up their vision for a minute or two. Now I don't want anyone using the radio again until you've made visual contact."

Will could see the lobby just ahead, lantern light flickering across the wall and the floor. He thought he heard Kalyn whispering, wondered if she was sending up prayers against whatever was coming.

Will turned around, jogged back toward the alcove, practically tripped over Rachael in the darkness.

"Just me, honey."

"I can't see a thing, Will."

"Get your flashlight out."

"I'm already holding it. Should I turn it on?"

"No, but be ready when I say. I'll handle the shotgun. You be my light source." Will found his radio, just a red dot in the darkness. He pressed TALK. "Suzanne and Lucy? Copy?"

Suzanne's voice came back: "Yeah?"

"Don't turn it on yet, but one of you operate the flashlight while the other mans the shotgun. Better than each of you fumbling with two pieces of equipment at once."

The radio went quiet, and Rachael and Will stared at the alcove, waiting for their eyes to adjust, to begin picking out form and shape in the darkness, but they never did.

SIXTY-FOUR

Roddy hated Fidel and Javier. They'd controlled every aspect of this job. Told him where to go, how to go, talked down at him like he didn't know what the fuck he was doing out here in the bush in his own state. This wasn't Mexico or the Arizona borderlands. This was his block, and he resented being treated as a foot solider under their command.

Of course, he didn't utter a word of that dissatisfaction. Didn't venture an eye roll, display a single millisecond of outward frustration. He and Jonas had agreed: They want to run the show? Fine. Because what outranked Roddy's frustration with Fidel and Javier was his fear. You did not fuck with Alphas. They were mythic. Doing business with them, regardless of how lucrative, entailed severe risk, since the possibility existed that things wouldn't work out, that you might insult them or be perceived as trying to take advantage.

He thought it strange—the Alphas were here on principle, didn't give a shit about the money, the women, said Stoke could have whatever they found. They'd spent tens of thousands to come up here just to deal with that ex-FBI agent. Stoke had warned Jonas and the boys not to upset them, said flat out. "You piss them off, *your* problem. I'm not getting involved. Certainly not intervening on behalf of your ass. You're their bitches, so grab ankle, grit teeth, and pray you come back."

At least the Alphas had brought some killer toys and been nice enough to share. And despite his inner griping, he had to admit that they certainly seemed to know what they were doing. Roddy felt like a fucking SEAL on some badass spec ops gig.

So here he stood, freezing his ass off in waist-deep snow, waiting for the signal, acknowledging the irony that what scared him more than anything was that he might accidentally kill the ex-FBI agent or Mr. Innis. They'd been cautioned several times against making that mistake, which meant that on top of everything else, he had to worry about who wound up in his sights.

A wolf howled. With the moon rising over the Wolverines and that milky smear of stars, it was almost too bright for night-vision goggles. But Roddy went ahead and slipped them on, figured the signal would be coming soon, and from what they'd seen, it would be total darkness inside the lodge.

Kalyn was up now, moving in slow circles around the freestanding hearth. She kept debating whether to start with the Browning or the twelve-gauge, decided finally on the 9-mm, since the shotgun felt cumbersome hanging from the strap around her shoulders. She slipped it off, set it on the stone in front of the dormant fireplace.

Wolves were howling outside, on their way back to the lodge.

From where Fidel stood, the view was spectacular—the black lake and the hills and a moon edging up on the horizon. Nothing like Sonora or the industrialized desert waste of Phoenix.

His parka and snow gear lay in a pile nearby.

He crossed himself and waited for the signal.

The snow was deep on the veranda, almost to the man's waist. The large wooden door stood thirty feet from where he squatted by the railing, protected from the snow by a steep overhanging eave.

Javier reached into his pocket and sent the signal, then pulled out the walkie-talkie. He pressed TALK, said, "Get ready."

The deep anticipatory tingling in the pit of his stomach was spreading like wetness across a napkin. He'd mapped everything out, nailed it down so cold, he had but to execute the movements, the choreography. He felt like a ballerina in that regard, waiting backstage before the curtains opened.

Devlin sat on the floor in Ethan's room. She was cold.

In the opposite corner, the newborn cooed.

The head of a woman named Theresa rested in her lap, and Devlin stroked her hair and whispered into her ear that everything would be all right.

. . .

A shaft of moonlight passed through the west-facing window of the south-wing alcove. It illuminated the floor, the walls in lunar light. A wolf howled, much closer now, and received no answer.

Lucy's walkie-talkie coughed up a loogie of static, Kalyn's voice squeaking through the speaker, "Lucy, come see me for a second."

"Be right there, K."

Will reached out, located Rachael's hand in the darkness, squeezed.

Lucy walked quickly down the corridor, the vast darkness of the lobby looming just ahead. The shotgun she carried in her left hand was so heavy, and she couldn't imagine actually firing it at someone, the bruising recoil, the earshattering report, the killing.

Ten feet from the lobby, she spotted something out of the left corner of her eye. She stopped, staring at the door to 114. It was wide open, which shouldn't have been the case, considering they'd locked every room on every floor that afternoon.

Lucy hurried on.

Three steps from the lobby, her legs melted.

She hit the floor, head pounding and consciousness fading as someone dragged her back into 114.

SIXTY-FIVE

The pager in Roddy's pocket vibrated. He inhaled the spike of adrenaline, moving now toward the east-facing window at the end of the north wing, wading through the snow. He reached the window's base, took a moment to calm himself and rack the slide on his suppressed Beretta 93R, slipped his finger into the trigger guard.

He peeked over the windowsill, peered through the glass, the night-vision world green and grainier than a B horror movie. He spotted a man sitting against the wall, not ten feet away, at the opening to a stairwell, with what appeared to be a shotgun across his lap. Roddy ducked down, listened. No sound of movement. He hadn't been seen.

Three, two, one. This time, he stood upright, the detachable stock pressed tight against his shoulder, squeezed the trigger twice, half a dozen 9-mm rounds piercing the glass.

The man with the shotgun shook like the epicenter of a tiny earthquake, his body riddled with bullets, and fell over. He hadn't made a sound. Only the shatter of glass could have compromised Roddy's presence, and he didn't think it had been that loud.

Never saw that coming, did you, my man? I'd have made a helluva Special Forces solider. It's gonna be so much fun to talk about all this with Jonas and the boys. After *the Alphas are gone.* He pictured them having beers, laughing in Stoke's poolroom at the Fairbanks warehouse, each taking turns telling everyone how they'd stormed this lodge like it was fucking Normandy.

Kalyn's walkie-talkie chirped.

Suzanne's voice: "Kalyn, you there?"

"Yeah, what's up?"

"Where's Lucy?"

"She's not with you?"

"No."

"She left the lobby at least a minute ago, heading back your way."

"Well, she isn't here," Suzanne replied, in tears now, "and I don't hear her coming."

"Just sit tight. I'll find her."

Kalyn slipped her radio into her pocket and stared down at her sister, who lay unconscious on the floor. "Sorry, Luce," she whispered, "but I didn't come all this way to see you killed."

All right, buddy, time to focus. Roddy played the move several times in his head. *Stand quickly. Both hands on the windowsill. Leap through. Roll twice across the floor and sight up the corridor while lying on your stomach. Extra clips in your pocket. Use controlled bursts. Don't freak out, and remember to breathe. Three, two, one.*

He came to his feet, gloves on the windowsill, such an adrenaline charge running through him that he swung both feet over at once, clearing the sill by several inches, with enough energy to jump a mountain.

Screaming, something gone terribly wrong, like he'd landed in the mouth of a shark, then realizing what it was with a crushing desperation, saw in that gray-green light the rusty metal teeth of a grizzly snare sunk into his shinbones, clamped halfway up his throbbing tibias.

He tore his gloves trying to pull the jaws apart, grunting, teeth gritted, veins rising from his forehead. *Oh God, I fucked up. The Alphas are gonna kill me.*

But the jaws didn't budge. He could hear his legs splintering as he stared at the man he'd shot, the teeth burrowing deeper, closing slowly, and through the bone-fracturing pain, he realized there was something wrong with the guard—longhaired, pajamaed—and it was this: He had rigor mortis. He was stiff, rigid, dead for hours, maybe a day. *What the fuck?*

And the grainy green turned to blinding white as a shotgun boomed. His vest caught most of the pellets, but the force knocked him back onto the floor. He ripped off his goggles, reached for the Beretta, footsteps coming toward him and the unmistakable horror of a twelve-gauge pumping, thinking, *The vest will buy me time to spray them.* He aimed at the light, but the time wasn't there. They don't make a vest for your face.

SIXTY-SIX

J onas could tell right away that the man was already dead, his face polka-dotted with buckshot. Besides, he wasn't sitting right. His head tilted unnaturally to one side and the shotgun looked as if it had been propped up against him. *Means there's probably someone sitting a little ways down the corridor with some firepower trained on this spot.*

If the Alphas hadn't vetoed the use of radios, he'd have warned Roddy's dumb ass, since they probably had the same setup at the end of the north wing.

He slipped off his goggles. Didn't really need them yet, the moon bright as all get-out and lighting up the alcove like Christmas. He heard something in the distance behind him, glanced back across that long, narrow lake lathered in moonlight. At first, he thought they were men running toward him, then realized it was the wolves he'd been hearing, their heads rising and falling as they bounded through snow.

Why the fuck were they moving *toward* him? Ever since coming up to Alaska from L.A., all he'd heard was how skittish they were, and you were supposed to have an orgasm if you saw them in the wild. Fuck this Grizzly Adams shit. God, he missed the Valley. He turned back toward the lodge, raised the Beretta, and squeezed off a burst.

Suzanne was looking over her shoulder for Lucy when the glass of the west-facing window fell out. She hadn't heard a gunshot, and from where she sat, she couldn't see either window. Suzanne slowly rose to her feet, reaching for her radio, and as she pressed TALK, someone screamed at the other end of the lodge.

She backpedaled, heard the crunch of broken glass—someone in the alcove now—realized they'd put the bear trap on the wrong side.

A shotgun boomed somewhere on the north wing.

There was a bright, quiet muzzle flash at the end of her corridor.

Will pressed TALK, breathing so hard, he could barely speak. "Guy just came in through the east window. He's dead."

Kalyn said, "Copy that. We've had a visual. Everyone check in."

"Devi, here. We're fine."

"Ken and Sean. We're fine."

After a moment, Kalyn said, "Suzanne? Lucy? Copy?"

No answer.

Will: "Kalyn, did you see or hear anything on the south wing?"

"No, just the glass breaking and the guy screaming at your end, so that had my attention. Look, everyone maintain your positions. I'll check it out."

Ken rose suddenly to his feet, as if he'd been resolved to stand for some time, his loops coiling, and just now worked up the nerve to spring.

"Dad," Sean whispered, "what are you doing?"

"You know, we don't deal in this currency." He shook the Mossberg. "We're gonna get ourselves killed sitting here." He threw the shotgun down.

"Where are you going?"

"Out there."

Ken strode twenty feet to the thick door and slid back the iron bolts.

"Dad!" Sean whispered. "You sure about this?"

"I love you, Sean. I'm sorry I brought you here." He pulled open the door, and Sean could see a meter of snow just beyond the overhanging eave, the railing of the veranda nearly buried. The cold that swept into the passage made his eyes water.

Ken stepped over the threshold and pulled the door closed after him.

Jonas put on his goggles, stood at the edge of the alcove, surveying the corridor. He saw the woman he'd shot a short ways down—motionless, sprawled, her shotgun unattended on the floor. He went and picked it up.

Looking down toward the end of the corridor, where it opened into the lobby, he saw bright green flares of light—lanterns perhaps. He could just make out the shape of someone sitting on the hearth.

He removed his white parka and snow pants, but instead of continuing down this corridor, he turned around and started for the stairwell.

Ken stood under the eave, feeling the cold infiltrate his down jacket. In the absence of lantern light from the passage, it took a full minute before his eyes picked out what detail the moon allowed—the veranda, buried under feet of drifted snow, the railing covered in places, poking through in others, the forest fifty yards to the east, out of which meandered a black stream, the snow dipping toward its banks in folds, something voluptuous about the curve, like white hips in the moonlight.

When he saw them, he wondered why the tracks paralleling the railing hadn't been the first thing to catch his attention, and, likewise, the figure who stood where they ended, perhaps thirty feet away in the farthest corner, pointing a gun at him.

Ken felt his heart trip over itself, but he managed to raise his arms.

The figure waved him over. Ken nodded, moving forward onto the snow, sinking to his waist, doing his best to negotiate the snowpack while keeping his hands above his head.

Ten feet from the masked figure, Ken saw a gloved palm extend in his direction.

He stopped, trying not to stare at the wicked-looking pistol aimed at his chest.

The figure wore a white mask to match his winter apparel, with a bar cut out that exposed his placid blue eyes, and the divoted bridge of his nose.

"What do you think you're doing?" the man asked.

Ken smiled nervously, ducked his head in greeting. "I just want you to know that my son and I are—"

"Where is your son?"

"Just inside that door. We're guests of this lodge. Or were, and we don't have any quarrel with you."

"How do you know?"

"Know what?"

"That we don't have a quarrel."

"Because I don't know you."

"I think it's safe to say I have laxer prerequisites for having a quarrel." The man raised the suppressed pistol to shoot Ken in the head.

"Oh God, please. I'm rich. That's what I came out here to tell you."

"You came out here to tell me that you're rich?"

"Yeah."

"Congratulations."

"No, not just that. Also that I would give you any amount of money if you would let my son and me sit out whatever's getting ready to go down in there."

"You have this money with you?"

"No, but I could—"

The man squinted his eyes, grimaced. "What? I leave you my address? You send me a check?"

"Or a bank account number. It would be seven figures."

The man seemed to consider this. "And we would operate on what? The honor system?"

"Please."

"All right, let's go."

"Back to the door?"

"Yes."

Ken turned away and started back across the veranda, his feet growing cold, snow having slid down into his boots. He felt a swell of pride at having walked out here and saved himself and Sean.

He said, "I'll even tell you where everyone is in—"

At first, he thought the man had pushed him, that he wasn't moving fast enough, and he tried to improve his pace, but something bloomed inside his right lung—a rod of molten pain—and he went down, kneeling in snow up to his neck, watching the man in white clean his blood off a piece of metal by running the blade between his gloved thumb and forefinger.

"I already know exactly where they are, Ken," he said, proceeding on toward the door. "But many thanks."

Ken stood up, accomplished three staggering steps in the snow.

The man in white had almost reached the door, but he stopped and glanced back, saw Ken standing there.

Ken heard the man sigh, watched him shake his head in annoyance.

He was coming back now, and two steps from Ken, he pulled the knife out of a hidden sheath stitched into his snow pants.

Ken reached out, put his hand on the man's right shoulder to stop himself from falling, and, as if in accommodation, the man grasped Ken's right shoulder and shoved the KA-BAR Marine Hunter eight times into his stomach.

Kalyn came to Suzanne and knelt in her blood, felt the guilt knocking, knew better than to let it take root. Any distraction could be fatal. She pulled out her radio.

"Suzanne's gone," she said. "So we know at least one of them has made it into the lodge." As she slipped the radio back into her pocket, a pack of shadows leaped through the open window into the south-wing alcove and disappeared up the stairwell.

A scream emanated from the lobby.

Kalyn grabbed her radio again, said, "Sean? Ken?"

Will's voice crackled: "You hear that?"

"Just sit tight. Stay where you—"

"No, I'm gonna check it out."

Rachael said, "You aren't leaving me here alone."

"I didn't say I was. Let's try to go without the flashlight, though. Might as well not advertise our position." He helped his wife to her feet and they progressed toward the specks of light in the lobby, dragging their hands along the wall, using it for a guide.

Jonas emerged from the stairwell onto the fourth floor. The corridor was empty, so he spent a moment unloading the shotgun, then dropping it on the floor. At the far end, lantern light shone from the lobby. He figured he'd claim a secure position and snipe from above.

He started down the corridor. The Beretta felt good in his gloved hands, but he didn't like passing all these doors, kept expecting one of them to swing open.

As far as he was concerned, the Alphas could fuck themselves. He wasn't putting his life in danger just to make sure he didn't kill the FBI agent or William Innis. They were storming this lodge in total darkness, no idea what they were walking into. Shit happened in this type of situation, and if someone jumped out of a corner, *buenos* fucking *noches*.

He heard screams somewhere in the lodge—definitely a man's.

The corridor suddenly filled with the noise of incoming footsteps. Jonas spun around, glanced back at the alcove, which was washed out in green light, the details obliterated by the flood of moonbeams. He knelt down, pulled off his goggles. The darkness was streaked with red, exploding with phantom light. His eyes struggled to adjust. He got the goggles back on just in time to see five wolves running toward him.

He squeezed off a burst. The one in front yelped and fell. The others leaped over their compatriot, still coming, unfazed, undeterred.

Two bursts. Another went down. *Fuck.* The slide locked back, three still coming.

He wasn't accustomed to automatic weapons—pull the trigger too hard, your magazine's spent in the blink of an eye. The Alphas had warned them about this. He ejected the clip, was going for another when the wolves reached him.

Jonas was a big man, 250 pounds, six three. He reminded himself of that and stood, bracing for impact, thinking, *I'll just snap some necks. Not like I haven't done that shit before.*

The two in front rammed into him at the same time, the force far beyond anything he'd expected, his head smashing hard into the floor.

He saw pricks of painful light. He was on his back, the Beretta gone, one wolf tearing into his right arm, the other two going for his face.

One of the wolves tore the goggles away. Teeth ripped through the parka around his neck, the down airborne like a shredded pillow. And it occurred to him, *They're going for your throat.*

Their slobber was warm, their breath foul. He tried to sit up, but they had both of his arms now, and a giant white wolf that seemed to glow in the dark was straddling him, teeth bared, inches above his face yet hesitating, as if to savor this moment. At some level, outside the fear and the pain, Jonas recognized its sadistic patience, the pleasure-delay, and he thought, *This fucker's a real killer. Doing this shit for fun.*

SIXTY-SEVEN

Kalyn followed the south-end stairwell up past the second and third floors. She held the shotgun, her finger in the trigger guard. As she neared the fourth-floor alcove, she heard something—slurping, snarling, ripping.

She stepped into the alcove. It was pitch-black. She held the shotgun in one hand, a flashlight in the other. Its beam shot through the dark and illuminated a shotgun, shells all over the floor, two dead wolves, and three feasting wolves. They looked up, their mouths slicked with blood, their teeth bared, protecting their kill.

Kalyn's right arm ached with the weight of the shotgun. The wolves glanced at one another, as if consulting; then the big white one started toward her. *Gonna have to fire it with one arm.*

She kept the light beam on the white wolf, leveled the shotgun, fired, the twelve-gauge recoiling, whipping back, the scalding barrel popping her in the face.

She fell. The flashlight rolled across the floor. Just darkness in the corridor and the patter of the wolves coming. She got to her feet, pumped the shotgun, pulled the trigger. Pumped again, fired. Pumped, fired. Something whimpering. Pumped, fired. Pumped.

The corridor reeked of gun smoke, and it was silent now. She walked to the flashlight, picked it up, blood trailing down her face from where the shotgun had struck her forehead.

The beam of light passed through the smoke. Now there were three dead wolves less than ten feet away, but the white wolf and the gray one weren't among them.

She moved carefully toward the body in the corridor—a large man slumped over on the floor, faceless and eviscerated. *Two down. Thank God. Wolves did my work for me.*

She continued on toward the stairwell that would take her back down into the lobby.

Will and Rachael crept through the candlelit passage. Where it began to curve toward the veranda exit, Will stopped, whispered, "Wait here. If they're dead, I don't want you to see it. You've seen enough already."

Will pushed on.

To his surprise, there was only one body—Sean's—encompassed by more blood than it seemed possible for a human body to hold. Snow pants, a mask, and a white parka had been discarded by the door.

Four shotgun blasts thundered out from one of the upper floors.

Will ran back to Rachael.

"What the hell was that?" she asked.

"I don't know."

"Are they dead?"

"Sean is. Ken's gone."

Will's radio squeaked.

Kalyn's voice: "Bad guy number two is dead."

"How?"

"Wolves. They got into the lodge through a broken window in the south-wing alcove. I killed one of them and two were already dead, so that leaves a pair running around here somewhere. Watch yourself. They're mean as hell."

Will pressed TALK: "Sean's gone. Don't know where his dad is, so another one of them got in."

"Just get back to your post in the north corridor."

Devlin's voice: "Guys?"

"What, baby girl?"

"Are any of you up here? I hear footsteps outside the door."

"Get the shotgun ready," Will said. "That isn't us, but we're on our way."

SIXTY-EIGHT

Kalyn moved across the stone floor of the lobby and sat down on the hearth in front of the giant fireplace. She kept looking up and down the north- and south-wing corridors, watching the exposed stairwells that climbed fifty feet toward the rafters on each side of the lobby, the passage behind her, the adjacent library door, closed and locked. She set the shotgun on the stone, fished four shells of buckshot out of the pocket of her fleece jacket. As she reached for the Mossberg to load the shells, a pair of black boots emerged from the flue into the enormous hearth behind her and lowered silently toward the grate.

Devlin illuminated her face with the flashlight beam and held her finger to her lips so the women could see.

She mouthed, "Shhh. Someone's out there."

She traded the flashlight for the shotgun but couldn't remember if she'd pumped it, opted to wait, as the slightest noise would give them away. She crept up to the door, strained to listen. Thought she heard something like a soft exhalation on the other side, perhaps the scrape of fabric against fabric.

She dropped quietly to her knees, lowered herself onto the floor, the right side of her face flush against the carpet. Their room was dark, but a lantern flickered outside in the hallway.

Through the crack under the door, the strand of lantern light was broken in two places. She saw the tips of a pair of boots, could have poked a finger under the door and touched them.

Ten feet away, invisible in the darkness, the infant began to cry.

· · ·

Will and Rachael slipped out of the passage and into the stairwell. No lanterns or candles here, the darkness absolute.

Rachael whispered, "Should I turn on the flashlight?"

"No. Just go slow and keep one hand on the wall like we did before."

Even as he said it, Will knew they might be walking blindly to their death, couldn't stop himself from picturing a man crouched on the next flight of stairs, outfitted with night-vision goggles, just waiting for them to stumble past.

They proceeded carefully, one step at a time, Will's heart knocking so hard he feared he'd faint. This was far worse than the wolves. At least you could see your attacker coming outside.

They reached the landing. Will traced his hand along the wall, letting it guide them to the next flight of stairs. Three steps up, he stopped.

"What is it?" Rachael asked.

"I see a light up ahead. Wait here."

Will ascended the remaining nine steps. At the top, he reached an archway, and from there he could glimpse the corridor, where a lantern mounted to the wall threw shadows and light on a man dressed in black, standing at the door that opened into Devlin's room.

Will glanced back down the steps, waved Rachael up. She came, stood beside him as the corridor filled with a baby's wailing. They raised their shotguns.

The man leaned against Devlin's door, his ear pressed to the wood. Will felt an eerie chill radiate down from the base of his neck into his spine.

Will and Rachael eyed each other, and she could barely see his lips moving in the low light.

Will mouthed, "That's Javier."

The man spun, bullets striking the walls of the stairwell, the iron railing sparking.

The Innises returned fire, then dived back into the archway, ears ringing. Will pressed Rachael up against the wall, whispered, "You hit?"

"No, you?"

"No. Don't move." Will peeked around the corner, gun smoke drifting through the corridor. The door was splintered with buckshot but still intact. No one there, just sprinkles of blood. Will motioned for Rachael to join him, and he spoke into her ear, "I think he's pinned down at the end of the corridor, maybe fifteen feet away. All the doors are locked, so I don't think there's anyplace—"

Will heard a door squeak open.

SIXTY-NINE

Kalyn pushed the last shell of buckshot into the twelve-gauge and pumped it. She set it beside her, took out the Browning. The shotgun was good if you didn't know how to shoot, but you could easily get yourself killed in the time it took to absorb the shoulder-bruising recoil, pump it, and take aim. Her head was bleeding again, and she was dizzy from the blow.

As she wiped away the rivulet of blood trailing down her nose, the Browning flew out of her hand and slid across the stone, hitting the library door. She went for the shotgun, and as she realized it wasn't there, she felt its barrel, still blazing hot, push into the back of her neck.

"You will tell me your name."

She stared at the floor, said nothing.

"Are you the ex-FBI agent?"

"No, I've been imprisoned in this lodge for five years. But I can take you to her right now. She's just through that passage over—"

"Stand up." Kalyn stood. "Take three steps forward and slowly turn around, leaving your hands up, fingers open." Kalyn moved toward the doors, her arms raised. She stopped and turned.

A man garbed all in black stood in the hearth, covering her with her shotgun. Where his face wasn't streaked with soot, she saw that his skin was reddish brown, wondered if perhaps he was half Mayan.

He looked at Kalyn, said, "I'm afraid you resemble the photograph I have of Kalyn Sharp. Are there any other weapons on your person?" She shook her head. "Remove your jacket and your pants." Kalyn didn't move. "Take them off now, or what's going to happen to you will only last longer and involve more pain."

A pair of shotgun blasts tore out of the passage.

. . .

Will yelled into the corridor, "*You wanna walk out of here, Javier?* Two of your friends are already dead."

A small explosion around the corner shook the floor beneath Will's feet.

After a moment, another noise filled the passage—a zipper in motion, followed by the sound of something dragging across the floor. Will didn't risk taking a peek.

"Hello, Will. Were you able to locate your wife?"

"Yes."

"I hope the very short amount of time you've had together was worth the pain that is coming your way."

"Look, you have nowhere to go, and there're two of us here with shot-guns."

Something went *whisk* in the corridor.

"What was that?" Will asked. The sweeter smell of tobacco smoke mixed in with the cordite. Will was thinking, *Maybe I should just go for it, poke out mid-sentence, hope to catch him off guard.*

"Do you remember, Will, the substance of our last conversation?"

"Yes, you—"

"I extended you and Kalyn the opportunity to improve the outcome of our inevitable future meeting."

"Javier—"

"And you did not accept my offer."

"Jav—"

"What? *What,* Will? What are you about to propose? That we call things a day? Do you believe I have traveled all these miles, at great expense, suf-fered cold and snow, the myriad wrongs to me and my family, only to turn right around and go home now that I have found you? Please answer me."

"No."

"Well said."

Will looked at Rachael, whispered, "We're gonna have to kill him."

"Will, I know your daughter is behind that door. Would you care to know my plans involving her?"

SEVENTY

Fidel finished patting down Kalyn. She was already sweating, her hands restless with nervous tremors.

The man began to shift back and forth on the balls of his feet like a prizefighter. He grinned. "We go a few rounds? Hand-to-hand combat?"

Kalyn backed slowly away. He pursued.

She asked, "Where's Javier?"

"Don't worry. He'll be along."

Fidel faked a lunge, drew back into a boxer's stance, and jabbed, his reach longer than what seemed commensurate with his height.

She slipped the punch, thinking, *Next time you better fire back.*

He smiled. "You're quick. Still, I am going to knock all of your teeth out of your mouth and shatter the bones in your face. Do you know what's going to happen after that?"

Fidel charged. Kalyn sidestepped, his elbow catching her above the left eye. She staggered back, blood sheeting down her face in a flood of warm pain, then turned, sprinting for the Browning. She could see it against the library door, glinting in the firelight.

Fidel whistled. She froze. He came forward, holding the Mossberg at waist level.

"*¡Vamos!*"

She was twenty feet away, point-blank range for a shotgun, no way to miss unless you set your mind to it.

"*¡Vamos!*"

Kalyn walked back toward the hearth.

He said, "Get down on the floor."

She complied, watched him jog over to the library door and pick up the Browning. Fidel pocketed the clip, ejected the live round, then dropped the empty pistol on the floor. He returned and stood over Kalyn, pumping the shotgun again and again. For a moment, she thought he was fucking with her, then wondered if he was confused, unsure of how to operate the weapon. When she saw the shells falling on the stone, she understood.

He slung the shotgun across the lobby, where it slammed into the wall. "Get up."

Kalyn struggled to her feet, her head in agony.

The blade caught a sliver of lantern light as the Alpha moved toward her.

Will inched the shotgun barrel toward the corner as Javier spoke.

"I will disarm you, your wife, and Kalyn, immobilize you, and let you watch me slowly and methodically take her apart."

"What has my daughter done to you, Javier?"

"She is loved by you. That is plenty."

Devlin gripped the shotgun. Nothing to do but trust she'd pumped it several hours ago. She stood at the door, found the lock in the darkness, slowly turned the dead bolt.

She grasped the doorknob, trying to remember if it had squeaked when she'd opened it before. *Turn it slowly. Slower than you've ever done anything in your entire life.*

The knob turned. Painstakingly, she pulled the door open—just an inch so it could clear the frame. A ribbon of light stretched across the floor, and Devlin let the doorknob ease back into place.

The man's voice sounded close, a few feet up the corridor.

She pulled the knob again, opening the door another inch, light texturing the exterior. It was chewed up by buckshot—a swath of damage near the floor, another at the top of the door frame. She peeked around the corner, glanced up the corridor. Javier was squatting down along the wall beside a black duffel bag, his back to her, a cigarette dangling from his lips. In one hand, he held a pistol fitted with a silencer and a long magazine. In his other hand was a small device that reminded her of an oversize PEZ dispenser. Javier crouched ten feet from the stairwell, where, under the archway, Devlin's father was hunched down with a shotgun.

When he saw her, his eyes went wide and he shook his head and mouthed, "Get back inside that room."

SEVENTY-ONE

Kalyn held out her hands as she backed away from Fidel, realized she hadn't heard anything from the Innises since the shotgun blasts a few minutes ago, wondered if they'd managed to get themselves killed.

Fidel's knife didn't look particularly menacing—a black plastic handle with finger grips supporting a four-inch blade, each side slightly serrated, the end curving to a nasty point. He held it in his right hand, moving nimbly on his feet, a hard, focused determination pulsing in his black eyes.

"This makes you proud? To fight a woman this way? You know I'm outmatched." She was backpedaling toward the opening of the south-wing corridor, Fidel's face becoming less distinct, more shadowy than firelit.

"This has not a thing to do with my pride," he said. "This is only about causing you pain." He lunged, swiped—a fluid, lightning motion, and before she could react, Kalyn's right arm felt suddenly cold, blood running under the sleeve of her fleece jacket, dripping off the ends of her fingers, but no pain yet, only that awful metallic cold. Next came a ripping sound: fleece splitting. Another flash of ice, this time spreading down through her abdomen.

"Javier warned me not to touch you, but I don't think he'll mind a little innocent necking."

She felt light-headed. The instructor in a grappling seminar at the Academy had said something that now banged around inside her head like a prophecy fulfilled. *The most dangerous adversary you'll ever face is an opponent who's skilled with a knife. Avoid these confrontations at all costs.*

She backed into the corridor, her legs weakening, blood streaming down her thighs, her shinbones, into her socks. It wasn't supposed to happen like this.

They will take you slowly apart if you don't know what you're doing.

She could barely see Fidel now—just a silhouette against the low light of the lobby.

He advanced on her again and she felt the draft from knife wipes passing within inches of her face.

He sliced her right hand. Carved a two-inch line across her cheek, just missing her nose.

They were midway down the corridor now, and every passing second, it hurt more to breathe, the cold transforming into a glow in her chest.

She tripped over Suzanne's body, fell, scrambled back onto her feet. Fidel slipped on the blood but caught himself. He was close again, within three feet, and cornering her into the alcove. In the bright moonlight that came through the broken window, she saw her fleece pants slicked with blood.

Fidel said, "You are not bleeding too much I hope. This is foreplay. Don't come yet. Javier would never forgive me."

He opened the top of her left leg, but she didn't respond to the pain, turning instead, as if to break for the stairwell, heard the floor creak as he lunged after her, Kalyn spinning to face him, catching Fidel in the exact mistake she'd prayed for—a wide, careless knife swipe—which she parried, now palming his elbow, her other hand grasping his wrist. A quick jerk broke the man's forearm, just a soft snap followed by a howl of pain that was squelched when she punched him in the throat, a solid, direct hit, the hardest blow she'd ever landed, powered by hips and fear and rage.

With all her strength, she grabbed Fidel's arm and shoulder and hurled him toward the east-facing window.

The springs squeaked.

Fidel screamed.

In the moonlight, she saw him pinned between the rusty jaws of the grizzly trap, his wrists caught, the teeth burrowed into his stomach, his back, and still struggling to close, the hinges creaking.

Through clenched teeth, he screamed Javier's name.

Kalyn moved toward him, saw the pool of blood expanding within the circular boundary of the snare.

She reached down for his knife.

"*Por favor,*" he begged. "I can't feel my legs."

Kalyn smiled through her own pain. He spit at her.

"I want you to make this easy on me," she said. "And on you. Tilt your head back. Show me your throat."

He said something in Spanish that she didn't understand.

"Look, I've got things to do. Wanna sit here? Bleed out slowly while the trap finishes its supper?"

"*Dios,*" he whispered. "*Dios.*" He couldn't even cross himself.

Fidel stared at the ceiling and thought of a woman named Maria.

. . .

Devlin shouldered the shotgun, trying to remember what Kalyn had told her several hours ago. *Kicks like hell, so lean into it. Aim at the head or below the waist.* She was standing in the threshold, one foot in the room, one foot in the corridor.

Devlin aimed at the man's head, slipped her finger into the curve of the trigger.

She squeezed.

Nothing happened.

Oh God, I didn't pump it.

The baby screamed.

Javier glanced over his shoulder, spotted Devlin standing in the doorway.

As Will stepped out into the corridor and leveled his twelve-gauge shotgun on Javier, something rolled across the floor, between his legs.

Will was absorbing a slide show of images: Devlin struggling to pump her shotgun; Javier diving away, shielding his head; Rachael's quizzical face as she stared at the black device that had come to rest against the toe of her left boot.

Then Will's world exploded in a flash of brilliant, deafening light.

SEVENTY-TWO

Kalyn heard the explosion as she swiped the magazine for the Browning back from Fidel. She limped through the darkness of the first-floor corridor, desperate for some decent light to see how badly she'd been cut. It hurt terribly, particularly through her midsection, though she didn't seem to be bleeding as profusely as before.

She stopped thirty feet from where the corridor opened into the lobby. The white wolf moved past the freestanding hearth, trotting in her direction, toward the south-wing corridor. At first, she thought it hadn't seen her, that perhaps it was heading for the staircase, but its head was already dipped, hackles rising, and she could hear the deep, guttural rumbling in its throat—a low, malicious growl. The Browning was in the lobby, she'd left Fidel's knife in the alcove, and there was no time to reach the only unlocked door in the vicinity—the room where she'd left her sister, unconscious.

There are weapons on the fourth floor—a shotgun and a machine pistol.

The wolf passed into the darkness of the corridor, and she turned and ran as hard as she could up the passage, every step sending a shock of agony through her abdomen.

She reached the alcove, heard the wolf panting behind her, closing the distance between them with every stride. She was telling herself she'd outrun him in the stairwell, thought for some reason he couldn't move as quickly up the steps.

She turned into the stairwell.

The gray wolf was coming down the last flight of stairs, and it snarled when it saw her, its teeth wet in the moonlight, black with blood.

The white one was fast approaching.

She saw the window, the glass broken out, rushed over, climbed up onto the sill, glanced back, the wolves right there, yellow and pink eyes raging.

No other choice. She jumped down into the snow—a rush of cold—thinking, *The front entrance is locked, but I can bang on it, get him to let me in. If I can get there, I can make it back inside.* But it was a long way, the entire length of the south wing, through deep drifts.

She was practically swimming through the snow now, clumps of it falling down her collar, melting on her neck, and the wind had kicked up, blowing powder into her face like a swarm of tiny pins.

It was a bright night, with a huge moon and loads of stars, but her vision seemed to be darkening. She looked back, having already gone thirty feet out from the window, saw one of their heads emerge from the snow, the wolves fighting their way through deep powder in a movement that resembled swimming dolphins.

Will thought, *I'm not dead.* He sat up, unsure of how long he'd been unconscious. For a moment, he could see only a single frame of white. Someone, presumably Devlin, was calling out to him, but her voice was distant and muddled.

His vision restored—washed-out tones of lantern light and shadow, Rachael sitting up behind him, conscious and intact, her pants blackened from the close-range detonation.

Rachael asked, "Are you okay?" but his voice seemed trapped in his head.

Devlin was kneeling in front of him, and he tried to read her lips, but the disorientation stymied his effort.

Will climbed to his feet and careened into the wall.

Kalyn moved faster now, groaning with each step, focused on nothing but her legs powering through the snow. The next time she looked up, she realized she'd veered off course, away from the lodge, and was actually heading downslope toward the lake and the floatplane dock.

The wolves were still coming. She could see nothing of the white one but its eyes.

She reached the lakeshore, the moon's reflection in the water disturbed, waves slamming into the snowy bank.

The wolves kept coming.

She looked up toward the lodge entrance, and there he was, wading toward her through the snow, a black duffel bag slung over his shoulder, a machine pistol in one hand, a Mossberg in the other.

The sound of the Beretta and the bullets ripping through the snow was lost to the wind. Kalyn only saw the wolves disappear under the snowpack, where they would remain until next June, when the snow broke and the scavengers came.

Javier stopped a few feet away, the black fabric over his right shoulder shredded by buckshot.

"You're bleeding," he said.

Kalyn stood shivering in the cold, bracing against the wind. "Your friend had a fairly liberal interpretation of 'don't touch her.'"

"You killed him."

She nodded.

Javier glanced back at the lodge. "Just you and me and the Innises now."

Kalyn felt lines of blood trailing warmly into her boots.

"So," Javier said, unscrewing the silencer from the Beretta's barrel, "shall we?"

"You can barely stand, Will."

"My balance is coming back." He took the shotgun out of Devlin's hand. "You both stay here. How's your leg?"

"It hurts bad."

"I know, but you're lucky, Rach. That flashbang went off right underneath you."

"What's a flashbang?" Devlin asked.

"Stun grenade."

Somewhere beyond the walls of Ethan's room, a shotgun thundered.

"Is that inside?" Rachael asked.

"I can't tell."

Staccato shots responded to the Mossberg, automatic gunfire, which from inside the lodge sounded like beads dropping on a glass table.

Will staggered out into the corridor and closed the door behind him, his ears still ringing, unable even to hear his own footsteps as he hurried down the stairs and into the passage.

The wind shrieked under the brilliant Alaskan moon, building towers of snow against anything in its way.

Will saw the blood briefly—black smears by the lakeshore—before the wind concealed it with snow.

Waves of dizziness washed over him.

He spotted what appeared to be bloody tracks leading away from the lake toward the woods, though in the brutal wind, they were vanishing before his eyes, and would certainly be gone before he could reach the trees.

He collapsed, struggled back onto his feet, and started toward the woods as the tracks filled in, smoothed over and erased by the coldest wind ever to sting his cheeks.

Nine days ago, Kalyn Sharp had come to his home in Colorado. Nine days.

Is it over? he wondered. Nothing would have surprised him now.

He tried to deny the relief lurking in the nether regions of his conscience, but there was something so inescapably fitting about them killing each other, if that was in fact what had happened out here.

Will stopped after ten agonizing steps. He didn't have the strength to walk into those woods and dig through four feet of snow to find their bodies. He scarcely had the balance to stand. But he went on—tired, so very tired—when all he wanted was to make a fire in the library and fall asleep with Devlin and Rachael in his arms, wake up someplace else.

Talisman

SEVENTY-THREE

Devlin felt the g force push her down in the seat as the seaplane lifted into the air, the inner lake falling away, the lodge and the floatplanes dwindling into toys, accessories to a child's train set.

The sound of the props intensified, the De Havilland Twin Otter roaring south.

It was four hundred miles to Anchorage. Two hours to civilization. Devlin glanced around the cabin at the surviving women. She reached down, took her mother's hand in hers, laced their fingers together. Rachael smiled. Between the pair of 620-horsepower engines and no headphones, it was too noisy to talk.

Staring out the window, Devlin said a prayer for Buck Young. The bush pilot had landed on the inner lake yesterday morning, found them, and then flown back to Fairbanks for help.

Devlin turned her attention toward the world below, thinking, *Somewhere down there, under all that snow, lies Kalyn.* Her father had searched until dawn for their bodies, but the wind had tucked them away for a long hibernation. She registered a flicker of relief and sorrow, would always remember flying out of this wilderness because of the tension inside her, the unresolvable contradiction she would just have to live with, and for years to come would mark this moment, in all its emotional complexity, as her first breath, first heartbeat as a grown-up.

Soon the Wolverine Hills had diminished into forested ripples of earth. She turned away from the window, from this wilderness she would not see again, swallowing to release the pressure in her ears.

. . .

Cook Inlet opened into the Gulf of Alaska, a universe of glittering dark blue water that stretched to the horizon. Devlin watched the paths of ships and oil tankers moving south toward the Pacific and continental America.

The De Havilland banked and descended. They were over land again, and looking out her window, Devlin could see the skyline of Anchorage and, just beyond, the shining, glaciated sprawl of the Chugach Range.

SEVENTY-FOUR

They touched down at Lake Hood Seaplane Base just shy of 1:00 P.M., after taxiing for several minutes over the choppy water. Two seats ahead, a woman began to sob uncontrollably, so loudly that everyone could hear, even over the drone of the props.

A second woman started to cry, then a third. They were all on Devlin's side of the plane, and when she peeked over the seat in front of her, she saw them staring out the windows.

She looked, too, the glass streaked with windblown lake water. They were approaching a series of docks, and right away, she picked out their destination. A dozen ambulances had backed up to the one on the end, the rear doors thrown open, paramedics standing by with stretchers. Devlin spotted a procession of police cruisers behind the ambulances, lights flashing, waiting to escort the women to Providence Alaska Medical Center. Two fire engines idled beyond the cruisers—they would lead the motorcade. A nearby parking lot was filling fast with cars, vans, three news trucks—giant satellites perched on their roofs, transmitting the scene across the world.

A crowd had formed along the shore. People were taking pictures, shooting videos. Firemen and police officers stood guard behind a barrier of yellow crime-scene tape.

The woman sitting two rows back suddenly shouted, "Oh God, there's Jimmy! It's Jimmy! He's a teenager!"

Devlin noticed that a handful of people had been allowed past the police barrier. They were gathered at the end of the dock—husbands, sisters, brothers, children, parents—and Devlin could see that every one of them stood crying, hands cupped to mouths, some outright weeping and prostrate, others signing "I love you" toward the seaplane.

The engines quit.

Devlin looked at her mother, her father, saw tears running down their faces, too. There was no stopping it, the emotion so sharp, so intense, it seemed to suck the oxygen out of the cabin. The women on the other side of the plane were unbuckling their seat belts, leaning across to look out the windows that faced the dock, searching for their loved ones amid the throng.

The pontoons bumped into the wooden pylons. The base crew went to work tethering the plane, tying down the props.

The families of the women pressed up to the end of the dock, and Devlin watched a man kneel down and reach out over the water, his hand just able to touch the window that framed his wife's face.

His voice was muffled, but Devlin heard him say, "Oh God, Melinda! Oh God!"

"Jeff!"

A police officer walked over and patted the man's shoulders, said, "Sir, I know it's emotional, but we have some women on the plane who need immediate medical attention."

"I'm right here, Melinda!" he yelled. "Right here!"

The officer led him and the others a little ways back from the plane.

The pilot opened the De Havilland's door. Light streamed in. Devlin felt the frigid air, thought she smelled the ocean. A paramedic ducked into the plane—a young man with a goatee and stylish sideburns—his face darkening at the sight of the passengers.

He steadied himself and said, "We have ambulances waiting outside for everyone."

Rachael stood up, said, "Take that woman in front first."

The paramedic knelt down. "What's her name?"

"Natalie."

He was staring at an eighty-pound woman, severely malnourished and catatonic, who'd suffered so much trauma, it had destroyed her mind.

"My name's Rick," he said. "Your family's here, Natalie. I'm gonna carry you out, okay?"

He unbuckled the safety belt and lifted the woman from her seat, turning around carefully in the cramped space near the door and the cockpit. Through her window, Devlin watched another paramedic take Natalie out of Rick's arms. He was cradling her like a child, her eyes open yet seeing nothing. Someone draped a blanket over her.

A man emerged from the crowd, staggered toward Natalie. He was pale and shell-shocked, like he'd encountered a ghost or become one himself.

Rachael grabbed Devlin's and Will's hands. "Guys?" she whispered. "You see what you did? It isn't just about our family."

Outside, the paramedic said, "Is this your wife, sir?" The man had no voice, could only nod.

"Why don't you come with me. You can ride with us to Providence."

SEVENTY-FIVE

Will dutifully tread and retread his story, from start to finish, so many times that he could tell it without thinking, without feeling, to the special agents in charge with the FBI's Phoenix and Anchorage field offices, to Inspection Division agents from the Bureau's headquarters, to Border Patrol, ATF, even a detective from the Pima County Sheriff's Department, successor to Teddy Swicegood, who had died of a stroke two and a half years earlier on a golf course in Sierra Vista.

The FBI had been looking for Kalyn Sharp for the last year, since it had come to light that she'd defrauded the Bureau, absconding with $150,000, which they suspected she'd used to track down her sister. They called her "a rogue agent, mentally unstable," said that had she not been killed in Alaska, serious prison time would have loomed in her immediate future.

"Just to be clear, you do understand who this character was?" Agent Messing said, his big West Texas accent filling the drab hotel room.

It was two days before Rachael's scheduled release from the psychiatric hospital at the University of Colorado, and this young DEA agent from the Phoenix Field Office sat on the couch in Will and Devlin's suite at the Oxford in downtown Denver. Will had been staring out the window toward the Front Range, his patience worn ragged by the steady stream of agents from more law-enforcement agencies than he cared to keep track of.

He replied, "Kalyn told me he was with the Alphas."

"Not *with*. Number-two honcho. We had a bug in a Tempe warehouse they'd been using. One in Jav's car. One in his mansion. I could put my hand on the Bible and say he's the scariest sumbitch I ever encountered."

"You met him?"

"Once. At a Starbucks in Scottsdale. I'd been tailing him for a few days, and he made me while he was ordering."

"What happened?"

"We had espressos on the patio."

The agent unbuttoned his too-tight Belk suit, ran his fingers through a blond crew cut that let too much of his oily scalp shine through.

"What is it?" Will asked.

Agent Messing shook his head. "This ain't for public consumption, and in fact, it can't walk out of this room."

Will got up, went over to the open door that led into Devlin's bedroom, where MTV blared from the television.

He closed it, returned to the chair, and when he was sitting down again, Messing said, "I had reason to believe, and this is coming from a reliable source, that Javier wanted out."

"Out of what?"

"Everything. His marriage. The Alphas."

"Why the Alphas?"

"Greed probably. Whatever the motivation, it wasn't rooted in goodness. Wasn't 'cause he found Jesus. Nothing like that. The man is pure evil. But the point is, you don't leave the Alphas. It's blood in, blood out. Know what I mean?"

Will shook his head.

"You kill to join, and the only way to leave is through death. In light of this development, we really, really wanted to catch up with Mr. Estrada. For whatever reason, he was unhappy with the Alphas, and he could have made a devastating witness, blown the whole thing apart. Now, his widow's a stone fucking wall, but if there's anything else you might know or remember . . ." Will shook his head. "Well, here." Messing reached into an inner pocket of his jacket, produced a card. "Anything surfaces, call me. Day or night."

"I will."

Messing stood and Will rose to shake his hand. "I'm guessing you've had a revolving door of visitors from every federal agency under the sun."

"Yeah, it's been taxing."

"Then I won't keep you. I'm glad you've got your family back, Mr. Innis."

Will walked Messing out, decided as they stepped into the hallway just to go ahead and ask him.

"Tell me something," Will said.

"Shoot."

"Should I be worried?"

"Worried about what?"

"A visit in the middle of the night."

Messing let out a soft sigh and studied the carpet under his dull shoes in a way that made Will nervous, like he wasn't going to like the answer. He was half-wishing now he hadn't even asked.

"I don't know, Mr. Innis. It's sketchy territory, trying to predict what the Alphas will and won't do. I guess what it'll probably come down to is whether or not you're on their radar."

"Do you think I am?"

"No way to know. I understand that's not the piece of comfort pie you want to hear, but it's the truth, I'm sorry to say."

"What would you do?"

"If I was in your boots?"

"Yeah."

Messing cracked his thick linebacker's neck. "I'm gonna tell you something that's gonna be both horrifying *and* freeing. There ain't nothing you can do, short of move your family to some overpopulated Third World shithole and disappear. If the Alphas decide to come calling, you won't stop them. Not with a shotgun under the bed. Not with different names. They're just plain the nastiest motherfuckers anyone's ever heard of. So live your life, Mr. Innis. Don't look over your shoulder or buy a home security system or anything of the sort. Just pray you were a blip on their radar that has long since disappeared."

SEVENTY-SIX

It had been a little over two months since they'd landed in Anchorage, weeks that had taken years to pass. For five of them, Rachael had undergone treatment and counseling at the psychiatric hospital in Denver. But these last few weeks, leading up to Christmas Eve, they'd been together, seeing if the pieces still fit in that quaint farmhouse in Mancos, Colorado. Devlin wasn't sick, and Rachael was eight and a half months pregnant. They'd hired a midwife out of Farmington, New Mexico, to attend the home birth, expecting to have a little one in the first or second week of the new year. Will was coming to terms with the fact that the child in that enormous belly of Rachael's didn't possess a single chromosome of his DNA.

He remembered Devlin's birth, sixteen years ago, could still recall the lightning that had struck when she'd come screaming into the world, still teared up thinking about it—that fierce, inexorable love that had altered everything he thought he knew about priorities. What kept him up lately, these long December nights, was the fear that he wouldn't feel those things when this baby came, wondered how you faked a thing like that, how you raised something you didn't feel belonged to you.

He prayed to God every night that the lightning would strike again.

It had been a cool, dry Christmas Eve, and much to the Innises' delight, little snow had fallen so far this season in the Mancos Valley. You could see patches of it gleaming under the sun or the moon on the rim of Mesa Verde, and the La Platas were buried above ten thousand feet. But the pasture out back stood bare; the river slacked off to a trickle. No snow lingered under the spruce trees that enclosed the farmhouse. There wasn't even a fading patch to be found in the north-facing shadows—Devlin had gone looking that afternoon.

She was thriving, out of school for Christmas vacation and spending all her time with her mother—hoisting Rachael out of chairs, cooking for her, cleaning, helping to prepare the nursery in what had been an empty bedroom when she and her father were on their own.

It was only at night when she thought of Alaska, in bed, buried under covers, listening to the wind blow through the firs. A few nights ago, a pack of coyotes had moved through the pasture. Their yaps woke her at 3:00 A.M.—evil, mocking laughter—and she sat up in bed, thought for half a second she was back in the Wolverine Hills, saw that huge white wolf with raging pink eyes standing at the foot of her bed.

She'd thrown back the covers and walked into the kitchen, poured herself a glass of water, and sat down at the table, listening to them howl until her hands quit trembling.

One of Rachael's therapists in Denver had said something that applied to them all. If you let fear take hold, if you let it own you, your life ceases to be your own. She'd even given them a motto, a creed—concise, profane, and unforgettable. Devlin had glanced at the refrigerator clipboard where Will had scribbled it in black Magic Marker, thrice underscored.

Fuck the fear.

SEVENTY-SEVEN

*D*evlin is already rubbing her eyes. It's nine o'clock, late for a six-year-old. She stands on her tiptoes and hangs the last ornament on the tree—a clear glass cactus. Her parents are sitting on the couch, sipping hot toddies—Arizona-style: fresh-squeezed orange juice, hot water, Grand Marnier, honey, dash of cayenne.

It's a warm December night. Devlin climbs onto the sofa between Rachael and Will.

"Everybody up for It's a Wonderful Life?" he asks.

"I'll probably fall asleep before Harry falls through the ice, but sure," Rachael says. Will walks over to the television set, finds the video in Devlin's movie cabinet, pops it into the VCR. He brings the remote back with him. "Will, I'm cold," Rachael says. "Would you get my sweatshirt?"

"I'm not sure how I feel about touching that hideous thing."

She grins. "Back off my alma mater." Will had gone to law school at Carolina while Rachael was finishing her undergrad work at Duke. The schools were only seven miles apart as the crow flies, but a more malicious rivalry you could not find in all of collegiate America. The sweatshirt was a badly faded navy blue, the letters—D-U-K-E—having long since peeled away, leaving only a less faded palimpsest of the word.

Will retrieves it from the sweater chest in their bedroom, brings it back into the den.

"Thanks, honey." He sits down with his family, presses PLAY. His dark-haired girls snuggle up on either side of him, and whether it's the holiday or this movie that always makes him cry, Will is briefly overcome, keenly aware of what he has. There is only the small white lights of the Christmas tree, the glow of the FBI warning on the television screen. And for a moment, before the movie begins, the house is so quiet, they can hear the wind blowing out on the desert.

SEVENTY-EIGHT

A decade later, in a different state, in what felt to each of them like a different life, the Innises were decorating another tree—a blue spruce Will had chopped down in a small grove by the river two days ago. Rachael lay stretched out on the couch in the living room, watching her husband and daughter hang unfamiliar ornaments and makeshift tube-sock stockings from the mantel. A fire was petering out in the small stone hearth. The farmhouse smelled of wood smoke, hot cocoa, the sap from their Christmas tree.

"You remember those hot toddies we used to make?" Rachael said.

Will smiled. "God, those were good."

"What's a toddy?" Devlin asked.

"It's a hot alcoholic drink. We used to make ours with orange juice, Grand Marnier. . . . I forget what else we put in them."

"Cayenne," Rachael said. "Most important ingredient."

"Maybe we can make them next year?"

"Definitely."

Devlin sat at the end of the couch, opposite her mother, massaging Rachael's feet. "I've got a great idea," she said. "Let's watch *It's a Wonderful Life*, like we used to."

"Do we still have that video?" Rachael asked.

"No," Will said. "It got left in Ajo with everything else. But I guess I could drive into town, see if the video store's still open."

"No, don't leave," Rachael said. "We'll remember it for next year."

"Yes. Next year. We'll do all our old traditions."

"But I don't want to go to bed yet, Dad. Can't we stay up together a little longer?"

"Sure, baby girl. Of course we can."

Rachael suddenly shivered, said, "Will, I'm cold."

Will's socks slid on the dusty hardwood floor as he walked down the hallway into their bedroom. He was already untucking the quilt from the corners when he happened to think of it. He let go of the cover and climbed across the mattress, knelt down on the floor on the other side, opened the deep drawer on his bedside table. There it was. Eight weeks and he hadn't even thought about it until now. Hadn't needed to. He reached into the drawer, pulled out Rachael's navy blue sweatshirt.

He smelled it. The garment no longer carried her true scent, hadn't for years.

He sat for a moment on the floor near the window, a view of the moonlit pasture through the glass, just holding Rachael's shirt to his face, sliding his hands over the soft fabric, feeling the cloth between his fingers. He'd slept so many nights alone, this sweatshirt wrapped around his arm. When it had finally lost Rachael's smell, he'd gone out and bought the perfume she'd worn, sprayed the sweatshirt with the fragrance.

I don't need this anymore, he thought. He stood, wiped his face, took Rachael's sweatshirt with him, and walked out of their bedroom, back down the hallway, stopping where it opened into the living room.

They were still together on the couch in the light of the dwindling fire.

His daughter. His unborn child. His wife.

And he thought of all the women who'd been rescued from that lodge, imagined them in this moment, this Christmas Eve, back in their homes with families they had never expected to see again.

He delivered Rachael's sweatshirt, saying, "We're gonna need more wood to save this fire. I'm gonna go out and grab an armful." Will walked into the kitchen. Devlin could hear him stepping into his boots, the doors opening, the screen door banging closed after him. She sat down on the cool hardwood floor beside her mother.

Rachael said, "So what were Christmases like for you and Dad while I was gone?"

"I don't know. We didn't do much. They were just, like . . . sad, you know? Really sad. Last year was the first time we actually put up a tree. What were yours like?"

"I never knew when Christmas came, honey. Usually, I didn't even know if it was December, although there were days when I remember thinking, *This feels like Christmas.* Honestly, I'm glad I never knew when it came.

I think that would have broken me." Rachael sucked through her teeth and winced. "Ooooh."

"What? What's wrong?"

She was rubbing her stomach. "Nothing. Just a little contraction."

"Is it time?"

"No, honey. These are just Braxton-Hicks. You'll know when it's the real deal."

"How?"

"I'll be swearing like a sailor."

SEVENTY-NINE

It was a cold night, windless, starry. The gravel crunched under Will's boots.

The woodpile stood against the stone chimney at the side of the house. He filled his arms with logs and carried them to the front porch, dropped the first load at the foot of the steps. On the way back to the woodpile, he stopped. He could see the pasture in the distance, glowing under the full moon. There were shadows moving across it.

He froze. The thudding of his heart seemed to pluck at the silence like a guitar string as he counted half a dozen deer sauntering over the turned earth, working their way toward the river for an evening drink. They looked albino in the moonlight, so bright out there, he could see their breath clouds.

Will exhaled slowly as the fear receded, and he wondered if it would always be this way—that breathless anxiety as he rounded corners, listening for clandestine footsteps in the silence, looking for movement where none should be. He could tell himself a thousand times that the Alphas would never come for them, but that didn't mean it would or wouldn't happen. Messing had been right. These things, he couldn't control.

Live your life, Mr. Innis.

Fuck the fear.

Will reached into his pocket, pulled out Javier's BlackBerry, which he'd taken from Kalyn's pack two months ago, before they'd flown out of the Wolverine Hills.

He kept it charged and always with him like a pocket time bomb, waiting for a call—from whom, he did not know. Maybe Jav's wife or an Alpha compadre.

He turned it on, stared at the glowing screen. There had been no calls.

The BlackBerry wasn't going to vibrate. He'd been holding on to this device as an obsessive-compulsive talisman—he checked for messages every hour—as if before the Alphas came for them, they would call first, as if nothing could happen to his family without advance warning, as long as he religiously checked for incoming communication.

"I should throw this piece of shit at the chimney," he said aloud, his grip tightening around the BlackBerry, his finger inadvertently pressing a button on the side.

The screen changed to show a list of folders, SMS OUTBOX drawing his attention, and he clicked the icon to open the folder containing sent text messages, wondering why this hadn't occurred to him before. Maybe he could find some phone numbers and addresses of Javier's associates, forward them on to Agent Messing.

The last two text messages had been sent to the same phone number, Phoenix area code:

> FRIDAY, OCTOBER 19, 2007 • 10:41 A.M. AKDT
>
> J—Arctic Skies, Buck Young. We leave at 1:00 P.M. today
> for the Wolverine Hills: 200 miles west of Fairbanks. K.

> THURSDAY, OCTOBER 18, 2007 • 11:03 P.M. AKDT
>
> J—Fairbanks, Alaska. Here in one piece, but barely. K.

He opened a calendar on the BlackBerry, his heart accelerating, mouth running dry. Eleven P.M., on October 18, would have been the night he, Devlin, and Kayln spent in Fairbanks at the Best Western. October 19, the day they'd flown to the Wolverine Hills. The BlackBerry had been in Kalyn's possession both days.

What the hell? You told him where to find us?

And a barrage of pieces that had been needling Will ever since he'd met Kalyn started to fall out of orbit and assemble themselves—things that had bothered him subconsciously, that had set up shop under his skin while he'd been too distracted, or unwilling, to pay them credence.

So you wanted out, he thought. *You and Jav. And you brought us along for what?* He smiled as it hit him. *Because just disappearing wasn't enough. You needed witnesses to your deaths to get the Alphas and the FBI off your backs.*

He stood in the shadow of his house, trying to fit it all together, his mind passing through bewilderment, anger, then coming to rest in a state of awe as everything at last made perfect sense. *What performances.*

They'd put his life, and his daughter's, in danger, but he'd gotten Rachael back, returned twenty-two women to their families, and for that, perhaps, he could play along.

Will hurled Javier's BlackBerry into the stone chimney, the device exploding on impact.

He walked into the backyard, stood looking through the windbreak of spruce trees into the pasture, spotted the herd of deer still scrounging the banks of the Mancos River.

He looked up at the stars in the navy December sky and wondered where Kalyn was tonight, trying to make some kind of sense of her, but like a prism, each memory gleamed from a different facet, and all he arrived at was, *Who* are *you?*

The FBI agent who showed up at my house, all business, on a crisp October night?

The femme fatale who kidnapped a family and interrogated an Alpha at gunpoint?

The woman who showed kindness and warmth to my motherless daughter, and sacrificed herself in the back of a semi to find her sister?

The deer had caught wind of him, six heads raised, two of them antlered, the racks the color of the moon where the moonlight struck them.

The broken woman with scarred wrists I almost made love to in a Fairbanks hotel?

Will sat down slowly in the dead grass and watched the deer evaluate his scent, lose interest, and go back to their nighttime wandering.

May you find your peace, Kalyn.

Looking over his shoulder, he could see the adobe glow of firelight on the walls inside his house and the strands of white lights that Devlin was wrapping around their pitiful spruce. It was filling him up now, this sense he'd come to the end of something, that he was turning out of a bad corridor, though into what, he didn't know. Just that it was someplace new, and he had his family with him.

That was more than enough.

EIGHTY

He'd been trying to catch the bartender's attention for five minutes, with no success. The club was packed, the music appalling, and all he wanted was a nightcap, something strong and classic that you didn't have to slurp out of someone's navel.

The hard bump jolted him from his annoyed reverie, and he turned, ready, but it was just a very drunk young man—twenty-one, twenty-two—holding a Corona with lime in each hand, taking full advantage of the all-inclusive amenities. He wore a baseball cap turned sideways on his head, and no shirt, for the benefit of anyone who might desire an unencumbered view of his magnificently sculpted abs.

"Watch out there, bro, 'kay?"

Javier glanced down at his boots, spilled beer foaming on the iguana skin as a surge from the dance floor pushed the college boy within range.

"Watch out? You just bumped into me," Javier said. "Why are you telling *me* to watch out?"

One of the young man's friends grabbed his arm, "Come on, Brian, I found that piece of ass we saw at the pool today."

But Brian jerked his arm away. "Nah, man, nah." His face becoming flushed with rage. "What the fuck is *your* problem, bro?" He poked a finger into Javier's chest, *cerveza* sloshing onto Javier's black silk shirt, so close now, Javier could see his pupils—booze-dilated into huge black plates.

"Nothing," Javier said.

"What?" Brian turned his head, displaying his ear to Javier in an exaggerated fashion.

"Nothing," Javier said, louder.

Brian nodded. "That's right. That's what the fuck I thought."

"What did you think?"

"What?"

"You said, 'That's what the fuck I thought.' Like you had already formed an opinion prior to my response."

"Yeah," Brian said, pointing in his face now, "I could tell you were a little bitch and that you wouldn't do shit."

Javier nodded, smiling, "Very perceptive of you, Brian."

Then he turned toward the bar, the bartender coming his way now, raised a finger to catch her attention as the college boy drifted back toward the dance floor.

He strolled the Fun Ship's Empress Deck, the glasses pleasantly cool in his hands. Though he could still hear the bass pulse of the Christmas Eve rave at the Galax-Z dance club on the upper deck—a trip hop remix of "Silent Night"—it felt good to be walking away from that madness toward the bow.

They were thirty miles off the eastern bulge of South America, and the stars shone in clustered swarms. Farthest he'd ever been from Sonora.

He'd been planning to kill her tonight, but he figured he might as well play it safe, wait until they reached Rio. There was such joy in the anticipation.

She put her hands on the railing and leaned over the bow, the dark water six stories below, tropical air clinging to her skin like sweaty satin.

Kalyn turned at the sound of approaching footsteps. Javier passed through the illumination of a deck light and handed her a glass, Kalyn registering the sour waft of tequila.

"Patrón," he said. "Sorry, best they had."

They clinked glasses, stood leaning against the railing. Somewhere out in all that dark lay the coast of Brazil. They would dock in Rio de Janeiro on New Year's Eve.

"How is Kalyn tonight?"

"All right, I guess. Missing Lucy."

Javier sipped his tequila. "I've been thinking a lot about Raphael."

"You'll see him again."

"I hope."

She said, "We did a good thing, you know."

"I'm aware."

"Doesn't it feel good to you?"

"I suppose."

She looked over and smiled, thinking of that night just a year ago, when she'd finally caught up with him. He'd wanted a way out—they both had—

and she'd shown him a door. Now they were standing here together at the bow of a cruise ship, en route to South America, with $425,000 between them that Javier had taken from the safe in that Alaskan lodge. He still scared her, something diamond-hard and unknowable in those blue eyes, but she liked that he scared her, and she liked his heat.

"Merry Christmas, Jav."

"*Feliz Navidad*, Kalyn."

The engines of the cruise ship hummed beneath them, a low, steady bass line, and Kalyn leaned over just enough so their elbows touched.

Javier said, "What are you doing?"

"This." And she kissed him for the first time, for a long time.

When they came apart, she said, "But you know something?" The corners of her mouth and her tongue were tingling. "You still hurt my sister, you fucking psychopath."

Javier smiled at this, but the smile faded and he stared in disbelief, watching Kalyn bend down, her knees grazing the pool of blood, and wrap her arms around his thighs.

Then she hoisted him up onto the railing, grabbed the handle of the knife she'd embedded in his gut, and pushed him into the Atlantic Ocean.